COUNTER TO MY INTELLIGENCE

Book 7 of The Dixie Wardens MC

BY

LANI LYNN VALE

ISBN-13:
978-1519658944

ISBN-10:
151965894X

Dedication

Readers, this book is for you! You asked for Silas, and you got Silas! Enjoy him!

Acknowledgements

FuriousFotog — You're a genius. That's all.

Alfie – I can't believe how you've made this character come to life. Thank you.

Asli – Once again, thank you.

Dani- Thank you for help, I couldn't have made this beauty shine without you.

Leah- my enforcer and pep talker, thank you!

CONTENTS

Other Titles by Lani Lynn Vale:
The Freebirds

Boomtown

Highway Don't Care

Another One Bites the Dust

Last Day of My Life

Texas Tornado

I Don't Dance

The Heroes of The Dixie Wardens MC

Lights To My Siren

Halligan To My Axe

Kevlar To My Vest

Keys To My Cuffs

Life To My Flight

Charge To My Line

Code 11- KPD SWAT Series

Center Mass

Double Tap

Bang Switch

Execution Style

Charlie Foxtrot

Kill Shot

Coup De Grace

PROLOGUE

Rules are meant to be broken...just not quite like that.
-Coffee Cup

Sawyer

"Bristol, please let's not do this!" I pleaded with my best friend.

Bristol looked over at me with a raised brow. "Finals are over. You don't have volleyball practice for two months. It's time to stop being such a hermit and just be a college student like the rest of us."

I shook my head. "I don't think this is a good idea. I'm freaking out, and I'm not even there yet. I really don't want to go."

Bristol looked unimpressed.

"I'm going whether you want to or not. The decision is up to you," she left that hanging in the air as she walked out of our shared dorm, closing the door quietly behind her.

"Shit," I sighed.

I really, *really* didn't want to go.

But it was more than apparent that Bristol did.

I wasn't one for parties. I was more comfortable curled up with a good book rather than going to a party or hanging out with friends.

I loved Bristol with all my heart, and I knew she loved me right back.

We had been friends for as long as I could remember, and I knew that she'd always be there for me. Even if I wanted to be left the hell alone.

Bristol had done her best to 'get me out of my head,' as she liked to call it, but it would help if I actually *wanted* to be out of it.

Which I most certainly did not.

I was a very shy person.

Between her and Isaac, my boyfriend, I was doomed.

Something he proved in the next minute when a text showed up on my phone.

Issac: Going 2 the party w/Bristol. You better be there.

Fuck!

I looked longingly at the new book I'd picked up at the grocery store earlier before I sighed and walked to my dresser, pulling out a pair of pants as well as a black spaghetti strap shirt.

It wasn't the greatest, but it'd do.

I wasn't going there to impress. I was going there because I was being forced.

***

"No, Isaac. I don't want any," I growled four hours later.

I'd already had a beer, and it was one more than I'd wanted to have.

I was a lightweight. Any more than four drinks, and I wouldn't wake up for a very, very long time.

Which was why I always stayed with one and one only.

Isaac, though, didn't seem to care.

"Seriously, I don't want one!" I said, shoving it away.

After this night was over, so were Isaac and me.

He'd tried to publicly grope me and have sex with me, which was something we hadn't done before, and now it was something we wouldn't *ever* be doing.

He'd tried to get me to play beer pong, and when I wouldn't, he played with a couple of other college coeds.

When I drank that first beer, he thought he'd hit the lottery and kept trying to force-feed me more.

"You're such a fuckin' downer, Sawyer. Get the fuck away from me," Isaac slurred.

I wanted to nut punch him.

Repeatedly.

"Well, I think I'll go home, then," I hesitated. "Do you want me to give you a ride?"

His eyes narrowed, and he took a look around.

The party had been a 'bust,' or so he'd said. I didn't know if it had or not.

Seemed there'd been a lot of people there, but they'd slowly drifted out of the main room until there were only about fifteen of us left in it.

"Yeah, I'll go home. Let me go get one more drink."

I wanted to tell him no, but I knew that that was probably the only way I was going to get out of here.

We were in his truck, after all.

"I'll go get Bristol," I said, wandering away from him.

I found Bristol in the kitchen doing things that I didn't think were possible.

Mainly those 'things' were drinking upside down with a tube shoved down her throat while a few of the football players yelled, '*chug, chug, chug*' over and over. She even managed to look good doing it, too.

"Um, Bristol?" I called to her worriedly. "It's time to get going, are you ready?"

The football players looked up at me with open curiosity in their eyes.

They'd been doing that all night, and I had no clue why.

I wasn't anything special, but they were staring at me like I was the biggest, juiciest steak they'd ever seen.

"Bristol?" I called again.

The closest football player finally lowered Bristol's legs, and she hit the floor while spewing beer out of her mouth through her laughter.

Beer covered her from head to toe.

"I think it's time to go," I said softly.

Bristol nodded, so glassy eyed that I thought for sure she was going to fall over any second.

With the help of the football players, I loaded a very boisterous Bristol, and a very touchy Isaac into his big three-quarter-ton truck.

Isaac's truck wasn't my favorite thing to drive on the best of days, but it being night and slightly rainy, I knew it wouldn't be fun *at all.*

Regardless of my apprehension, I got into the driver's seat, pulled the seat up so I could reach the pedals and the steering wheel, and started it up.

"Remember, it pulls to the left," Isaac slurred, leaning over the console to run his mouth along my neck.

I cringed and pushed him slightly to fall back into his own seat.

"Let me drive, please," I said pleadingly.

Isaac laughed as he turned to Bristol who was sitting in the middle of the backseat, staring at us giddily.

"I knew y'all would make such a great couple!" She cheered, clapping her hands like she was a seal at Sea World.

I wanted to flip her off, but it took both of my hands to maneuver Isaac's huge truck.

Did I mention I hated driving it?

He had huge tires on it.

They were so big that the top of the tire came up to my waistline.

His truck was the size of a tank on steroids.

His daddy bought it for him the day he turned eighteen.

Now, two years later, it still looked brand new because he took such good care of his 'precious baby.'

When I got my first car, it'd been because I'd saved up the money for it since I started working at fifteen.

Although my parents were great, they weren't the richest folks.

In fact, they weren't even middle class.

We were the 'barely making it' class.

Even now, with me out of the house, they were still struggling to make ends meet.

They did have more kids besides me, so it was understandable.

But it was also probably why I'd be in debt until I was fifty.

Paying for my bachelor's degree in nursing wasn't very easy. Thank God for student loans.

Although they wouldn't be my friends once I graduated.

"Why are you going so slow, Sawyer? I feel like we're crawling!" Bristol yelled, leaning forward on the console.

"Put your seatbelt on or I'll pull this truck over," I said with as much venom as I could.

Neither one of them ever wore seatbelts, and it drove me absolutely nuts.

I heard two clicks, and I turned accusing eyes onto Isaac.

He knew my rule!

"Why is it so hard for y'all to follow that rule? I mean, seriously, it could save your life if we were in an accident!" I growled, turning back when I saw lights flash in front of me.

I couldn't stop.

A Ford Bronco pulled out in front of me and did it at the exact wrong time.

Under normal circumstances, had he done that, I would've missed him.

But I was in Isaac's huge truck, which was hard to slow because it was so big.

I was also driving at night. In the rain.

So, instead of stopping or even slowing when I slammed on the brakes, it slid.

Then the brakes locked.

The tires squealed.

Isaac, Bristol and I screamed.

And we hit the Bronco with a deafening, blood-curdling crash.

It was terrible.

I saw the whites of the man's eyes before the truck T-boned him.

Saw the woman in the front seat turn to someone in the back.

Then nothing.

Absolutely nothing.

I couldn't get my brain to make any sense of what had just happened, and wouldn't know until days later that I had killed every single person in the vehicle.

And it was all my fault.

***

Six months later

"After considering all of the evidence and hearing the defendant's testimony, we find the defendant guilty of four counts of manslaughter," the spokesman for the jury said.

My world came screeching to a stop.

All of my time.

All of my dreams.

Gone.

Every single one of them.

Four counts of manslaughter.

I looked at my mother with tear filled eyes.

She looked back at me with the same sad expression.

I closed my eyes, a single tear slipping down my cheek.

"Sawyer Ann Berry, you are hereby sentenced to eight years in Huntsville. Dismissed," Judge Abbott declared, finalizing this entire nightmare with the slam of his gavel.

My heart hurt.

I couldn't breathe.

Eight years.

I'd be nearly thirty when I got out!

"Don't worry, Sawyer. I'll get you out. We'll appeal it. I promise you," my father's good friend and my attorney, Donald Barber, promised.

I looked at him and shook my head. "Just…just take care of my parents. They're going to need you."

He smiled at me sadly. "I will, pumpkin."

My only hope, once the appeal was denied, was that I'd make parole.

I looked over at my best friend, who understandably felt horrible, and my boyfriend…whom I hadn't broken up with because he'd become my rock.

Maybe not so much of a boyfriend anymore, more like a huge part of my support system.

The two of them had become my sole source of strength through this nightmare. I couldn't have made it through without them.

They'd stayed with me, despite what I'd done.

And I couldn't thank them enough.

***

Four years later

"Parole denied."

My eyes closed, and my heart ripped in half.

The last thread holding it in one piece was gone.

Most likely forever.

CHAPTER 1

If she chooses a day on the back of your bike to a day of shopping, then she's a keeper.
-T-shirt

Silas

"I'm sorry, Silas. It just happened. I never thought we would get back together. But with Sawyer getting out next week, we started talking a lot again, and we've come to the decision that splitting up wasn't something that either one of us wanted to do," Reba said softly.

My brows rose.

"Reba, honey. We've never really had anything exclusive. I understand that you'd want to get back with your old man. Hell, that's probably why I never did anything past kiss you and spend time with you. I knew your heart belonged to another man." I shook my head, but raised my hand to rest softly on the side of her face. "It's okay, darlin'. It's time to put you first and not that girl of yours. She's a grown woman now."

Reba smiled at me sadly.

"You don't know Sawyer, though. These past eight years have changed her. She's not the same bright, happy book nerd anymore. My baby is gone, and she needs me now. She needs her family even more now than she ever did. Plus…when she finds out about Isaac, she's going to be heartbroken," she whispered.

"What?" I asked.

I didn't really want to know, but the fucking brothers had turned me into a fuckin' gossip whore.

Not to mention that this had been huge for our little community.

Everyone knew what had happened.

Knew Reba, her husband, and their four kids.

Had prayed right along with the rest of the city that what had happened wouldn't get any worse for the poor woman.

Then Reba had to go on and prove that the loser Sawyer had thought was hers was a big piece of shit.

"Isaac got some woman pregnant," Reba said, slicking her hair back. "I've been telling Sawyer for years that she shouldn't have expected Isaac to wait." She shook her hair. "Isaac is getting married to that woman next weekend. The fucking week after Sawyer is set to get out, no less."

What a fuckin' chicken shit.

"Well, let me know if you need anything, okay?" I told her softly.

Reba smiled.

"Thank you, Silas. You're very sweet," she said, giving me a hug.

I hugged her back and gave her a kiss on the forehead.

"Gotta go, sweetheart. Let me know if you need me."

Reba nodded and waved as I straddled my bike.

Starting it up with a deafening roar, I rode out of the parking lot and headed straight to the clubhouse.

My mind wandered to that night eight and a half years ago.

I'd been on the volunteer fire department, and had been there in time to see the three kids in the big truck get taken to the hospital by three separate ambulances.

I'd noted almost immediately that the occupants of the other vehicle weren't going to make it.

They were all dead.

The two in the back hadn't been wearing seatbelts.

They'd been ejected from the Bronco and laid under sheets to protect their privacy.

The two in the front seat were also dead. The Bronco had caved in like an aluminum coke can crunched under a boot.

The driver's seat was in the passenger's space, and blood could be seen everywhere.

Sometimes, being a first responder wasn't a fun job.

I passed the truck that'd hit them and instantly smelled all the beer.

It was obvious that the Bronco had pulled out in front of the truck.

But the truck, had the occupants not been drunk, might have been able to stop had they been sober.

What a fuckin' mess.

My phone rang, breaking me out of my thoughts and that horrific night.

"Hello?" I answered.

My helmet had a Bluetooth setup for it.

Then I laughed at the realization of what a sucker I'd become.

My daughter had bought the helmet for me because she hated when I 'put myself in danger unnecessarily.'

"Hey, dad. Will you watch the kids for me this weekend?" My daughter, Shiloh, asked.

I smiled, knowing I'd do it without question.

I, of course, had to tease her a bit, though.

"All of them?" I asked playfully.

My daughter laughed. “Yeah, all of them. Even Sam’s and Sebastian’s.”

Now that, I couldn’t do.

“You know I can’t watch all of them. They’d eat me alive,” I told her honestly.

Shiloh laughed again.

“Can’t you ask Reba to help you like she did last time?” She questioned.

I grimaced as I swung into the parking lot of The Dixie Wardens MC clubhouse.

“No can do, baby. Sorry. Reba and I just called it quits about twenty minutes ago,” I informed her.

There was a moment of shocked silence as my daughter processed that.

“I thought y’all were doing good?” Shiloh asked quietly.

I shrugged. “She’s getting back with her ex. The daughter gets out soon.”

Shiloh knew the story.

Reba had been very open with her daughter’s struggles.

We all knew the whole tale.

I’d been new in the Benton area, so my daughter hadn’t been here when it’d all gone down.

She was aware of the talk, though.

The town was stuck in the past, reliving memories of that night often.

It’d been a big deal for the town.

The family that had died that night had been celebrating their daughter’s graduation by going out for ice cream.

The parents of the girl, and the girl’s boyfriend had been in the Bronco, with the boy driving.

It'd been raining and visibility had been poor, and the accident had been brutal.

I'd remembered that clearly.

The aftermath had been what rocked the town.

The girl had just been accepted to Columbia University and would have been leaving later that month.

The girl's boyfriend had already been attending Columbia University on a scholarship for football.

He'd been a star quarterback, and the college community had felt that loss throughout their world.

The real reason, though, that the community kept bringing it up, was because of the parents.

The father had been a teacher at the high school, and the mother had been a teacher at the elementary school.

The same teachers who'd taught the girl who'd killed those four people.

"'Yo!" Loki called, interrupting my thoughts. "What are you doing?"

I looked up in surprise to see four men staring in my direction.

Loki, Trance, my son, Sebastian, and Cleo.

"What the hell do you care what I'm doing, boy?" I asked.

It was a decent question, though, so I'd give him that.

But I was the president of The Dixie Wardens MC.

If I wanted to sit on my bike in the forecourt of our clubhouse in the rain, then I fucking would.

Simple as that.

"You got a call a couple of minutes ago from a man named *Bonus*," Sebastian said from his position under the porch roof.

I nodded.

Bonus was my contact/handler.

I was a retired CIA asset, but occasionally they had need of my… services.

I didn't offer them lightly, so they knew to call me only when they well and truly needed it.

I'd earned that right.

And the agency knew it.

I also had a kid that hated for me to prove it.

"Thanks," I said, getting off my bike and pocketing the key in my jeans.

They all nodded at me as I entered the clubhouse, and I walked straight to my office.

I called 'Bonus' back immediately.

"It's about time," the man on the other end of the line said.

I laughed. "You told him your name was Bonus?"

Lynn laughed. "Well, you lot seem to like going by funny nicknames, so I decided to give it a whirl to see how I liked it."

I rolled my eyes.

"Lynn," I said, taking a seat in my office chair and punching on the computer. "What the fuck do you want?"

Lynn sighed and leaned back.

"You told me if the name 'Shovel' ever came back online again, I was to let you know immediately. So here's your call letting you know immediately," Lynn said dryly.

The breath in my lungs froze, and my eyes went far away as I tried not to vomit at hearing that name again.

"Tell me everything."

CHAPTER 2

If the trailer's a-rockin', don't come a-knockin'.
-Bumper Sticker

Sawyer

Officer Donner's hands ran longingly over my hair, and I squeezed my eyes shut and I prayed.

I'd made it eight years without being raped.

Please don't let it happen in the last twenty minutes I'm here.

A fight broke out in the yard, and the sirens started to wail as the security personnel started to swarm the area.

"Don't worry, darlin'. Maybe we can meet up on the outside, make this real," Officer Donner whispered.

I wanted to puke.

"See you soon, sweets," he said as a parting gift, then left me to finish packing my few belongings.

"You're welcome, bitch," my cell-mate, and second best friend in the world, said to me.

Ruthie, Ruthann Comalsky, had been my cell-mate since I'd entered the wonderful world of Hunstville Women's Correctional Facility eight years ago.

She'd had my back when guards tried to rape me the first day I was there.

And I had hers when they tried to do it to her later that night in retaliation for helping me.

Ruthie was in jail because her husband had tried to beat her to death, and instead of taking it lying down, she'd shot him while he was peeing during one of his breaks from hitting her.

Something that almost anyone would've done.

Ruthie was thirty-one to my twenty-nine, and she had four months left on her nine-year sentence.

And I felt horrible leaving her alone.

"Ruthie," I said softly. "I'm so sorry."

Ruthie's face melted as she took me in.

"It's going to be okay, Sawyer. I promise. You'll see," she whispered.

I should've known when those words came out of her mouth, that they would only bring bad luck.

Those words gave me hope when I damn well knew I shouldn't have had any.

"Get out of here already. They called for you over an hour ago," she urged quickly.

I put one last thing in my trash bag and walked up to the one thing that had saved me these last eight years. The one woman I owed my life to, over and over again.

"I love you, Ruthie," I whispered to her. "I'll be waiting the day you get out."

She hugged me tight.

"I'll look forward to it. We'll go for burgers and a beer. Okay?" She asked hopefully.

I nodded weakly.

She grinned, and I let her go.

She tossed me my bag, and I walked out behind the guard that'd be walking me to the front gates.

I felt lost.

Really lost.

I had no clue what I'd do once I got out.

I knew my mom was willing to take me home… but I didn't have a home.

Not anymore.

I was staying at a halfway house in town, much to my parent's annoyance.

But I just didn't think they needed to hear me at night when I woke up from my nightmares.

The scenes that played out in my mind, over and over as if in a loop, night after night.

Although, now, they weren't all the same horrid one of the night I crashed into that Bronco.

Now there were new ones… more vivid ones that didn't have eight years on top of the memories.

"Hurry up, girl," the guard at my side said. "They're about to come in from the yard, and I don't want to be caught with my pants down."

I checked the eye roll.

Apparently, I was the 'pants down' portion of his problem.

Then he'd have to protect me since I was technically no longer a ward of this prison.

I hurried anyway, though.

I had a date with Isaac. And I couldn't wait to see him.

I was blessed to have him.

He'd been there for me through thick and thin.

As had Bristol.

They were two of the best friends ever.

We arrived at the final door that would lead me to the final hallway that led outside, and I swear my heart was about to beat out of my chest.

Not necessarily from happiness, though.

From fear.

I'd spent eight long years on the inside, and I wasn't sure I would ever be the same.

I'd always be registered as a criminal.

Finding a job would be hard.

Really hard.

I already knew my nursing career was gone.

You couldn't be an ex-con and be a nurse. You had to have a clean record.

Fuck, but I'd had an extensive background check to even get into the program in the first place.

Now, the entire year and a half I'd spent on my bachelors of nursing degree was useless.

As were many medical field jobs that might be willing to take my college credits.

"Sign here," the guard behind the glass window ordered, shoving a paper in my direction and a bag of my belongings.

There wasn't much there.

An old cell phone that was so outdated that I'd never be able to turn it on again, let alone use it.

A key to my old dorm… something else I didn't need anymore.

A wallet with my driver's license in it.

My expired driver's license.

And a watch.

That was it.

The extent of the belongings I had arrived here with.

"Here's all the Certificates of your Release for timed served. Here's your post bail money, as well as a bus ticket," the guard muttered.

I smiled. "I won't need the bus ticket, I have someone meeting me."

I hadn't told my mom the exact day I was getting out.

I wanted to get changed out of these horrid clothes first.

They were mine, but they fit my twenty-two year old self. Not my twenty-nine year old self. They were too tight, and I was fairly sure that if I bent over, the button on the front of my pants would burst off and shatter the glass in front of me.

He shrugged and threw the ticket down onto the table beside him.

"Thanks," I muttered, putting the watch on.

It felt weird.

Like really weird.

I hadn't worn jewelry in well over eight years.

Belly flipping summersaults, I walked out the door of the long hallway and stepped into the sunshine.

To find nobody there.

It was just that, the end of the road.

I looked to my left, noting the huge red fence that marked my captivity for the last eight years.

Then to my front to see the very empty parking lot.

Then to my right, seeing more of that same red brick.

I didn't dare go back in and ask for that bus ticket.

It'd be like admitting defeat. And I wasn't a fucking quitter.

Far from it, actually.

With no other recourse, I started to walk.

The duffel bag I had in my arms was heavier than hell.

It held fifteen books, two pairs of clothes and photos.

My whole entire life was packed into that one single bag.

As I got to the main road, I turned left, noting the buildings off in the distance.

That would be the way to go then. The other way only had trees.

About a mile and a half into my walk, I lost my books, dumping them into the first trashcan I came to right at the edge of town.

Even though it killed me to do it, I walked away and didn't look back.

The first restaurant that I came to was a Whataburger, and I immediately turned into the parking lot and walked inside and straight up to the counter.

"Can I help you?" The woman behind the register asked.

I nodded, and bit my lip as I looked over the menu boards above her head.

"Umm, I want a number one with cheese and ketchup only, please. Large fries and a Coke," I said softly.

The woman blinked, looking me up and down, and I just knew she was thinking 'how are you going to fit all of that into your tiny body?'

Luckily, she didn't say it aloud. Instead, she handed me a number on a little orange triangle.

"Have a seat, we'll bring it out to you shortly," she said, smiling.

I wondered if she knew I was coming directly from the prison?

Did the duffle bag give me away?

It was fairly simple. Just a black canvas bag with a black zipper.

I could be anyone, I decided.

"Thank you," I said softly.

She nodded and handed me a cup that was the size of my head.

I blinked, taking the cup.

Holy shit! The cup was freakin' *massive*.

Shrugging my shoulders, I walked over to the drink fountain and stared at it.

"It's new," a little girl, probably about twelve, said.

She was wearing pink capri pants and a pink flowered shirt.

I watched her as she filled her cup up with ice, then started punching buttons on the screen.

"You can put whatever you want into it. It's pretty stinkin' cool, if you ask me," she chattered as she filled her drink up with at least seven different flavored drinks.

A suicide.

I hadn't had one of those in years.

So what did I do?

I followed suit, filling up my massive head-sized cup with grape flavored soda, Dr. Pepper, and a cherry vanilla Coca-Cola.

"That's gross," I heard said from behind me.

At first I didn't comprehend what I was hearing, but it didn't take long for my brain to come back on line.

"Bristol," I said breathlessly. "You came."

She smiled. "I did. I was late, I'm so sorry. I meant to get there earlier, but my kids had a meltdown this morning before I left, and it made me late. I got to the parking lot I was supposed to be picking you up in, and the guard at the gate pointed in this direction to where she saw you walk. It's only understandable that you'd want something to eat."

A tear slipped from my eye as I placed my drink and bag on the closest table, and then I walked right into my best friend's arms for the first time in eight years.

She smelled like strawberries.

She always had.

She loved strawberries.

And I'd forgotten.

Bristol had visited with me hundreds of times in the last eight years, but I'd never hugged her.

We weren't allowed to touch.

For the visitor's safety, I sneered.

"I'm so glad you're out, honey," Bristol whispered roughly, her throat clogging with tears as she did.

I nodded. "Not that I'm not happy that you're here," I said, pulling away from her when my food arrived. "But what are you doing here? I thought Isaac was picking me up. At least that's what his last letter said."

Bristol looked down at her hands.

"Isaac," she hesitated. "Isaac has a lot of stuff to explain."

I blinked.

"What do you mean?" I asked as we both took our seats. "Is he having trouble at work again?"

Isaac worked with his father. His father owned an oil business that allowed him the free reign to be the big boss, living large on the money his men made for him.

His son was also privileged that way as well.

Not that Isaac saw it that way. He didn't like that his daddy was the boss of him. He wanted to be his own boss.

The problem was that his father dominated the market in our small community.

Anybody who was anybody knew who Doral Roans was.

Nobody would cross Doral for Isaac. He wasn't worth it.

Something I'd been trying to tell Isaac for years. No one was going to leave Doral and start doing business with him just because he's a nice guy. Doral had been the dominant supplier in this market for years. Not to mention that he was not a nice man, and he was definitely not a man you'd stop doing business with to do it with his son instead.

"Jesus," Bristol said, distracting me. "Do you want me to go get you another burger?"

I moaned at the way the juicy morsels filled my mouth with heaven.

And the fries.

Oh, my God, the fries.

They were divine.

"No," I said, washing the fries down with a suck on my Suicide. "I'm probably not going to eat all of this."

Bristol stayed uncharacteristically silent as I polished off my hamburger, only making the odd comment about people that walked through the door.

"We'll have to go find you some clothes," Bristol said, surprising me.

"I don't have any money to buy clothes," I informed her bluntly.

She blinked. "I have money."

I shook my head. "You're not buying me clothes. I'll just get the ones from my mom's house. It'll be okay."

She looked at the shirt that I was wearing and raised her brows.

"And will they all fit you like that?" She asked teasingly.

I looked down at the baby doll T-shirt that was something closer to a half shirt rather than a shirt, and shrugged. "It'll work out. I'll sew some new ones when I get home."

She shrugged.

"We have an apartment over the garage that I want you to stay in," she said softly, looking at me with sincere eyes.

I shook my head before the words had even finished coming out of her mouth.

"Why not?" She asked, crossing her arms across her chest and sitting back into her chair.

"You have nothing to make up for, Bristol," I said honestly.

She closed her eyes. "If it wasn't for me, you wouldn't have gone to that party in the first place."

I shook my head, a small smile tipping up my lips.

"No, but you would've called me to bring you home, and I would've come. And the same outcome might've been possible," I answered her.

She closed her eyes.

"I want you to stay. Dallas wants you to stay. Please, stay," she whispered.

Dallas was my younger brother, by exactly thirteen minutes.

He and Bristol had gotten close once I'd been taken away.

Bristol lost her best friend, and Dallas lost the sister that he told everything to.

It was inevitable that they'd find solace in each other's arms.

I looked into her sincere eyes and felt myself caving.

"You'll let me pay rent?" I confirmed.

A muscle ticked below her right eye.

"Yeah," she said very begrudgingly.

"And you'll let me babysit for you whenever I want?" I asked her.

She laughed.

The sound was sweet.

And I loved it.

"Of course, anytime you want."

I smiled. "Good. Now, how about you tell me what it is that you've been avoiding telling me."

She looked down at the piece of paper that had lined my straw, she picked it up and started to pick it apart into tiny little pieces.

"Isaac," she started, then stopped again.

My brows rose.

"Isaac," I encouraged her.

She dropped the paper onto the tray and reached for my hands.

"Isaac is engaged to someone else. He got one of his secretaries at work pregnant, and he's marrying her next weekend," she said in a rush.

I blinked.

"You're…he's…*what*?" I asked, flabbergasted.

She nodded.

"Yeah, you heard me right," she confirmed.

I looked down at the cheese that'd fallen from my burger earlier and cringed.

"Wow," I said unsurprisingly. "I always thought he'd give up on me… just, not for it to happen the day I got out of prison."

Bristol licked her lips, and I knew she had more to say.

She just didn't want to hurt me anymore.

"What is it?" I asked softly.

She took a deep breath, and then gave me the full force of her brown eyes.

"He's been doing it since the beginning… I just didn't want to tell you when you had enough things to worry about," she admitted.

I froze, but Bristol continued to speak.

"I've debated telling you for years now… it's just… how do you tell your best friend that the man she thinks she's going to marry is actually with someone else? You've given me your life, and I owe you everything. If it weren't for you, I wouldn't have my family right now. And it breaks my heart that you had to have something so god awful happen to you for me to accomplish my dreams," Bristol cried softly.

I grabbed her hand. "Bristol, I've already told you a million times that it wasn't your fault. How many times do I have to do that before you understand? What happened that night… that was all me. Every bit of it. I hit that person. Those *people*. I chose to drink. I chose to go to that party with you. Everything is my fault, not yours. I love you, but you need to give it a rest. Let your heart heal."

She looked at me with tears in her eyes.

"And when will you heal?" She asked forcefully.

I shook my head.

There would be no healing for me.

There would just be existing.

And that's all that there would ever be.

Existing, alone.

CHAPTER 3

I hate when people accuse me of lolly-gagging when I'm quite obviously dilly-dallying.
-Coffee Cup

Sawyer

"I don't have much experience with anything office related," I told the receptionist at the vet's office where I was applying. "I'm good with dogs, though."

The woman smiled. "Well, that's definitely a plus!"

I smiled back.

The woman's smile was infectious.

Her name was Joanie, and she reminded me a lot of my mom.

"Joanie, I'll need you to input this into the computer and order some meds for Diesel so Mr. Coby can take him home," called an older man with a smile on his face.

I watched him walk into the little counter area and hand Joanie a piece of paper before turning to look at me.

He offered me his hand.

"Zack Deguzman," he introduced himself, offering me his hand.

"Sawyer Berry. It's nice to meet you. I've heard a lot about you," I shook his hand.

"Are you kin to Dallas Berry?" He asked.

I froze for a second. If I said that I was related to Dallas, he would know exactly who I was, but how else could I explain how I'd heard about him?

There was no guarantee that he wouldn't judge me like others had.

"I'm…" I hesitated, looking for a good way to phrase it. "Yes. I'm Sawyer Berry. Dallas's sister."

I could tell the minute he realized just who I was.

I saw the surprise in his eyes, followed by the pity.

What I didn't see, though, was disgust.

Something I saw on quite a few people's faces when they realized who I was and then remembered just who it was that I'd killed.

"Ah," he said, nodding his head. "I understand. Come, walk with me to the exam room so I can see one of my favorite patients."

I blinked in surprise.

"Really?" I asked.

Now that he knew, he didn't act any differently, and I was really surprised.

Most people acted differently, almost as if I had an infectious disease after being released from prison.

I hurried behind Dr. Deguzman, who was walking rather quickly.

"Gosh, Dr. Deguzman, you have long legs," I panted as we arrived at the room in the very back of the office.

His eyes sparkled as he turned to look over his shoulder at me.

"Call me Zack. And get ready for some fun," he said, opening the door slowly.

The moment it was open wide enough, a wiggly little body slipped out, darting like a brown missile straight towards me.

I dropped down onto my knees and picked the little cutie up before he could scurry any further past.

"Gotcha," I cooed, bringing the wiggling, wagging, excited little dog up to my face and giving him a kiss. "Aren't you just the cutest thing I've ever seen?"

"That's my dog," a cute, little voice said softly.

I looked up into a beautiful pair of green eyes and smiled.

"This is your puppy?" I asked. "What's his name?"

"He's actually a she. And her name is Lou," she said, crossing her hands across her little chest and glaring at me.

"A girl named Lou," I nodded. "Got it."

I handed the dog back to her, and she wrapped her thin arms around its wiggling body and started to struggle back into the room that Zack had closed once he'd realized I had caught the little bundle of energy who had managed to escape.

I opened the door for her and bent down to stop any more wayward escapees. I could hear the fun they were having beyond the door, and, sure enough, I managed to catch two more as they tried to dart out.

"Here you go, daddy," the little girl with the beautiful blonde hair said to the most beautiful man I'd ever seen in my life.

He was literally captivating.

And very obviously taken if the gold wedding band on his hand, as well as the three kids at his feet, were anything to go by.

"Thanks, baby," the man said, gesturing to the floor where he wanted her to put the dog.

Dr. Deguzman… Zack… was on the floor running his fingers along the scruff of the puppy at his feet. A little black dog that was just a smidge smaller than all the others.

The mother of the dogs, a gorgeous German Shepherd that reminded me of the very thing everyone thought about when they hear 'German Shepherd,' was on the floor in the corner of the room, watching the comings and goings with sharp eyes.

"That's Tequila," the man said.

I blinked and looked up at him. "What?"

"The dog. Her name is Tequila," he rumbled again, clarifying his earlier information.

I swallowed thickly, so caught up in the two different colors of his eyes that I kind of forgot to breathe.

I nodded in understanding. "Gotcha."

His eyes studied me closely, watching me while I interacted with the dogs.

I tried my hardest to ignore it.

Out of my peripheral vision, though, I took him in.

He was wearing what most bikers would wear, since that was what he ultimately was.

Or, at least, that's what I figured him for from the biker's vest he was wearing.

I vaguely remembered a biker gang being here the few times that I'd come to Benton, Louisiana with my parents, but I didn't remember them looking like *that*.

"Well, they all look fairly healthy, Trance. I don't see a thing wrong with them. I also think they can be weaned from their mother now, too. That means your training can start as soon as you want to. They're perfect," Zack informed Trance.

"Shit," Trance said, sighing and rubbing his face with his hands.

"Daddy sad," the boy said.

The boy looked a lot like his father with his blue eyes and curly blonde hair, and you could definitely tell they were father and son.

The littlest, though, was all of two year's old at most.

He didn't look like his father.

My best guess was that he looked like his mom.

Because he was the only one with curly black hair and pale skin. He resembled a porcelain doll, and he was currently looking me in the eyes, his the most brilliant green that I'd ever seen, and my heart stuttered in my chest.

"Daddy sad?" He asked me.

He touched my cheek, then leaned forward and threw his arms around my neck.

Stunned momentarily, I had to wait a few seconds for my heart to stop breaking.

If I had a kid, I would have wanted him to be just like this child.

But that wouldn't be happening for me, and I'd decided to let it go.

"I don't know why your daddy's sad, baby. Maybe you should ask him that when you're alone," I told him gently.

He squeezed me tighter, pulled back, and gave me a toothy grin that consisted of large amounts of drool.

"Cookie?"

I smiled and shook my head. "No, I don't have any cookies."

"Daddy has cookies in the car," the little girl reprimanded the boy gently. "And he told you not to talk to strangers."

I decided not to point out that she'd done the same thing only moments before with the dog. Instead, I chose to stay silent as I stood and put some distance between me and all that cuteness.

The kids… not the man.

Not that he wasn't hot as hell, either.

He just wasn't my type.

Not that I had a type anymore.

I'd been thinking that Isaac was my type all these years… yet, here I was, single with no desire for *any* type.

"Good," the biker man said. "I can't wait to share that news with Viddy. She'll cry."

Zack snorted. "Your wife will have to let them go eventually. Aren't you going to start training them for the police officers in Shreveport and Bossier? Seems you can't do that if you don't start giving them a little leash to run on."

The man sighed.

"When our old dog, Radar, died… she never got over it. She still cries when she sees pictures of him, and she's devastated that he'll never get to know his grandbabies," the man said softly.

"Well, Trance, I really would like to see these boys getting out for a little social attention. I'd love you to bring them to the puppy party this weekend. It'll be good for them. If you end up deciding you'll come, just give us a call the day before, so we can have enough food for all of them," he said, standing up and offering his hand.

Trance took it and shook Zack's back once before dropping it and saying, "Alright, guys, let's start hauling 'em out to the truck."

One of the seven dogs was dropped unceremoniously into my arms, and I smiled at the little runt that Zack had been cooing over earlier.

"I like this one the best," I said to no one in particular.

"He's for sale if you want him," Trance mumbled as we all walked out the door.

"What? Why?" I asked.

Hadn't I just heard that he was going to train them to be police dogs?

"He's the runt and the sickly one. We won't be training him to be a K-9 officer. The other six will be. They have that drive. That one just likes to lay there and sun himself all day. Not saying that's not a good thing, but it's not a trait that makes a good K-9 officer," Trance explained.

I blinked. "Really? So, how much for a lazy dog that likes to sun himself?"

"You can have him for nine hundred dollars," Trance said as he started loading them up into the back of the truck.

I handed the one in my arms over reluctantly.

There was no way in hell I could afford nine hundred dollars.

"Ah," I said as Trance took him without looking at my face. "I can't do that right now. Plus, I'm not sure my brother'll want another dog at his house."

He nodded. "If you change your mind, Zack has my number."

The kids were the next thing he loaded into his big 'ol truck before he backed out of the vet's office with me watching them leave.

That man had everything that I wanted out of life.

And it sucked that I'd never have what he had.

***

"Well, I'd love for you to take the job, Sawyer. It's completely up to you, but I think you would really fit in well with our team," Zack said as we walked out later that night.

I smiled.

"Thank you, Zack. I look forward to spending more time here and helping any way I can," I said honestly.

He smiled.

"Why didn't you say anything to Trance about training dogs?" He asked as he walked with his hands in his pockets. "I'm sure he could use the help."

I grimaced. I had explained to the vet that I had trained dogs, but not that I was in prison while I did. I loved that part of my life, but I'd still been incarcerated while I'd done it, and it wasn't something that I was comfortable talking about. At least not yet.

"Because it would've gone into why I know how to help train dogs," I answered. "And then he would've looked at me differently."

Zack snorted.

"He knew who you were without you telling him. He's a cop and a member of The Dixie Wardens MC. I hate to break it to you, honey, but everyone knows who you are. You haven't changed much in the last eight years. As soon as you said you were related to Dallas, I knew exactly who you were. But I'm old. Others that have a sharper brain will figure it out instantly. I think it's time to give yourself a little break. Maybe they won't have a problem with it like you think they will," Zack said, coming to a stop beside his Ford truck.

I'd admired it as soon as I pulled into the parking lot.

It made sense that the most expensive vehicle there belonged to the one that got paid the most.

I looked over at my bike that was leaning against the side of the building we'd just come to a stop next to and sighed.

"What time would you like me to be here?" I asked softly, avoiding the subject of me telling people who I was and what I'd done, completely.

"Eight sharp, Ms. Berry. I have a couple foals to go check on in the morning, and I think I'd like you along to help me," he answered immediately.

I gave him a thumb's up and started walking to my bike.

I'd had a car a long time ago, but when I'd had to get a lawyer… the car had to be sold to pay for lawyer fees.

Now I had to save up some money again to pay for a new one.

At one time, I had money saved, but my entire life savings had been sunk into our lawyer.

I was literally starting from scratch.

"Be careful, Ms. Berry," Zack called as I started pedaling out of the parking lot.

At least the exercise would be good for me.

I wasn't 'fat.'

Far from it, but I also wasn't 'in shape' either.

Well… roundish was a shape…just not the shape I wanted.

I'd nearly pedaled all the way to the county line when I saw the first biker pass me.

Then a second. And a third.

Until I'd been passed by at least ten of them.

I blinked as they kept pace with me as I rode down an impressively steep hill.

I'd had to walk up it this morning, pushing the bike. It was too steep for my out-of-shape legs.

One biker, though, caught my eye above all the others.

He was older than the rest.

He had on blue jeans that were so faded that I was sure they'd be as soft as silk.

He wore a red t-shirt under the same black biker vest that the man at the vet today, Trance, had been wearing.

His helmet only covered the very top of his head, and I wondered what the point of wearing it was when it only covered half of it. Was the bottom half unimportant?

Then I thought about the fact that I wasn't wearing one at all, and I was going just as fast as they were, and snickered to myself, turning my attention back to the road in front of me.

I felt the vibrations from the motors in my teeth as they slowed even further, letting me pass, before they all turned into a parking lot.

The building was pretty new.

The outside of it was incredible.

The exterior of the building was made of a shiny tin, made rustic looking with wood framing the entire thing. Huge glass windows. Large wooden door.

It was then that the sign caught my attention. *Halligans and Handcuffs.*

Nice.

I'd heard about the place from Dallas.

He'd written about the impact that this place had had on the city of Benton.

How it'd turned into a local hangout for not just cops and firemen, but the entire community.

I turned my head back around and kept on pedaling.

Then I started to hold my breath.

Because I was coming up on the spot where *it* happened.

The exact spot where my whole life had changed.

The spot where I'd taken the lives of four people.

I willed myself not to stop, to keep going, but my feet and hands wouldn't listen.

My hands pulled the brake, and my feet stopped pedaling.

I came to a stop on the road where there was still, to this very day, flowers and four crosses.

And I started to cry.

I couldn't help it.

My God, I'd taken four lives!

Me!

I was a horrible, no good, very bad person and not a single day went by that I didn't wish it was me that'd died that day instead of them.

If I could go back to that moment in time, I would've prayed for God to take me instead.

I would've done anything to change places with them.

Pleaded.

Gotten down on my knees and begged.

Not because I didn't want to spend my life in prison, paying for my crimes.

But because those four people didn't deserve to die.

Mr. and Mrs. Neesen had been educators.

They'd been making a difference in children's lives.

Their daughter and her boyfriend had futures so bright ahead of them that even my previous dream of a nursing career didn't compare.

I hadn't realized that I'd dropped to my knees until I heard a motorcycle again.

I didn't look up.

Hoping that, if I didn't move, nobody would notice me.

I should've known it was a stupid wish.

Especially when I looked up to see the bike stopping not even five feet from me.

It was the older biker.

The one I couldn't stop looking at earlier.

And, Sweet Baby Jesus, was he ever hot.

He certainly didn't look 'old.'

He looked…sexy. Distinguished. Mature. And very, very male.

The only reason I could really tell that he was 'older', as I was calling it, was because of his hair.

It was salt and pepper.

A silver fox, I thought to myself.

Even his beard.

"You okay?" The man rumbled.

Oh God, his voice was sexy.

Deep.

Alluring.

"Yeah," I sniffled, wiping my eyes with the backs of my hands. "I'm fine."

He nodded. "Did you fall?"

I looked down at my bike, realizing that he thought I'd crashed or something with the way I was crying and on my knees, my bike at an awkward angle from where it'd fallen.

"No. I didn't fall," I said, looking down at my hands. "I'm okay."

That 'I'm okay' was more for my benefit than his.

I needed to get up.

To get away from here before I went into one of *those* moods again.

The type that sucked me in and wouldn't let me go until morning.

I could feel the panic rising. Could feel the tears pouring down my cheeks.

But I couldn't stop them.

I didn't know how.

And then I said something stupid.

"I killed them," I whispered brokenly.

CHAPTER 4

Hold on to me. Never let me go. If you do, I can't promise I'll be there when you come back.
-Sawyer to Silas

Silas

"I know," I told her.

She clenched her eyes shut, and the apples of her cheeks, the only part of her face that had any color left in it, paled.

"I never meant to," she whispered. "I wish it would've been me."

My gut clenched.

This was most certainly not how I wanted to meet Reba's daughter.

I'd hoped it'd be under different circumstances.

Maybe while she was visiting her parent's house.

Or maybe while at the grocery store.

I didn't do tears.

Tears did things to a man.

Made him feel sorry for things he couldn't control.

Made him do and say things that he never would've said had there not been tears.

"Life doesn't work like that," I told her, wishing it did, in fact, work like that.

I would know.

I could recall five such instances that I could offer myself instead of another person being taken from me. And it never got any easier.

"I know. I know. I can't stop myself from thinking it, though. It's like a burn in my gut, and a bullet to my brain. It never stops," she whispered, leaning forward so her hands were crossed tightly around her stomach.

No, it didn't.

"You want a ride?" I asked.

She finally gave me her eyes, and I felt the shock all the way through me.

It pierced my brain, traveling to the tips of my fingers and toes.

Her hair was down.

Long, curly, black, and down to her ass.

It was beautiful.

But what made her absolutely stunning were her eyes.

A deep shade of blue, nearly indigo.

Her eyes were captivating, and I found myself extremely disappointed when she looked away and went back to staring at the cross.

The cross that was changed with the seasons like clockwork.

New flowers were put on the spot once a month by lord only knows who, and it bothered me at times.

The town wasn't letting it go.

And I feared that this meant bad things for Sawyer.

Especially when it came to making friends, once again

"No, I don't want a ride," she said, startling me.

"How far do you have to go?" I persisted.

She pointed in the direction.

"That's helpful."

She shrugged, uncaring.

Then, without another word, she got up, mounted her bike and rode away.

She looked back three times before she was too far away for me to see her, and I cursed as I looked over at the cross one last time before I started the bike up with a roar.

I was meeting Lynn to talk to him about the possibility that Shovel could be near the town.

My town.

A town that I told him, under no circumstance, was he ever allowed to show up in again.

He'd been in jail now for over twenty years and had been released just two days ago, according to Lynn.

When I'd first gotten into The Dixie Wardens, Shovel had been the vice president of The Dixie Wardens MC.

He'd been the president's right hand man, and the one man that was steadily pushing more and more drugs through the small town of Benton until it drew the attention of the CIA as well as ATF.

The CIA wanted an inside man, and I'd been put into place as a prospect. I worked for an entire year to get into that club, and I had to endure torture upon torture in the process.

And I fuckin' hated every single minute of it.

Mainly because of the man named Shovel and the fact that he thought giving drugs to kids was an okay thing to do.

Not to mention he was the one to push all the other illegal activities.

Which meant *I* had to do illegal things.

I followed the girl at a safe distance until she was nearly on the road to a nicer subdivision on the outskirts of town.

When she was safely within the confines of said subdivision, I pulled over, shut the bike off once more and pulled out my phone.

"Yeah?" A male voice answered.

"Dixie," I said. "Is Berry there?"

Dallas Berry was Sawyer's brother, and I had a feeling that he'd want to know what had just transpired.

"Yeah, him and Kettle are sitting right here," Dixie said, the music from the bar thumping loudly across the line.

"Tell him his sister needs him. She's at his house."

"Got it."

The phone clicked, signaling the end of the conversation, and I shoved the phone back into my pocket before I started the bike back up.

With one last look into the subdivision where she'd disappeared, I put all thoughts of Sawyer Berry, her captivating blue eyes and her beautiful black hair out of my mind.

Instead, focusing on what was to come.

***

Three hours later I wasn't in any better of a mood.

In fact, it was worse.

"What do you mean that's all you can tell me? So he got out of prison, walked down the street, got on a bus, and you haven't seen him since? What about his parole officer?" I questioned him, pinching the bridge of my nose.

Lynn shrugged.

"Hasn't seen him either. Neither has his doctor," Lynn confirmed.

"Fuck!" I yelled, bringing the attention of the bartender to me.

I'd ridden two hours to get to this little hole in the wall bar, and then spent another hour waiting on this fucker to get here. This was really pissing me off.

He'd just shown, and in no uncertain terms, had said that he had no clue where Shovel was.

Nor did he think he could spare any resources on finding him.

"How about this," I said, leaning back in my chair. "You tell that boss of yours that he'll help me, or he'll fuckin' regret it? Do I make myself clear?"

This would've never happened with the old director.

The new one felt he was too good to help out old colleagues.

Even if I wasn't technically a colleague of his anymore, it didn't mean that I didn't do the odd job here and there.

It also didn't mean that I didn't still know some people.

Or that I couldn't get to the fucker.

"He's not going to like that," Lynn cautioned.

I shrugged. "I don't really give a fuck. I can find Shovel myself, of course, but old Crotch Rot isn't going to like it."

Lynn rolled his eyes. "Crotch Rot? You're still calling him that?"

I nodded.

Crotch Rot was really Crotchet. And he didn't much like being called Crotch Rot. Which was why I did it.

Crotchet didn't like me, and I made no bones about not liking him either.

He was a selfish prick who only looked out for himself and his own advancement in the company, rather than the men under his wing.

"Just tell him," I sighed, standing up and paying my bill.

The bartender nodded his thanks for the tip, and Lynn walked with me out to my bike.

I scanned the parking lot, as I did automatically every time I entered a different environment, and straddled my bike.

"I'll tell him, Silas. But you're going to have to be careful. He's not a dick. He won't care what you did to get where you're at. He sees it as you being over entitled. Something he's been spouting off for months," Lynn offered.

I smiled.

I'd been offered Crotchet's position more than once. Had I wanted it, I could just go take it from him. And maybe he needed to know just what he was dealing with.

"Fine," I said, smiling lightly. "I'll talk to Rosenthal."

Lynn blinked.

Slowly.

"You'll… you'll what?" he stuttered.

I nodded, firm in that decision. I had been considering going over his head.

Maybe I should just go over right now.

Maybe that was the way to take care of this… to nip this thing in the ass before it got to where I could see it going if it got out of hand.

"Yeah, I think I'll do that. Don't worry about telling Crotchet a thing."

CHAPTER 5

Some days are harder than others. But those other days I usually drown myself in wine, so I'm not quite sure if they're actually easier or if I'm drunk.
- Fact of Life

Sawyer

"You can't take a baby into a bar," I said in mock outrage as Bristol pulled into a parking spot directly in front of Halligans and Handcuffs. I was referencing one of my favorite movies – *Sweet Home Alabama.*

"It's not only a bar... and besides, it's one o'clock in the afternoon," Bristol said as she got out.

Since Bristol and Dallas' youngest was on my side, I got the car seat and carried her inside, *warily.*

"Whatever you say... I won't be the one going down for child endangerment," I muttered under my breath.

By the time I made it to the front door, Bristol was there holding the door open for me.

I winced when the car seat dug slightly into my arm, and I handed the baby off to her mother.

The baby was probably all of eighteen pounds, but that was enough to make her feel like a million in the car seat.

Bristol took the seat and slung it into the crook of her arm like it was second nature... which it probably was seeing as this was her second child.

Their other baby, Latham, was at pre-school until three this afternoon.

Latham didn't even know me, and I was his aunt.

I shut down that thought before it could morph into anything worse.

I studiously avoided looking at the cross on the way to and from work today.

It'd been only a half-day today since Zack had Friday afternoons off, and I was grateful.

Riding my bike back and forth to work, as well as putting in a whole eight hour shift, was tiring.

And it was more than I'd done in ten years; it was going to take some getting used to.

"Just two?" A man asked.

I looked up to find the man behind the bar, a man that had a long white beard down to his chest, and a pot-belly to rival a sumo wrestler, staring at us.

"Two and a baby. A booth will be fine," Bristol said, holding up the arm that was holding the car seat.

The man nodded to a booth towards the middle of the room, and I grinned.

I loved how they incorporated all the firefighter and police memorabilia.

It was tastefully done, not ostentatious like it could've been.

"This place is nice," I said, sitting down across from where Bristol sat Danni's car seat.

Bristol took her own seat, and we both looked the menu.

It was the, "What can I get for you ladies?" That had me looking up.

It was the man.

The same one from the other day that'd stopped to make sure I was okay.

The older one.

I licked my lips.

"Dr. Pepper," I said roughly.

My voice sounded scratchy, as if I'd been gargling Jack Daniel's and chain smoking.

The old man smiled, and I was taken by his appearance once again.

I'd never seen an older man as hot as him.

He was just as fit as any other man in the room, if not even more so.

"I want a water with lemon," Bristol said, smiling at the man.

I felt an irrational surge of jealousy when the man turned his attention to her. "You got it, babe."

Bristol smiled as the man turned and left, and I was left wondering how well they knew each other.

"You know him?" I asked softly.

Bristol nodded.

"Everyone knows him. He's the owner," she whispered back.

My eyes widened. "Really? How old is he?"

She shrugged. "We always get mixed numbers. His son, who I'm sure you'll see around, says he's in his fifties. But the man doesn't look a day over forty. He's seriously beautiful, and I can only hope that Dallas ages that well."

"His hair looks like that man's on the commercial… you know the one for 'Touch of Gray?' The one that you said looked fake?" I whispered back.

She nodded. "He shaved off his long beard a few months ago. He looked a little bit older then. Now he looks like a fuckin' cover model for Harley Davidson. They could seriously use him on all their ads and women would go buy Harleys just in hopes that their husbands might look that cool."

I rolled my eyes.

"He looks good now, though. I like his beard that size."

His beard was trimmed close to his face and outlined his jaw, upper lip, and midway up his cheeks perfectly.

It was the type that would feel great against the inside of your thighs… you know…if I had to guess.

I'd only had one lover in my lifetime, and that was when I was seventeen.

And he was as baby faced as they came.

It was incredibly disheartening and had been the only experience I would have… probably ever.

Which was the saddest part.

"What are you getting to eat?" She asked.

I looked down at my menu, noticing that they didn't have anything that wasn't fried.

My mouth watered at the plethora of foods.

"Chicken fried steak, fried okra, French fries, and fried pickles."

Silence.

I looked up to see Bristol staring at me with wide eyes.

"You're going to give yourself a heart attack," she mumbled, going back to her menu.

I shrugged.

"Maybe."

What did it matter?

I had no life.

And my family had already proved that they could live without me.

There was nothing keeping me here.

"She doesn't look much different," the whispered voice had me tensing.

I didn't look up from my menu as I listened to the two ladies across the aisle from me discussing me.

"Do you think she had to become a dominant in prison to get her jollies off?" Another voice whispered.

"No. She's too small. She's probably the one that was on the bottom. Isn't prison a good way to get AIDS and stuff like that?" The other one countered.

My eyes closed and my cheeks flushed with embarrassment.

Yes, it was a good way to get AIDS.

AIDS was high in the male population.

It wasn't as easy for women to spread it to other women.

That wasn't to say that women didn't do things to each other in prison.

Women got just as desperate as men.

I didn't, though.

I was too busy hiding from guards to worry about the other prisoners. Thank God for Ruthie, or I'd be just another person on a list of women that the guards tried to, *and did*, hurt.

And the other prisoners liked it that way.

More attention on another inmate meant less on them.

Ruthie and I had been the 'beautiful ones' according to the other inmates.

We'd had to become quick, smart and imaginative to protect ourselves against the guards.

I'd like to say they were all perfect gentlemen, but they weren't.

Far from it.

"I'll bet she sold her vagina out to the police officers that worked there to get more privileges," the nasty woman continued.

I was done.

I scooted out of my seat and started to run.

I didn't realize I was running away from the bathroom, not toward it, until I came to a hallway that led nowhere.

Fuck!

It came to a line of doors off the back hallway.

One was marked as a supply closet.

Another as an office.

The last was unmarked.

Then there was the emergency exit.

Although I didn't push out of it since it said that an alarm sounded when the door was opened.

Tears welling up my throat, I went to the very end of the darkened hallway and turned my back to the wall before sinking down to my butt, using the wall at my back as leverage so as not to fall over.

Wrapping my hands around my knees, I buried my face into my legs and tried to will myself not to cry.

But it didn't work.

Tears soaked through my clenched eyelids and my breath started to come out in pants.

I felt, more than heard him.

He dropped down in front of me and placed both hands on my arms.

"I kicked them out," that deep, sexy voice said to me.

"You didn't have to do that," I mumbled into my knees.

"Yeah, I fuckin' did. I don't want bitches like that in my restaurant. Fuck that," the man said eloquently.

I laughed through my tears, sniffling delicately as I raised my head from my knees.

Jesus, the man was really close to me.

"We should stop meeting like this," I told him, wiping my tears with the back of my sweatshirt.

He grinned, showing off a smile that was brilliant.

The left side tilted up more than the right, making it more of a grin rather than a smile.

But he totally worked it.

"Your friend's concerned," he told me.

I closed my eyes and leaned my head against the wood paneling behind me.

"Yeah, I'm sure she is," I said tiredly.

I was exhausted.

I knew I shouldn't have come out today.

"Come on," he said, picking me up by my elbows.

Easily, I might add.

He didn't even strain.

Then he took both of his hands and wiped my tears off of my face before smoothing them down either side of his thighs.

I blinked.

"Thanks," I said.

He shrugged. "Anytime."

Then, with the man's arm around my shoulders, he led me back into the main part of the restaurant.

And nobody took notice.

Not one single person.

They were all looking down, doing their own thing.

Which was surprising to me.

Normally, when a hysterical woman runs through the restaurant, when she comes back you'd expect them to stare.

But not one single person did.

Bristol smiled sadly at me as I was helped into my seat.

"Food will be out shortly," he mumbled as he walked away.

I watched him go, impressed with how well those jeans fit his ass.

And still, not one single person looked up.

"Holy shit!" Bristol said, leaning forward and capturing my attention from the man who'd just walked around the bar.

I raised my eyebrow in question. "What?"

She blinked.

"You didn't hear him?" She asked in surprise.

I shook my head.

"No, why?" I asked.

She bit her lip and leaned forward.

"He ripped the whole fuckin' bar a new one. Those two ladies that were talking about you ran out of here crying. And he sent one of his men after them to make them pay their bill!" Bristol informed me.

I blinked.

"What'd he say?" I asked.

She smiled.

"That you were a human being, not a 'fuckin' circus sideshow' and that everyone needed to 'leave the girl the fuck alone and let her live her fuckin' life.' It was *awesome!*" She crowed.

That got a few looks, but they all just as quickly turned back to their plates and their own conversations.

"Wow," I finally said.

Bristol nodded. "Silas is infamous. He's like the most badass of all badasses! If you're going to have anyone stick up for you, and it's him, it means you'll have the entire Dixie Warden Motorcycle Club at your back if you ever need it."

I smiled sadly.

That would be awesome… if I were worth having that.

But I wasn't, so I wasn't going to look too much into it.

What was the point?

They didn't know me.

And they didn't need to. I was worthless.

"Here's your food, ladies."

I looked up to see yet another hot guy passing out food.

He didn't look like he should be delivering our food.

He looked like he should be on the cover of a fireman calendar.

"Thanks Kettle," Bristol said, pushing her food in front of her. "You're not usually doing this. Are y'all short today?"

Kettle, was that really his name?

He answered to it, though.

"Yeah, Silas fired one of the men today because he said something he didn't like," Kettle said.

So the man's name was Silas.

I liked it.

Kettle didn't go into details, but for some reason I just knew that the man had been fired for saying something about me.

Fuck.

"Thanks," I said, smiling at my plates that were placed in front of me.

I didn't look at the man, though.

I could feel his eyes on me, studying me, and I knew that I wasn't ready to be inspected so deeply yet.

Tears were still clinging to my lashes, and I just knew that Kettle would see right through me.

Especially if what I guessed was true about him being another member of The Dixie Wardens.

Although he wasn't wearing the vest, but with his a firefighter shirt with blue tactical pants, I just knew he had to be a part of them.

My suspicion was confirmed moments later when he left.

"He's a part of The Dixie Wardens, too?" I asked, popping a piece of fried okra into my mouth.

Bristol nodded as she delicately cut her grilled chicken into tiny, bite-sized pieces.

Awkwardly, I wielded my knife and fork, cutting into the chicken fried steak in front of me with a hacking motion.

See, we didn't have food like this in prison. Which meant I hadn't had to use a knife in eight years.

Knives of any kind, plastic or metal, were not allowed in prisons.

Nor was metal anything.

If it could be used as or turned into a weapon, it wasn't allowed.

Plastic cutlery, mainly sporks, were all we were allowed to use, no matter what we were having.

And, God, was the food awful.

I moaned when I took my first bite of the chicken fried steak.

It tasted like heaven, breaded and fried.

And the gravy was delicious.

Then again, it could've been just above subpar, and I'd still think it was heaven.

Anything was heaven compared to what I had to stomach for eight long years.

It was nothing less than what I deserved, though.

"You suck," Bristol said, eyeing my food with a longing eye.

I offered her a bite.

She shook her head.

"No, I'm trying to get all my baby weight off," she said, gesturing to her stomach.

I rolled my eyes.

"Bristol, you have no baby weight. You have boobs. And you're using those," I informed her.

"Yeah, I like your boobs. Let's just forget about losing weight," my brother said as he dropped down into the seat beside me placing one arm around my shoulder and snatched a fry.

I leveled a glare in his direction.

"Don't eat my food. Order your own," I said haughtily.

He laughed and stole another fry.

So I stabbed him with my fork.

"Oww!" He yelled, cradling his hand to his chest and moving away from me.

"I said, don't eat my food," I reminded him none too gently.

He narrowed his eyes.

I shrugged, not caring.

He didn't understand.

Nobody did.

Not unless you'd had to do time.

You didn't realize how precious the freedom to eat what you wanted was.

They really had no clue.

And hopefully never would.

"Can I get you something, Berry?" That sexy voice rumbled from my side.

I looked up when I popped a fried pickle into my mouth, crunching down on it in time for Silas' eyes to move to me.

The pickle crunched under my teeth, and I moaned.

So good!

His eyes flared, and he looked away to address my brother once again.

My face flamed as I thought about the show I'd just inadvertently put on.

Shit, Sawyer! Could you be any more embarrassing?

The reprimand stayed on my mind as I polished off the rest of my fries as Dallas ordered his food.

"I can't believe you didn't wait for me," he said once Silas was gone.

I kept my eyes on his retreating form until he disappeared into the kitchen to place Dallas' order, and I smiled.

"What are you smiling at?" Dallas asked, putting his arm around me again.

I laid my head on his shoulder as I relished the touch.

God, it felt nice to have human touch.

Wanted human touch, anyway.

"I like him," I mumbled, gesturing to Silas, who'd come out of the kitchen to stand at the bar.

Dallas squeezed my shoulder. "Yeah, he's pretty cool."

I pulled out of his arms when Danni, their daughter, started to cry.

"Past her lunchtime, baby," Dallas said to Bristol.

Bristol pulled Danni out of her car seat and handed her over to Dallas with a bottle she pulled from the diaper bag at her side.

I smiled as I watched my brother cradle the small girl in his arms and place the bottle up to her crying lips.

"You're so cute holding her," I said, smiling at him even wider.

He winked. "I'm cute all the time. Being a daddy just makes me even better."

I rolled my eyes.

The arrogance!

"Sure, whatever you say," I said, dipping a piece of steak into the gravy and smothering it.

Not intentionally, though.

My eyes were on the man behind the bar.

I watched Silas move.

The way the muscles in his shoulders shifted with even the tiniest of tasks.

Such as wiping down the bar in front of him with a white rag.

Or when he poured a beer from the tap.

I licked my lips, and he looked up just in time to catch me staring at him.

He winked and went back to pouring his beer, but my heart was frozen in my lungs at being caught.

Shit.

That wink, though, that was sexy as hell.

Oh, man.

I needed to get a life.

"So what happened to you last night? I went to the garage apartment, but the lights were out," Dallas said casually.

Too casually.

"I went to bed," I lied.

What I really did was get into the bathtub full of water that was so hot that my skin still burned from the heat and attempted to boil away my memories.

It didn't work.

I sat in that water for two and a half hours while I stared at my toes lit only by candlelight.

I thought about that night.

Then all the subsequent nights since.

And wished I'd never said yes to going out.

"Oh," Dallas said, looking down at Danni.

I could tell he thought I was lying, but I didn't care.

I wasn't fit company last night.

And he didn't need to see me like that.

Hell, *I* didn't want to see me like that.

"What time do you have to go into work tonight?" I asked, trying to change the subject.

“Six. I work C-shift this week,” he answered, looking up when his food was brought out.

I popped the last fried pickle in my mouth and held my hands out for my niece.

Just as she farted, and then filled her diaper with lord knew what.

“Uhhh,” I said, hesitating.

Bristol and Dallas started laughing.

“Oh, no,” Dallas said when I started to take my hands away. “You wanted her, you have to take her as she comes.”

Dallas got up and ushered me out of the booth.

I rolled my eyes, scooted out of the booth and stood. I took her and the diaper bag that Bristol held out to me.

I took it, looping it over my shoulder and walked with the now smiling little girl to the bathroom.

Where I realized they didn’t have any baby changing stations.

I looked at the non-existent sink area where there was no room to change a kid, let alone set anything down.

“Family establishment my ass,” I mumbled, pulling the door to the bathroom open and walking straight to the bar.

I knew the moment Silas realized I was making my way towards him because his body that was relaxed, stiffened.

Then he turned in my direction, crossing his arms over the top of the bar and watching me come.

“Need something?” He asked, taking in the baby and the diaper bag.

I nodded.

“You have no diaper changing station.”

It was meant to come out as a question, but instead sounded more like an accusation.

He blinked.

"Huh," he said, turning and making his way around the bar.

I watched him come until he stood in front of me.

"You can use my bathroom. It has a big sink area," he said, gesturing with his hand for me to follow.

I did, right into the same hallway that I'd found myself in from earlier.

I could smell him over certain *other* things, and it was wonderful.

Like pine needles and leather… the latter might be explained by the leather vest he had on.

A picture of a creepy woman was on the back, with *Dixie Wardens* over the top of the figure, and *Benton* under the bottom of it.

I wondered if he was really as important as everyone was making him out to be.

I doubted it.

A man that was supposed to be important wouldn't be serving people food at a bar.

He hired people to do that.

Not to mention he didn't mingle with the masses.

"Bathroom's through there," he said, gesturing to another closed door.

Danni made a cooing noise when she saw the lights above her eyes, and I nearly did too.

They were pretty cool.

He had a chandelier in his office.

Sure, the chandelier was made of beer and whiskey bottles, but it was still pretty awesome.

"Nice," I said, gesturing to the light with my head.

He grinned.

"Made it myself," he said as a way of thank you.

I smiled, but refrained from asking, 'did you drink it all yourself, too?'

He was waiting for the question, but I wouldn't give him the satisfaction.

Walking to the bathroom, I shut the door so he didn't see anything unsightly and laid Danni down on the cleanest bathroom counter I'd ever seen.

The bathroom matched the office.

It was pretty straight-forward.

Black granite. White tiles. White toilet.

There was a shower, though.

Something I wouldn't expect in a restaurant office, but whatever.

"Oh, yuck." I said, as I unsnapped the onesie Danni was wearing.

Shit had crawled out the top of her diaper and started to mingle with her shoulder blades.

Thank God I'd been holding her with a blanket underneath or I'd have it all over me, too.

"Hey!" I called. "Do you mind if I, ah, borrow your shower for a minute?" I called.

"Have at it. Since I'm in here I'm going to do a little paperwork," came his mumbled reply.

Well, he probably didn't mumble, but the door was shut, so it was inevitable.

I got the shower turned on, then thought, 'fuck it.'

I rinsed her off, onesie and all.

Setting her down carefully in the bottom of the tub, I unhooked the showerhead and started to spray her off.

"Wow, kid. What did you eat?" I asked.

She smiled and giggled as I used the man soap on the ledge to wash her down thoroughly.

And I knew immediately where the smell of pine came from.

Yummy.

By the time I was finished with Danni, she smelled like a Christmas tree with a hint of man and leather.

It was a very nice smell, and I couldn't help myself as I pulled Danni up into my arms, ten minutes later, fully dressed in a new set of clothes, and inhaled her scent.

I came out of the bathroom with Danni cradled to my chest.

Seemed like pooping and eating had tired her the hell out.

The door to the bathroom opened silently, and what I saw when I walked out had butterflies taking flight in my belly.

"Do you have a bag or something I could put these clothes in? Trash bag, grocery sack? I just don't want to drag all of this with me through your bar," I explained.

Silas looked up from his desk, and my breath caught in my throat.

He wore glasses perched on the end of his nose.

Ones in which he ripped off the moment he saw me standing there.

"Yeah, I think I got one when I brought my extra clothes a few weeks ago," he muttered, pulling open drawers.

He found what he was looking for and yanked it open before dumping the contents on the desk.

My eyes fell on the underwear that were on top, and I nearly let out a moan.

He wore tighty whities.

Holy shit.

Sweet baby *Jesus*.

"Here 'ya go," he said, holding out the bag to me.

I took it, then looked at the bathroom before looking back down at Danni.

"Do you…ahhh…mind holding her?" I asked.

His cool demeanor melted into a puddle of goo on the floor.

"Yeah, I can do that," he said, holding out his hands for me to place the sleeping Danni in them.

I handed her over, and her body was engulfed by his massive, scarred hands.

He cradled her to his chest expertly, and I was left staring at him dumbly for a few long moments while he looked down at the baby in his arms.

"She's cute. I can't even remember when my girl was this size," he mumbled. "My granddaughters though… they were cute like this. Now they're just shit heads."

I had to laugh.

No bullshitting from him.

Which didn't really surprise me.

He seemed the type to tell it like it was.

I smiled as I shoved the dirty clothes and the blanket into the little bag, and smiled even more when I came back out to see Silas still staring at Danni as if she were a piece of spun glass.

"How many kids do you have?" I asked softly.

He stood when he saw me with the things I'd brought with me and went to take them from me.

I shook my head.

"If you don't mind, I'd like you to hold her while I take all this out to Bristol. Then I'll go wash my hands," I said softly.

He nodded and walked with me out to the restaurant once again.

"I have three kids. They're all older now. Now I'm working on ruining the grandkids," he murmured softly as we walked down the darkened hallway once again.

My senses seemed to be honed as I listened to him.

The way his voice rumbled in his chest. The way he smelled.

I'd never felt like this around anyone in my life. It was an odd experience.

And when I got to the table where my brother and Bristol didn't even seem to care that I'd had their child for over twenty minutes, I was very disappointed.

I didn't want him to leave.

"Thanks man," Dallas said when Silas handed the baby over.

I set the bag of dirty clothes on the floor and offered the diaper bag to Bristol. "I have to go wash my hands. There are things on them that I'd rather not think about."

Bristol laughed, and I turned to find Silas gone, and nowhere in sight. Only the hint of pine in his place.

I couldn't figure out why I was so disappointed, but I was.

Really disappointed.

But it wouldn't be the last time I saw him. Nor the last time I smelled him.

CHAPTER 6

World's greatest farter…I mean father.
-T-shirt

Silas

"Get the fuck out of my sight," I hissed to Crotchet.

Crotchet narrowed his eyes. "Do you realize who you're talking to?"

I smiled. "Yeah, I realize exactly who the fuck I'm talking to, now move."

"You're not authorized to be in here."

"Crotchet, back off and let him through," Rosenthal ordered.

Crotch Rot froze and turned where his boss's boss stood behind him, ordering him to move when he hadn't even had the chance to meet him yet.

Everybody knew what Rosenthal looked like, though.

He was infamous… just like I was.

"You heard the man," I said quietly. "Move."

Crotch Rot's eyes narrowed, and he stepped forward. "You won't get what you want. Trust me."

I smiled. "Watch me."

Crotchet moved to allow me to pass, and I barely held back the urge to pop him in the face with the back of my hand.

Rosenthal didn't say a word until we were well away from Crotchet.

"You're making an enemy where you don't need to," Rosenthal said amusingly.

I shrugged. "Like I give a fuck. I'm old and on the downhill side of dead. I don't have to please everyone anymore. All I have to please is God and myself… and he's neither."

Rosenthal laughed.

"You never seem to lose the bad attitude," Rosenthal rumbled.

I sighed. "I got it from my mama."

"What can I help you with?" Rosenthal asked as we made it into his office.

He closed the door, and I took a seat and waited for Rosenthal to follow suit before I handed him a paper.

Shovel's name was the only thing on the paper, but he knew right off the bat what I was after.

"I haven't seen or heard anything from him. He fell off the grid the moment he got out," Rosenthal said before I could even tell him what I wanted.

"I know that," I leaned back in my chair and crossed my arms over my chest. "What I don't know is why he got out. There was no forewarning. No call to tell me he was out. No mention of parole at all, as a matter of fact. Why did something as important as this slip through the cracks? I check on this motherfucker once a week…then in between this week and last, he not only gets out…but then fucking disappears. Is that a coincidence? Because I'm thinking it's not."

Rosenthal's face hardened to stone. "I don't know what you want me to say to you, Mackenzie. I know you have a man on it. When I became aware of the situation, I started to follow the stepping stones, but I got nothing. Not a single thread."

I tilted my head back to stare up at the ceiling.

"Need I remind you that he tried to kill my kids… my wife? Which was why he was in prison in the first place," I said, not bothering to look at him.

"I know exactly what happened. I was right there with to you. Remember?" He reminded me none too gently.

I closed my eyes and let my mind wander back to that night. The night that my life changed forever.

***

"You're going to watch. Watch while I rape her. Watch while I rape your son. Your daughter. Your other son. That other trash isn't worth it… I know you don't care about her…but the other four…yeah, I know that'll get a reaction out of you," Shovel smiled manically.

Bile rose in my stomach as I watched him rub a hand up and down the thigh of my wife.

She was drugged.

Shovel had drugged us all.

I'd trusted the wrong person, and now they were all going to pay.

My mistake was going to probably kill everything I loved in one fell swoop.

And I didn't see a thing I could do to help me get out of it.

Then he snuck his hand into her panties, and my hands fisted behind my back.

Outwardly, though, I appeared calm.

God help him if he moved to my kids, though.

I couldn't do this for much longer.

They were never supposed to get to my family.

I never agreed on this.

I knew this one moment in time would forever alter my course in life.

Whatever I had to do, I'd kill this motherfucker.

It may be now…or it may be twenty years from now…but the fucker would die. And at my hand.

"Coming in hot," Rosenthal, my partner, said into my mic.

He was going to get here fast, I knew that.

But when Shovel started to run his hand along the side of my children's faces, I nearly lost it.

Shovel was never supposed to get this close.

All he was supposed to do was get to the front door. They were supposed to apprehend him…except Shovel had my other kids…the ones that were supposed to be in Galveston, eight fucking hours away.

So my partner had held off, and now the piece of shit had us all, with me helpless to do a goddamn thing about it.

This whole charade had been fucked.

I'd been undercover for years now.

It was never supposed to go on this long.

I wasn't supposed to get married.

I wasn't supposed to have kids.

And I sure as fuck wasn't supposed to have another wife.

Yet, I did every single bit of it for my fuckin' country…and look where I ended up.

Having four of the people I loved most in this world under the hands of a madman who couldn't see past his own fuckin' rage.

Thank God Rosenthal and the rest of my backup finally made it through the door, causing Shovel to freeze.

Because if he'd been even seconds later, I would've killed Shovel with my bare hands. Carved his heart out with only my fingernails.

"Freeze, put your hands up!" Rosenthal screamed.

Shovel smiled, and slowly lifted his hands up away from Sam's belly.

My throat convulsed as I thought about how much worse this could've been.

What he could've done to my other kids had he not been hell bent on revenge.

"I'll see you in hell," Shovel said as Rosenthal and another officer put him into handcuffs.

"No you won't, because there is no escaping to hell for you yet. You're going to live a nice long life, in a maximum security prison with no chance of parole, and I'm going to make sure you fucking enjoy the fuck out of it," I smiled.

Shovel glared as he saw that I was serious, and I stood, not sparing him another glance.

My family needed me.

But I knew one thing for sure.

I needed them...but there were still others in the club just like Shovel.

My job wasn't done...but my time as a good, attentive father, was.

And I'd pay for that decision every day for the rest of my life.

***

"I've got every available resource, computer geek, and field agent on the lookout for Shovel. Trust me, he'll be found, and when he is, I'll give him to you," Rosenthal explained.

I nodded and stood.

"Crotchet needs to keep off my case. You need to contain him – and keep him contained – and he needs to understand just what he's dealing with here. Maybe it's time you share those files with him," I said softly.

Rosenthal's eyes held mine and then he nodded once.

"Maybe you're right. I'll do that after you leave."

I nodded and offered him my hand, which he took.

His grip was just as strong now as it was thirty years ago.

"Be careful," he said.

I shrugged. "Got nothing left to lose, friend. Careful's not in my repertoire."

I'd lost everything thirty years ago…and even now with my kids half understanding what I'd had to do, it still wasn't enough to undo thirty years of damage and probably never would be.

CHAPTER 7

Is that your flashlight or are you happy to see me? Oh, that's really your flashlight? Bummer.
-Coffee Cup

Sawyer

"We've got to stop meeting like this," I said, plopping down in the seat across from Silas.

He winked.

"Was here first, girlie," he mumbled, leaning back against the booth he was in and taking a sip of his beer.

He was right.

I'd seen him the moment I'd crossed the threshold.

"What are you doing all the way out here?" I asked softly.

We were nearly an hour away from our hometown, in a place called Longview.

I knew why I'd come here. I just didn't know why he had.

"I think it's a little delicate for your ears," he chuckled, taking another drink of his beer.

My face flamed as I realized just why.

He was looking for a hookup.

At a bar that was not in his hometown.

Shit!

"Ahhh," I said, stumbling over something to say and coming up empty.

He grinned, and my nipples started to harden.

"That's why I'm here, too. Figured I had a better chance with a man that didn't know my life story," I murmured embarrassingly.

That, and I just wanted to feel something.

After a little bit of experimentation, I realized that alcohol just made me feel even worse about myself.

Made me relive the nightmares over and over until my drunkenness wore off.

This was the next logical step. Getting lost in someone's body for a couple of hours.

I was pretty enough.

And my outfit was perfect.

Black five-inch heels. Short skirt. Low cut top.

It was the exact outfit that women wore when they wanted to pick up a man.

When he didn't say anything, I took that as my cue to leave.

"Anyway…good luck," I said stupidly.

Jesus, but the man didn't need luck.

Every female eye in the room was aware of Silas.

He was just that *hot.*

I could feel his eyes on me as I walked away, could practically feel his phantom hands running up the outsides of my thighs to smooth over my ass.

Sweet baby Jesus.

I went straight to the bar and ordered a Jack Daniel's on the rocks.

I didn't have time to pussy foot around. If I was going to have the nerve to go home with a man, it'd have to be with a little liquid courage.

The bartender froze when he looked at me, a smile appearing on his face.

I already felt dirty.

So I drank to forget and hoped it'd work like it was supposed to.

After my second drink, I was finally loose enough to venture out onto the dance floor.

There weren't many dancing, but my devious mind was set on dancing…mainly because the dance floor was directly across from the booth that Silas hadn't moved from.

Not that he needed to move.

There's been a plethora of women stopping by his table.

Some had the courage to sit.

Some only walked past and waved.

He never waved back, eyes forward.

The ones that had the courage to sit, he spoke to, but only for a short time.

He was intimidating as hell, which I'm sure they realized after sitting for only a short time.

I weaved in and out of the tables on my way to the dance floor, very aware that I had the attention of many men.

Not the attention of the man I wanted, though.

But we'd just have to see about that.

***

Silas

I'm not a person known for his good decisions.

I knew I shouldn't take her.

Knew it was bad on way too many levels.

Yet my dick and my mind were in complete agreement.

And I was a big believer in fate.

We'd both been here looking for the same thing.

An hour away from our normal lives.

She's a baby.

She's younger than your kids.

She was younger than my kids…but she was older, too.

She had eight years of experience on the inside, and if there was one thing I knew, it was that prison changed you.

Made you grow up even when you didn't want to.

It was either live or die. There was no surviving when you had to watch your back twenty-four hours a day, three-hundred-sixty-five days a year.

I watched as she danced to a song that I hadn't heard in years.

She moved her hips enticingly, swaying from side to side, sliding her hands into her hair.

The men in the room were captivated.

But they wouldn't have her.

I would.

Downing the rest of my beer, I moved out of the booth, aware of everyone's eyes in the room moving to me.

A man that was set to make his move on Sawyer froze in his spot just by a simple glare from me in his direction.

He turned and moved away, the thought of trying for Sawyer dying an agonizing death once he looked into my eyes.

I moved up behind her just as the next song made its way in, and I smiled.

It was perfect.

Mostly because she stopped dancing and turned, seeing me standing there.

Her eyes widened, and she licked her lips.

I walked forward, coming to a stop only inches away from her face.

"You're sure about this?" I asked softly.

She nodded. "Yeah."

"You know who I am?" I asked.

She nodded. "I do."

"You know what I want?" I continued.

She nodded again. "Yeah."

"I don't do relationships. And whatever this is, it's not going to be hearts and flowers. I don't have time for that," he said again.

She shrugged. "I don't have time for hearts and flowers anyway. It's just not for me."

I didn't bother to contradict her.

She deserved the hearts and flowers. But I was a selfish prick.

It was wrong on so many levels that I couldn't count the ways…but my dick didn't seem to care.

"Your car or mine?" She asked as we walked past the front door.

I snorted.

There was no way I was squeezing into that tin can she called a car.

I'd seen her car.

It was the size of a shopping cart…or at least that was what it looked like.

It was a 1957 Volkswagen Beetle in a putrid shade of green.

I'd listened to Dallas complain about the car, just two days ago, after she bought it with her first pay check.

Though you had to do what you had to do when it came to your freedom.

"We'll take mine," I rumbled as I placed my hand on her back to usher her to my bike. "But mine's not a car."

She hissed in a breath when she realized what we'd be taking, and I watched as a shiver rolled over her.

"Okay," she breathed.

She wasn't drunk.

That I could tell.

Far from it, in fact.

She was loose, though.

Loose enough that she didn't care about getting on a bike with a man that was five years short of being twice her age.

"We're in for a long ride," I said as she came to a stop next to it. "Do you want to borrow my jacket?"

She looked at my leather jacket, then into my eyes, before she nodded. "Yeah, I'd like that."

First, I took off my colors, followed shortly by the jacket.

Then I wrapped it around her back and watched as she shrugged on the leather like it was a piece of silk rubbing along her skin.

Possession rolled over me as I realized how much I liked her wearing my coat.

It dwarfed her small body, but she didn't seem to mind.

Only pushing the sleeves up and smiled before she walked up to the bike and studied it.

"How do I get on without flashing the parking lot?"

I smiled as I walked up beside her and tapped the back of one thigh.

"Nobody can see what you got except me," I murmured. "Throw that leg over."

She lifted her leg, and I got the briefest glance of her pussy…*that wasn't covered by a goddamned thing*…before the skirt fell and covered her once again.

But it was enough to change my mind about going all the way back to my house; instead, deciding to hit up the safe house we had in Longview.

I didn't think I could handle an hour on the bike with her open pussy pressed up against my back.

Nor did I want to.

I was all for instant gratification, after all.

Lifting my leg to swing over the bike, I straddled the seat in front of her and started the bike up with a mutinous roar.

I lifted the helmet from the handle bars and offered it back to her.

"Put this on," I ordered.

She took it from my hand and put it on her head, scrunching it down tightly to fit on her head.

"Ready," she whispered.

I smiled. "Yeah, hold on to your titties."

She squealed in excitement as I made my way out of the bar's parking lot and into traffic.

I ascertained by five minutes into the ride that she'd never been on a bike before.

And, ten minutes into the ride, I'd decided to ignore my dick's insistence that we take care of him now, and drove all the way back home.

She was enjoying herself, and I found that I liked when she did that.

I'd not seen her laugh one single time like she had in the hour we were on my bike.

Then again, that's why I rode in the first place.

Riding a motorcycle was a freeing experience.

You let your mind wander and just let the road take your problems away.

It was like therapy, without the therapist.

A high without the drugs.

By the time we pulled up into my place, I felt like I had a completely different person on the back of my bike with me.

I hadn't forgotten about the way her very hot pussy felt against my backside…or the way her hands felt when they rubbed up and down my stomach, but I also found myself reluctant to get off the bike.

Something I had to do when I finally turned the bike off after backing it next to my house.

"I didn't realize you lived on the lake," she whispered, looking out over the view I had.

I reached my hand back to take the helmet she offered me, but neither one of us made a move to get off the bike.

"I've lived here for a couple of years now. My son lives across the lake," I said, gesturing in the direction of Sebastian's place.

It was lit like the Fourth of July.

Something I hated.

Not that I'd ever tell him.

I liked him being there, I just didn't like looking at the fact that he wasted money by leaving all those lights on, ruining my skyline with all those fuckers.

Then again, the same went for Kettle's place that was next to Sebastian's.

I wouldn't bring up the fact that her parents were just down the way from me, either.

I didn't want to ruin the mood after all.

Especially when I realized how sweet she smelled.

"Do you walk over there, or boat?" She asked me, leaning her head on my shoulder and wrapping her hands around my chest.

"I boat…or ride. Walking it would take a really long time. The lake extends quite a few miles that way," I said, pointing to the left. "It'd take hours to walk over there. And the other way is just swamp-covered land. Either way you go to get out of this lake, you have to cross bridges. So it's easier to ride more than anything."

Her hand started to do something with my lower belly, twisting my shirt in her fingers as she contemplated what I'd said.

And slowly but surely, her worrying pulled the hem up over my jeans, and I caught my breath when her fingers met the bare skin of my lower belly.

My dick started to throb the instant she touched me, and I had to grip my thighs with my hands to keep from throwing her onto the floor of my carport.

"Will you take me for a ride on the lake? I've never done that before," she whispered as her fingers dipped over the ridges of my abdomen.

"Yeah," I rumbled, closing my eyes when she shifted behind me to scoot closer.

Her nipples rubbed along my back, enticing me.

Her pussy wasn't helping any either.

"It's been a really long time," she said, letting her fingers drop until they played along the waistband of my jeans.

I inadvertently sucked in, allowing the tips of her fingers to dip below the waistband of my jeans until they encountered the wiry pubic hair surrounding my dick.

"I know," I told her. "Are you sure?"

She shivered at the huskiness of my voice, and I couldn't help the smile that ticked up the corner of my mouth.

"Yeah, never so sure in my life," she agreed.

I finally let up on my strangle hold I had on my knees and let my hand travel up and down the outsides of her thighs.

My hand traveled up and down, from knee to hip, back and forth, as she finally worked up the courage to start working at the buckle of my belt.

Her hands were shaky, and I let her do her thing so I didn't rush her faster than she was willing to go.

But when her hands yanked the zipper down, followed by the button, then dove straight for my cock, I was the one to freeze.

Her hands felt like silk against my length.

They were cold, but that didn't seem to matter to my cock.

Not even the slightest.

My balls were high and tight as she slowly started to work the length of my cock in her hand, pumping it fast and steady.

"I don't want to come in my pants," my voice cracked. "Pull me out."

She pushed my underwear down until my dick popped free of its confines.

The waistband of my underwear stuck under my balls wasn't the most comfortable in the world, but I forgot about it completely when her hand returned to my cock, pumping and massaging.

"I haven't come from a hand job in well over twenty years, but I'm about two minutes away from that," I informed her.

She laughed and let me go, my dick pointing straight in the air as she ran her hands up my torso.

I helped her by easing my cut off and then taking my shirt by the back of my collar and pulling it over my head, hunching my shoulders as I did so as to make it easier.

She sighed when she could feel my chest and back.

Her hands traveled up my belly to my nipples, circling them hesitantly.

Then further inside to run through the hair on my chest.

"I never really thought that I'd get turned on by chest hair, but I really wish I could rub my nipples against your…"

She didn't finish her thought before I'd twisted at the waist, hooked an arm around her, and maneuvered her until she was straddling the bike once again, but facing me this time.

Her ass rested on the gas tank, and my dick was only mere inches away from where it really, really wanted to be.

"So what's stopping you?" I asked, looking into her eyes.

The motion detection that'd turned on when we pulled in the driveway went out, and we were plunged into darkness.

I didn't so much as see, but hear, as she stripped first her shirt, followed shortly by her bra, from her body.

"I want you inside of me when I do," she whispered.

My eyes nearly crossed as I fished my wallet from my back pocket and quickly pulled out a condom from the middle of it.

I could hear her breath quicken as she heard me tear the condom open and remove it from its package.

Then I worked it down the length of my dick before I reached for her and yanked her forward.

The skin of her ass screeched as I yanked her across the gas tank, but she didn't complain, and I couldn't find it in me to care.

When my dick met the slick skin of her pussy, I hissed in a breath at the heat that was emanating from her.

Even through the latex of the condom I could feel it, and I'd never wished more for anything in my life, than to feel her skin to skin.

Alas, I didn't get this old by being stupid.

And she was a smart girl.

She needed the assurance that I was taking precautions.

Later, though, after we were both checked out, and I was assured that she was on birth control, we'd be revising this situation. I may not want a permanent relationship, but this? Well, let's just say that we would be doing this again.

She moaned softly when my cock met her entrance and then gasped as I slowly started to fill her up.

I wasn't a small man, and she felt like she'd never had a dick inside her before.

Couple the two, and I was so ready to blow that it was embarrassing.

But the moment I was seated fully inside her depths, and her breasts started to play along the hair on my chest, I locked my own pleasure down and started to focus on her.

"Lean back," I ordered her.

She moaned and clenched down on my length, but followed directions until she was laid out before me.

I fucked up into her as I moved my hands to play along her flat belly, moving up until I met the pebbled nipples on top of her beautiful breasts.

They were the perfect size for my hands. Not too big, but nothing to sneeze at, either.

I pinched one nipple and circled my thumb around the other, trying to learn what she liked best.

She leaned into the pinching, and I smiled.

So she liked it rough.

Good, because I did too.

Really rough.

"You like a little pain with your fucking, sweetheart?" I asked, pinching both nipples now, hard enough to cause her to cry out.

"I...I think so. It feels good," she whispered. "It's never felt like this before."

So whomever she'd been with hadn't had patience enough to find out what she liked. Typical.

All I could say about that was that he was a lazy fucker.

I took my time with my women...and I definitely would with Sawyer.

There was no reason on God's green earth that I couldn't get my women off before me, even if I had to put my own desires on hold to accomplish it.

I pinched one nipple with my thumb and forefinger while I leaned forward and captured her other one between my lips, effectively pushing me even deeper inside of her.

She cried out. From what? Could be the fact that I was deep as fuck inside of her, or maybe it was the way my beard played along the sensitive skin of her breast, I didn't know.

But I'd ask.

Later.

Right now I was too busy with feeling the way her hot pussy clenched around the length of my dick, and the way she was taking me deeper than any woman had ever been able to before.

"God, you feel so fuckin' good," I told her in between sucks.

Her hands came up to cup my head.

I was sure that if I had hair, she would've been yanking on it in her exuberance.

Especially with the way her hips lifted to receive each of my thrusts, or how she was exhaling one continuous moan instead of sighs like she'd been doing before.

"I need…" she hesitated. "I need something."

I pulled out suddenly, happy with the way she cried out in despair when I was no longer inside of her.

"You need what, honey?" I asked, helping her sit up until she was resting on the pad of the seat.

Then I helped her to her feet and turned her around until she was bent over, elbows resting on the seat.

But I thought better of it since I knew I wanted to do her hard, so I shifted her until she was bent over the hood of my '67 Charger.

Her hips met the cool metal, and she canted her ass, wiggling as she said, "Hurry."

I said a silent prayer for the fact that she was wearing such high heels, which enabled me to line my cock straight up with the entrance to her pussy, and slam inside.

"*Silas!*" She screamed. "Fuck!"

I grinned as I started to pound inside of her.

Hard, unforgiving strokes.

Each thrust had me hitting the end of her, battering her cervix with the head of my cock.

She didn't complain, though.

In fact, she was doing quite the opposite. Pushing back against my thrusts so that I rammed inside of her even harder.

My hands were probably bruising her hips as I gripped her, holding her steady as I took her hard.

And when I felt her hand sneak down to cup my balls and play along the base of my cock, I had to tighten my belly to keep myself from coming.

I started counting to a hundred in my head when I felt her start to circle her clit with her thumb while keeping her fingers on my balls.

And I had never been more thankful than when I felt her pussy start to flutter and ripple around me.

When she burst into an orgasm, I finally let myself go.

My cum exploded from my balls as it shot out the end of my cock, filling up the tip of the condom with so much force that I feared for the integrity of the latex.

Then she started to clamp down on me even harder, one long clench followed the other, and I forgot to care about *everything*.

It was long seconds later when I finally came back to myself.

I was pinning Sawyer to the side of my Charger with my big body, holding her down as the sweat started to cool on our bodies.

"I'm thinking I need to do that again…a couple hundred times."

I chuckled as I held on to the base of the condom, making sure it stayed in place as I pulled out of her.

I was enjoying the sound of my withdrawal from her – one of the sexiest damn things I'd ever heard – as I listened to her juicy pussy try its damndest to hold on to me.

She moaned when I finally exited her body completely and turned around suddenly to slam her mouth down onto mine.

"That was incredible," she whispered against my lips.

I snorted.

"You make an old man like me feel like a fuckin' superhero," I muttered against her lips, pulling her in close.

My still hard cock pressed against the apex of her thighs, and I contemplated grabbing another condom from my wallet when I felt her start to laugh.

"Let's go inside and do it on a bed this time," she whispered.

"Greedy little bitch, aren't you?" I asked.

She grinned as I gathered her up in my arms, hand under her ass, and started to carry her to the garage door.

Her legs went around my hips, helping hold my pants up, as I walked.

I was thankful I still *had* my pants when I was easily able to take my keys from my pocket and insert it into the lock.

Sadly, we never made it to the bed.

We made it to the kitchen table before I lost the ability to fight my dick anymore.

CHAPTER 8

DO NOT READ THE NEXT SENTENCE.
You little rebel, you!
-T-shirt

Sawyer

It was hours later that I was finally able to catch my breath.

"Is that normal…I don't think that was normal," I said, eyes getting heavy as I thought about all that we'd just done.

Silas chuckled huskily.

"Yeah, Sawyer. That's normal."

"I think you're lying…sex can't really be that good all the time. I mean, I'm a little rusty, but I don't remember it ever being like that," I told him.

His arms around me tightened, and I realized that he didn't like hearing about my 'other time' while I was naked in bed with him.

"While we do this, there'll be no one else. Understand?" He asked quietly.

I could ascertain an underlying sound of menace in his voice, and I readily agreed.

"Yeah. I understand. And it's not like I'll ever be doing that again…I just wanted to see if it would wo…"

I froze on what I was about to say, but Silas picked up on it.

"Wanted to see if what would work?" He asked, rolling so he was on top of me.

I shook my head, really not wanting to bring up why I'd gone out searching for a one-night stand.

"My dress. I wanted to see if it'd pick up the guys like I thought it would," I lied.

He scoffed. "Honey, you were wearing a skirt, and you had to have known that anything that short, on anyone, would've garnered a man's attention. Now how about you stop lying to me and tell me what you really meant."

I paused thinking about what to say.

"Being out of prison for me is…hard," I finally said.

His eyes searched mine.

"Yeah." He nodded in understanding. "It's going to continue to be hard."

I closed my eyes, not liking what I heard.

"I don't feel like I deserve to be out," I admitted.

I could feel his eyes as he stared at me.

"Why not?" He asked softly, smoothing a piece of my hair off my forehead.

"I killed four people," I said, tears immediately rushing to the surface.

"What happened?" He asked.

I closed my eyes. "I had one beer," I whispered, tears starting to pour from my eyes. "One. And it ruined my life."

He blinked. "You had one beer? That's it?"

I nodded. "Just a single Solo cup full."

"I remember reading the newspaper article. It didn't say anything about only one beer. It said you were drunk, over the legal alcohol limit. You are a small woman, but you wouldn't have gotten drunk off of only a single cup full," he rumbled, sitting up and turning on the light.

I nodded. "I wasn't drunk at all. In fact, I was barely even buzzed. I used to drink a glass of wine every night back then, so it wasn't like I had alcohol intolerance. It was just a bad deal," I whispered.

His face, though, showed his incredulity.

"What did the police report say? What was your blood alcohol level?" He asked, sitting up in the bed and throwing the covers off his lap.

I watched as he walked to the bathroom and flipped on the light before shutting it slightly behind him.

"I never heard what my blood alcohol level was, but then again, I didn't really care at that point. I'd just killed four people, one of which I graduated with," I informed him.

I heard the sound of him using the bathroom, and I wondered if he even heard me.

But after I heard the toilet flush, and the sound of him washing his hands, he came out with a worried look on his face.

"If you don't mind," he said tentatively, "I'd like to look into your case."

I shrugged. "That's fine. I'd always hoped for parole at four years. That was what my lawyer promised me would happen. But I was denied."

I frowned.

That denial had hurt.

Badly.

I didn't even know why I was telling him all of this.

He'd asked, and I'd told him things that I hadn't even told my own mother.

“Who was your lawyer?” He asked.

“A family friend,” I told him instantly.

He frowned. “Was your family friend a good lawyer? You don’t fuck around with something like that. You needed the best. Not someone that would feel obligated to help you.”

“He’s dead now, so I wouldn’t really know. We got what we could afford, which sadly wasn’t much. Not that it matters now since it’s all over,” I whispered, looking down at my hands.

He looked at me like I’d grown a second head.

“It’s not all over,” he rumbled, getting back into bed beside me.

I blinked. “What do you mean? I served my eight years.”

“You’re telling me you don’t lie awake at night and think about how horrible you are?” He asked.

I snapped my mouth shut.

I *did* do that.

“And you don’t mind the whispers from all the townsfolk?” He continued.

I laid back down on the bed and pressed my face into the pillow.

I didn’t want to talk about this.

“I’m not hearing your answer,” he said knowingly.

I narrowed my eyes into the pillow.

“It’s understandable. I killed four people. What do you want them to do, thank me?” I snapped, turning my head and glaring at him from across the sheets.

Maybe I should go.

Except I couldn't really leave since I'd left my car an hour away.

Fucking great.

"You can check the fuckin' attitude, Sawyer, I'm only trying to help. I've been in law enforcement since I was eighteen years old; I know a thing or two about laws. And the fact that you killed four people while *not being drunk*, because they pulled out *in front of you*, is not something you go to jail for eight years for," he snapped. "All I'm trying to tell you is it doesn't make fuckin' sense. You didn't even take a plea deal. I can't figure out why you were even in jail."

I shrugged.

"I don't know," I said, duly chastised.

He placed his rough palm on my cheek. "I'll look into it…but it wasn't your fault, from what I remember of the wreck. They had no lights on, and they pulled out in front of you. Trust me, I think something's missing here, and I'm going to find out what it is."

I turned my head to run my lips over the palm of his hand. "Thank you, Silas."

I didn't really want him to look into anything.

But I could tell by the determination in his eyes that he wasn't going to let this one rest.

Besides, what could it hurt?

Silas finally plunged the room into darkness, and I closed my eyes in exhaustion.

Mostly because of the way I'd been so well and thoroughly used tonight, but also partially due to the fact that I can't talk about the past, about what happened without feeling emotionally drained.

God, I hated reliving the past.

And, sadly, I did it every night in my dreams.

Just, hopefully, not this night.

Especially since I felt so safe in the arms that'd just gathered me close.

"Go to sleep," he rumbled.

I pressed my lips to his hairy chest and kissed him softly before turning to rest my head on his bicep.

His fingers trailed through my hair, and my eyes started to droop.

Then, I was asleep.

My dreams haunted me still, but I had Silas and his badass self there to scare them away this night.

What I didn't realize, though, was that I'd only given him even more fuel for the determination he felt to find out what exactly had happened.

Although I'd had no idea I did it, apparently I spoke during my nightmares.

***

I woke up to sunlight streaming through the windows.

I rolled around in the bed, startled when I hit the masculine body only inches into my roll.

"Mmmm," I said, curling up into Silas' chest.

He hugged me tightly, but just as suddenly, got up to leave.

"Where you going?" I asked around a yawn.

"Gotta go to the office. And you'll have to come with me now, or I can come back for you at lunchtime," he mumbled.

I shook my head and opened my eyes, mouth going dry when I saw his bare ass slipping into another pair of tighty whities.

I moaned in sadness, causing him to look over his shoulder and wink at me.

"What?" He asked.

God, he looked so good.

Not one single inch of his body wasn't in perfect shape.

He had zero fat on him whatsoever.

That should be illegal.

I had fat, so he should have some, too.

"You look good," I informed him.

He smiled. "Yeah, thanks."

"Are you okay?" I asked, watching as he slipped jeans up his thick, well defined thighs.

He shook his head. "Fine. My brain wouldn't turn off last night, so I didn't get much sleep."

"Is this because of what we talked about last night?" I asked.

He shrugged. "Yes and no. Or, at least, it started out about that. Then I couldn't turn it off, and I started thinking about other things. But did you want to stay or for me to take you to your place?"

"What about my car?" I asked.

"I'll have it brought to you by this afternoon."

"I have to be at work at ten," I said to him, reluctantly getting out of bed and walking naked to the shower.

He didn't follow me, and I found myself greatly disappointed.

He seemed different today.

More distant.

Not at all like he was yesterday, or even this morning when we went to sleep in each other's arms in the wee hours of the morning.

I took a long, hot shower, relishing the way the hot water felt over my skin.

I was sore.

My vagina felt like it'd been pounded with a fist.

Silas wasn't a small man.

In fact, I would say he was on the bigger side of big.

Which explained why my vagina wanted to revolt when I pressed the bar of soap to it and slid it through my legs.

My nipples were just as sore, not because they'd been pounded, but because they'd been pinched.

Wearing a shirt today should prove interesting.

The lace bra that I'd worn last night was definitely not happening.

I'd just have to go home and put on a sports bra for the day.

Although I'd promised myself that I'd never wear one of those torture devices again since that was all I was allowed to wear while in prison, I couldn't think of anything more comfortable to wear right at that moment.

Especially with the way that even the slightest of water hitting the tips caused a little sting of pain.

I cataloged the rest of my injuries.

Bruises in the shape of fingers ringed each wrist. Hand print bruises spanned each hip. Hickies on my chest.

I looked like I'd been through four rounds…not that I was complaining.

Last night had been just what I needed…all the way up until the retelling of what had happened that horrible night.

I forgot…and I felt again.

Something I'd been needing for going on eight years.

"I set some clothes out on the bed," I heard Silas rumble from the open doorway.

I looked over at him to see him looking straight at me.

"Thanks," I said. "But I can put my old ones back on."

He laughed. "We left them outside, and they're soaked. It rained last night."

"It did?" I asked in surprise.

He nodded. "Hard."

"Okay," I said, smiling at him through the glass.

He stared at me for long moments, and I let him, pressing my chest up against the slick surface as I leaned my forehead against the glass.

His eyes seemed to darken, but I heard the doorbell, and he growled.

"Hurry, we need to leave in ten," he ordered before slipping away just as silently as he'd come.

I turned off the water, happy that I would now smell like him, and pulled a towel off the rack beside the shower.

It was as I was drying my sore breasts that I heard it.

A sound that you never, *ever* want to hear when you're naked in a man's house that you barely even know.

"Hey, Silas. I was wondering if you could spare another beer. I'm making a roast today," my mother, Reba Berry, asked sweetly from the other room.

I froze mid nipple drying, and stared in horror at the wall.

I hadn't realized that my mother and Silas knew each other.

And well enough for her to ask him for a beer, at that?

Why wouldn't Silas have said something last night?

I wasn't a secret.

He had to know I was related to her.

I mean, if she was comfortable enough to come over here like that, than he had to have seen the resemblance between the two of us.

I mean, I looked just like her.

Long black hair, the same birth mark on our necks, in nearly the same place.

Same body type.

She was me, and I was her.

Only thirty years separated our ages.

So I sat on the bed and listened as my mother spoke with Silas about her roast and my father, all the while being *livid.*

It went on so long, in fact, that I got bored.

And started to look around.

Then I started to clean because, seriously, what was the deal with not throwing the clothes into the hamper?

So while I listened to my mother talk about her rose bushes that were lining the edge of her property, and the way my dad cooked steak last night for dinner, I started to launder Silas' clothes.

I started with the ones on his floor, picking them up and shoving them into the basket that had all of two things in it. A single sock, and a pair of his underwear.

By the time I was done, the entire thing was filled to the brim.

"Silas, my son tells me you called him the other night when you saw my girl on the side of the road…at the scene of that crash. I wanted to thank you. She really needs all the help she can get," my mother said, making me freeze in place.

I couldn't hear Silas' reply, but I didn't need to.

Mostly because my mom repeated his answer verbatim.

"Oh, I know you don't think you did anything, but you did. Dallas said he caught her crying, but decided to leave her alone. He also says there's been a lot of drinking going on. He finds all of her bottles in the trash the next morning," my mother said.

He'd been going through my trash?

What the fuck?

And I knew he had to be going through them.

I was the one who'd walked the fucking bags out to the trash can.

He'd have had to physically pull out the bag to know there were bottles in there.

Not like there were a lot of bottles.

Granted, there were some, but not enough to count as excessive.

This time I heard Silas' reply.

"She's allowed to drink, Reba. She spent eight years having her life dictated to her. Let her live her life without you all second guessing every single thing she does," Silas reprimanded her gently.

Then I heard the distinct sound of Silas' screen door opening.

Last night I'd remembered the grating screech, and I wondered how I'd not heard it when my mother had entered.

I heard the two of them talking more from the front porch and decided to go ahead and get dressed in the clothes he'd left me.

They looked new.

And in style.

All of my clothes were still what I wore in high school. Which meant I had a lot of things that probably wouldn't ever be acceptable on a twenty nine year old.

I wore them anyway, though.

Not like I had much choice.

Maybe I should make a stop by the Goodwill later.

They would surely have something better than what I had.

Like the pants and shirt he'd left me draped over the edge of the bed.

I picked through them, seeing that there were no bra or panties.

So I did what any normal woman would do.

Went to Silas' dresser drawers and pulled every single one of them open until I found the underwear.

I laughed when I saw how high up they came on my belly, giggling as quietly as I could as I slipped my feet into the jeans.

The pants fit a little loosely in the waist, but fit perfectly everywhere else.

The shirt fit everywhere but the boob area, but I didn't think that mattered as much as it could have since it was just a simple red, fitted t-shirt.

The only thing that was wrong with it was the fact that I had no bra to cover up my nipples.

And the tightness over the breast area was accentuating that fact.

"It fits," Silas rumbled from the doorway, causing me to jump and turn.

I had to smile when Silas' eyes automatically went to my breasts.

Such a typical man.

"How are you getting past that creaky porch door?" I asked, tugging my shirt down to cover my belly.

He smiled.

"Magic," he answered, starting to walk towards me.

"So you know my mom," I accused.

He nodded. "Yep."

"You knew who I was the entire time?" I asked.

He nodded. "Yep."

He wasn't ashamed that he hadn't told me at all. He just said 'yep' like it wasn't that big of a deal.

"She seemed friendly with you…do you hang out with my dad and mom a lot?" I asked.

His eyes widened slightly.

"Not your dad, no," he said. "Are you ready to go?"

I wondered what he meant by 'not your dad,' but he was gone before I could ask him.

So I followed him, shoeless, and came to a stop when I got to the living room.

"Wow," I said in awe. "This is nice."

The living room, kitchen, dining room, and what looked to be a study were all one huge, open space.

The walls were what looked like real tree logs stripped of the bark, and the ceilings had huge beams running along the rafters.

There was a large, brown leather couch in the middle of the room, facing what had to be the largest TV screen I'd ever seen.

And the kitchen was to die for.

Beautiful mahogany cabinets with black granite counter tops rounded off the living space with their simple but elegant addition to the large space.

All of it made me smile at the man who resembled that description to a T. Simple but elegant.

Silas was standing at the kitchen sink, putting water into a bottle.

My mouth went dry when I saw the look he aimed at me over his shoulder.

Sex and hunger.

Geez.

I took a step back, and his eyes changed, going to curious.

"Yeah, I put a lot of time and effort into this place," he said, screwing the lid down tight onto his bottle and making his way toward me.

He grabbed a hold of my hand on the way, walking and talking.

"I'll drop you off at your house so you can go change. I've already called one of my boys to get your car. They should have it there in time for you to leave for work," Silas said, leading me out to his garage.

I was thankful that he handed me a different helmet this time.

It was one that covered my face completely, the only thing anyone would be able to make out was my hair…but I tucked that into the helmet, too.

Perfect.

I smiled at Silas as he watched me do this with a small smile on his face.

"Embarrassed to be seen with me?" He asked as he tugged his own helmet on.

I shook my head. "No. I just don't want to see my mother."

And that was the God's honest truth.

I was tired of seeing her.

All she could do was go on and on about how sorry she was that I'd had to go to prison, and how she prayed for eight years, every single day, that I came out in one piece.

Seriously, I loved the hell out of my mother, but I didn't love her smothering me.

It was as if she was trying to make up for the eight years, but she couldn't, and instead it felt as if she was suffocating me.

He actually looked relieved when I said that.

"So you don't mind if you're seen with me?" He confirmed.

I nodded. "I wouldn't have left with you last night had I minded."

He grinned, and I was struck again by his handsomeness.

"Hop on, sweet cheeks," he ordered.

I winked at him, but it was lost on him since he'd turned around and started up his bike without watching me get on.

Which was probably good, because then he didn't see the way it hurt that he'd just dismissed me.

We made it out of his little lakeside retreat without seeing my mother, or anyone else for that matter.

Hell, we didn't see a single soul until we were nearly fifteen minutes into our drive.

I hadn't noticed how far out he lived yesterday on the ride to his home, but now that it was light out and I could see just where I was going, I was surprised.

He lived nearly fifty minutes away from my place, once it was all said and done.

And when we pulled up in front of my house, I had roughly forty-five minutes until I had to be at work.

Slipping my leg off the bike, I stood up and turned to him, holding out the helmet.

He shook his head.

"Keep it," he said, eyes on mine. "You'll need it later."

I blinked.

"Why will I need it later?" I asked.

He smiled, giving me those beautiful white teeth again.

"Because I plan on taking you for a ride again," he grinned.

My face blushed fifty shades of red.

Especially when he started to caress his bike in a loving manner.

"And I still have your ass print right here on my tank," he continued. "There's no way I won't want more of what I had last night."

My brows rose.

"Who said I was doing more than a night?" I asked, turning on my heels and going straight around the back of the house.

The garage apartment was detached from the rest of the house, thank God.

Because if I'd have had to go into the main house, I was sure I'd be asked why, exactly, I was panting, as well as the reason my face was so flushed.

And there'd be no way in hell I would tell them, seeing as my brother now reported my entire life to my mom.

Which reminded me.

Pulling out my phone from my pocket, I tossed a small wave over my shoulder at Silas as I rounded the corner.

It was time for my brother to hear exactly why his snooping pissed me off.

CHAPTER 9

Back in my day, a 'behavior disorder' was called being an asshole.
-Silas' thoughts on life

Silas

Four hours later found me heading straight for my office once I arrived at the clubhouse.

Lynn had called twenty minutes before and told me that I had the information I was looking for in my email, and I found that I really wanted to get to the bottom of this case.

Something about her case was bothering me…niggling away at me until I was on the verge of worried.

Sawyer hadn't lied when she said she wasn't drunk.

And I knew when people were lying. I had to know when people were lying to stay alive like I did.

I walked through my office and went straight to my computer.

Signing into my secure email, I clicked on the first email from Lynn and clicked *open*.

The subject line said *Sawyer Berry*.

The first two paragraphs were the particulars of the case.

Who was involved, details about the location, vehicle types, and the names of the occupants in both vehicles.

Alcohol level: .01.

My mouth dropped open.

What. The. Fuck.

I picked up my phone and called Lynn to make sure I wasn't seeing things.

"Hello?" Lynn answered three rings in.

"I need you to double check the numbers you sent over to me," I said without preface.

He snorted. "Knew you were going to ask that; I already had it pulled at BPD, too."

"And?" I asked impatiently.

"Same thing. .01. That's it," he answered immediately.

My jaw clenched.

"I need you to contact the lawyer and the judge. Pull me the…"

"…Already did it. Those files should be on your desk by the end of the day," he interrupted me.

"Thanks. Have you got anything else on Shovel?" I asked him before I hung up.

"Negative."

Shit.

"Thanks, keep me updated," I said.

"Will do," he agreed, and hung up.

I stared at the file some more, becoming more and more confused.

The police report clearly indicated the fact that the Ford Bronco pulled out in front of the Chevy Truck. It also clearly stated that none of the occupants of the Bronco were wearing seatbelts, which was a contributing factor to their being ejected from the vehicle.

It further stated that the two other occupants of the Chevy were drunk.

So drunk that they were nearly twice the legal limit.

“But she wasn’t drunk. What the fuck happened here?” I wondered aloud.

Knowing I wouldn’t be able to sleep until I found out more about this, I picked up my phone and keys from the desk and started to walk right back out the door without accomplishing any of my paperwork.

I guess that was one of the benefits of being the boss, though, getting to do whatever the fuck you wanted to do, when you wanted to do it.

I arrived at BPD less than five minutes after leaving my office, and I walked straight into the building, not even bothering to say hi to Loki or Trance as I went in.

The two of them were busy, though, and didn’t even notice when I passed by.

I walked straight into the Chief’s office and shut the door without asking.

“Silas,” Burke said, looking up at me with no surprise in his eyes.

Burke and I went way back.

I dropped a file on his desk, and he hesitated only briefly before he flipped it open with two fingers.

Leaning forward and grabbing his glasses off the desk, he pushed them on and started reading.

The more he read, the more stiff his body became until he fairly resembled a statue.

“You see it,” I surmised.

He nodded.

"Who was in charge of this case?" I asked.

He looked up, and his usually gray eyes were filled with menace.

"Harold Dunbar."

My brows creased. "He's been dead for eight years."

He nodded.

"Yeah."

Then a little niggle of worry started to slither down my spine.

"Who was the judge?" I asked, taking a seat across the desk from him.

He whirled to the side and started to peck away at his keyboard.

Much like I did.

"Escobar Giuliani," he answered after a few long moments.

My blood chilled. "Let me guess…he's dead."

Burke shook his head. "No. Retired."

My brows furrowed as I thought back to Escobar Giuliani. He'd been a young judge, and if I was thinking of the right man, he'd made quite a stir when he retired and decided to start a different career in the oil field.

At the time, I hadn't thought it odd.

I'd heard of cops and even some teachers leaving their jobs to go into the oil field. It was a high paying business. You earned a lot of money in a short amount of time.

It was demanding for a job, but it paid really, really well.

It was normal for any person to seek a higher paying job.

But Giuliani already *had* a high paying – and powerful – job.

And I didn't know a single judge, lawyer or even a doctor who left their high-paying jobs – jobs that had worked hard through higher education to earn – to take a position in the oilfield.

It was counterproductive.

“So, eight years ago, give or take, Giuliani retired?” I confirmed my suspicions.

He nodded. “Correct.”

“Alright, I think I’ll make a little side trip to see him. Give me his address.”

On my way out ten minutes later, I made eye contact with both Loki and Trance, urging them to follow me outside.

They did so without hesitation, Loki finishing up a phone call, and Trance gathering up Kosher.

When they met me outside, I had my phone to my ear and my second born son on the line.

“I need you to meet me somewhere,” I said without hesitation.

I didn’t really care if he had anything to do.

I knew he had the day off.

And to be honest, I’d dropped enough of my shit to help him that he could do the same for me.

“I have the kids,” he said.

“Call Baylee and get her there. I’ll text you the address. Meet me there in forty five minutes.” I ordered and hung up.

I texted him the address, knowing he’d call his wife and get her there, and I then turned to the two men at my back.

“Either of you remember that college kid killing the other college kids and the two teachers eight and a half years ago?” I asked.

They both nodded, but it was Trance's eyes that turned hard.

"I met her. She works at the dogs' vet."

I nodded. "Sawyer Berry. Dallas Berry's twin sister. Reba's daughter."

Understanding started to dawn in Loki's eyes.

But it wasn't what he thought.

In fact, it was quite the opposite.

This had nothing to do with Reba and everything to do with her daughter.

I handed the file folder over to Loki first and gave Trance the copy that I'd made while in the chief's office.

They both read, and I knew the exact instant that they got to the line where they read the alcohol level.

"What in the actual fuck?" Trance exclaimed.

I didn't say anything, waiting for them to read all the way through.

"So you have a dead detective and lawyer, a missing judge, and a girl in jail for eight years for a crime she didn't commit," Loki finally said, looking up at me.

I nodded. "Essentially."

"What do you need us to do?" He asked, handing the file over.

I waved him off. "Keep it. I've got my own at home. I want you to go ask some questions about the lawyer's death."

"And me?" Trance asked.

"You're coming with me. I'll need your…handiwork," I said, looking down at Kosher.

Kosher was intimidating as fuck.

I'd had my own trained narcotics dog about fifteen years ago, and Cujo – most aptly named, might I add – was intimidating as hell. But Kosher had Cujo beat by a mile.

He was the standard color of most German Shepherds, but he was the size of a Shetland pony on steroids.

And when he ran it sounded like a fucking Arabian horse barreling down on his unsuspecting prey.

Which was exactly what I wanted.

"I need to make one minor stop before we head over there," I said, straddling my bike and starting it up with a roar.

The others followed suit, and we were on our way in no time.

***

"Nice of you to show up," I muttered to Sebastian.

Sebastian shrugged.

"You can't really expect me to just drop the kids off with Baylee at work, now can you?" He asked.

I shrugged. "You have a babysitter."

He rolled his eyes. "Yeah, my sister who lives in Kilgore, which is nearly an hour away. You wanted me to be here within forty-five minutes. I did what I could with the time constraints you issued," he deadpanned.

Whatever.

"Here's what we have," I said, giving him the rundown of what we were about to do.

"So you think this guy knows something about why she was sent to jail?" Sebastian asked.

"Yeah, or I wouldn't be here," I said sarcastically.

Sebastian flipped me off, and Trance snorted under his breath.

"Let's go," I ordered them both.

I'd called on my way to Mr. Escobar Giuliani's place to verify that he was home, so I wasn't surprised when he opened the door.

The house was modest for what I suspected a former lawyer/judge would live in, but that was only another mystery I'd want to solve in the very near future.

"Mr. Giuliani," I said, offering the man my hand.

Escobar didn't take it, instead stepping back at the sight of me.

"What do you want?" He asked guardedly.

"Sawyer Berry," I said.

He blanched and started to close the door.

However, it was futile.

Sebastian stuck his foot out and stopped the door before it could close mere inches, and I pushed past them both to enter Escobar residence.

"I'll call the police!" Escobar echoed in outrage.

"I am the police," I muttered darkly.

Well...police…CIA…same thing, right?

Escobar blanched.

"He's also an officer of the law and works for Benton Police Department. He's here to make sure I don't kill you and hide your body if you do or say something I don't like," I told Escobar.

Trance snorted and stayed on the front porch, doing as I'd asked him.

Trance wouldn't be needed unless Escobar did something stupid, which I was hoping he wouldn't do.

“I want to talk to you about a few things,” I said, handing him a file folder. “How about you read this and let me know what you think.”

He took the file folder reluctantly and opened it, blanching at what he saw.

“I…I…I can’t do this. I have a wife and kids…please!” Escobar said, trying to hand the file folder back.

Suddenly, I just didn’t care.

And I didn’t care in a huge way.

I moved forward like a viper, striking at Escobar and taking him down to his back before he even realized I was coming.

Escobar’s breath left him in a whoosh as I pressed the bare palm of my hand against the man’s neck, holding him down as I spoke.

“Tell me,” I said, leaning into him slightly. “Tell me now, or so help me God, I will ruin everything you hold dear.”

He gasped as I put more pressure on his neck, then tears started to fill his eyes.

“I can’t. He threatened to kill them if I didn’t comply,” he choked. “You’re not the worst of the two evils.”

I laughed in his face. “You really think that?” I asked.

He nodded. “So you won’t tell me a word?”

He shook his head.

I got up until I was looming over him, then went to a picture that was on the mantle.

“So, this wife of yours…” I said, examining the picture. “You love her?”

“Yes,” he croaked.

I nodded. “And what will she do when she finds out that you had a hand in putting an innocent young girl in prison for a crime that she didn't commit? Will she be upset with you?"

Escobar didn't say a word.

I continued as if he'd confirmed my suspicions.

"Do you know what that poor girl went through?" I hissed at him through clenched teeth.

Remembering the dreams she'd had from last night, I wanted to shove my fist down the sorry fucker's throat and twist it around until his jaw broke from the pressure.

She'd woken not once, not twice, but seven times.

She'd cried out so painstakingly, that I'd thought something had been really wrong.

But then she'd started to mutter in her sleep.

The first time had been apologies for hurting the four people she'd killed.

As had the fifth and seventh.

The second, third, fourth, and sixth had been her telling her imaginary attacker to 'please don't rape me. I promise I won't complain again.'

That'd been when I realized she was talking about the guards from prison.

It had taken me a long time this morning, but I'd gotten the names from Lynn, along with the toxicology report from him about the accident.

And I was very appreciative of the information.

Because there was definitely some explaining that needed to happen.

"No," Escobar squeaked.

So I enlightened him.

"She was nearly raped every night for eight years. How do you think your child or wife would feel if that happened?" I asked, finally giving him my eyes.

Escobar turned over on to his side suddenly and vomited up his lunch.

Disgusting.

"I'd never do a thing like that, of course. Hell, I don't personally know a single man on this earth who would…or hadn't until now," I told him.

Then I looked up into the crying eyes of Escobar's wife, who stood at the entrance, and smiled.

"Do you love the piece of shit you married? Are you proud of this man?" I asked.

Escobar's wife sniffled, then turned devastated eyes to her husband. "I want you out of this house now. I want a divorce! Say goodbye to your children because I don't want you anywhere near them after what you've done!" She screeched at him

"No," Escobar said, making a grab for his wife.

His wife, having not been waiting for the grab like I was, fell when he grabbed her ankle to keep her from leaving.

She fell spectacularly, too.

Her hands went out to catch her fall, and I knew instantly that one of them was broken due to the harsh *snap*.

With nothing to support her weight, the rest of her body went crashing down, and her head met the edge of the coffee table.

The skin of her eyebrow instantly split open and blood started to pour from the wound.

And I knew I had him.

"Trance," I called as I hauled Escobar away from his now crying wife.

Escobar screamed. "I didn't mean to, Tawny. I swear!"

Tawny, however, was in too much pain to care.

"Get him out!" She screamed frantically.

Trance, doing the honors, took him out, cuffing his hands on the way.

Sebastian and I immediately dropped down to Tawny's side.

I felt horrible.

That wasn't how this was supposed to go down.

She was only supposed to make it look like she was assaulted, not actually *get* assaulted.

We had a fuckin' plan, damn it!

"Don't move, darlin.' My boy'll get you fixed right up," I said to Tawny.

She nodded, sucking in breath after breath.

"It was worth it," she breathed. "I can't believe he let that happen. I've been living a lie for over eight years now. I just can't believe it."

I smiled at her, pressing the palm of my hand up against her face.

"Time heals all wounds, darlin' girl. You'll just have to give it some time," I told her.

She smiled as tears started to flow down her cheeks. "Thank you."

I moved away from her as the paramedics entered the room, surrounding her.

Dallas nodded at me as we passed, and I nodded back, thinking about the woman I was doing this all for.

My stomach still hurt.

Those nightmares of hers were no joke, and I was going to track down every single guard in that prison and give them nightmares of their own.

“You have the right to remain silent,” Trance drawled slowly, reciting Escobar his Miranda Rights.

“I want a lawyer,” Escobar yelled loudly.

“You’ll get one…as soon as we get you booked,” Trance said.

When Escobar went to move, Kosher growled menacingly at him, keeping the little shit seated when I could see that he wanted to bolt.

“If you ever want to deal with me and not the prison system, let me know,” I said as I headed to my bike.

I didn’t spare anyone else a second glance as my bike roared to life, and I put it into gear.

My mind on what was lying ahead.

And that, my friends, was vengeance.

The cold, hard, *tear the fucker’s heart out*, type of vengeance. It’s a beautiful thing.

CHAPTER 10

A beard is like the magic key of the panty world. If a man has one, he can get into any woman's panties that he wants to.
-Fact of life

Sawyer

I arrived home from work in a fog.

It was storming, and I was glad that I had a car now.

That ride would've been difficult on my bike.

It was bad enough in my little car.

I'd had to detour four different times due to high water on the road.

I'd tried to call my brother, but the one time he wasn't up in my business, I couldn't get a hold of him.

The rain was so bad that I could barely see through my windshield, despite my wipers being on full blast.

I pulled into Dallas' driveway, annoyed to see the entire thing lined with cars.

I'd forgotten that he'd said that a few of the members of the fire department were coming over.

"Explains why he didn't answer my call," I muttered grumpily, as I pulled up to the only open spot on the curb, which happened to be two houses down from where I should be parking.

My phone rang when I was stuffing things into my bag to try to keep dry, but I left it there.

I'd check it when I got home…if it still worked.

It was a cheap one I'd gotten from Wal-Mart when I'd gotten my second paycheck from Dr. Zack.

Purse stuffed to the brim with my things, and two grocery bags in each hand, I bailed out of the car and slammed the door shut behind me, only realizing that I'd left the keys in the ignition.

Shit!

I spun around and yanked my door back open, pulling out the keys hastily.

This time, when I slammed the door shut, I locked it with the key and started to run to the house.

My tennis shoes were soaked through due to the ankle high water that was running down the street along the curb, but I kept going, in a full-out sprint.

I passed all the nice cars, as well as my brother's house, detouring straight to the garage apartment entrance.

I fumbled with the keys once again at the door to the apartment, but the door swung open without me having to do a thing.

"Get in here," Silas ordered through my surprise.

I went, dropping the grocery bags in the entranceway once I passed over the threshold.

"Shit, it's pouring out there," I gasped.

Silas snorted.

"Got here before the rain…guess it's good we're at your place so you'll be able to change clothes…after," Silas said.

I blinked, but not because of the water that was pouring from my hair into my eyes, but from surprise.

"What?" I asked.

He smiled, and I shivered.

"Cold?" He asked, taking a step forward and divesting me of the rest of my bags.

I nodded.

I *was* cold.

But it wasn't the cold that made me shiver, it was the smooth sound of his luxuriously deep voice and the way it seemed to slither down my spine.

"What'd you get?" He asked, placing the bags on the counter and looking through them

"Beer and stuff for spaghetti," I answered going to the bags and putting the meat away and handing him two bottles of beer.

Spaghetti was easy and filling, but also something I could have for the rest of the week for lunch.

Or would have been…had the power not went out twenty seconds later.

"At least the beer is cold," Silas said.

I heard the distinct sound of the cap being pried off my non-twist-off capped beers and blinked into the darkness.

"What'd you just open that with?" I asked, stunned.

Suddenly I felt the cool, sweating bottle of beer pressed against my arm, and Silas' deep, rumbly voice close to my ear saying "My hands."

I swallowed, taking the beer from him that was still touching my arm.

"Thanks," I said.

Then, as an afterthought, I said, "There's a bottle opener hanging next to the sink."

Silas laughed. "Got it."

Then he took off the cap of the second beer.

"Let's go take a shower," he rumbled.

I jumped, turning to face where I'd heard his voice.

"You scared me," I said. "And I can't. You just opened my beer. If I get in the shower, it'll get warm."

"So bring it with you," he said, taking a hold of my arm and pulling me in his wake.

"How do you know where to go?" I asked as I followed him. "And how are you missing all the things on my floor?"

He didn't answer.

My hand felt dwarfed in his, convulsing slightly when he said, "Take your clothes off."

I felt around for a flat surface, finding what I thought was the bathroom counter, but couldn't tell, and set the beer down.

Then I took my clothes off, as demanded.

The shirt came off easily, followed shortly by my bra.

But when I went to hook my fingers into the waistband of my jeans to drag them off, I froze when I felt the warm, wet mouth close around my erect nipple.

I hissed in a breath when Silas' beer bottle pressed against my back, making me push into him to escape the icy coldness of it.

He chuckled when I clutched at his head.

"Silas," I moaned. "It's cold!"

He left me then.

Pulling away from my breast with a soft ‘pop’, he turned the shower on.

I missed his presence immediately, audibly whimpering, causing him to chuckle darkly.

I started on my pants in the interim, pulling them with difficulty down my legs, and letting them pool at my feet.

I used my feet to step on the hem on either side, pulling my legs free of the restrictive, wet denim.

When I pushed my panties down, I felt Silas’ hands find a home on each of my hips, while his unclothed cock pressed up against the seam of my ass.

“Grab your beer,” he commanded.

I did.

The moment I had it solidly in my hands, I was lifted free of the floor and placed in the shower where the deliciously warm water started to seep over my chest and neck.

It flowed down my body in warm waves, and I held my beer up and away from the spray as, behind me, Silas’ hands started to run down my sides.

He was washing me as well as keeping his body against mine to keep me warm.

“How was your day?” I asked.

The question was immediately followed by a loud crack of thunder that startled me so badly, my legs nearly went out from under me.

Silas’ arm around my waist was the only thing that kept me from eating dirt…or shower tile, anyway.

The bar of soap in his hand didn’t fare the same treatment.

It fell in an echoing thud to the shower floor at my feet and came to a rest at the opposite part of the tub near the drain.

“Easy,” he said, bringing his lips to my neck.

I shivered once again as his beard ran along the cord of my neck, and his large palm, the one that wasn’t holding his beer, cupped my breast.

“That was a loud one,” I managed to squeak out.

“Mmm hmm,” he agreed, letting go of me to take a sip of his beer.

I followed suit and relished the bitter taste of the ale.

I hadn’t been a huge fan of beer until I’d discovered this particular brand.

“How do you like this beer?” I asked softly, leaning my head back against his chest.

Lightening flashed, followed only milliseconds later by another loud boom of thunder.

“It’s not bad. I’m more of a dark ale man myself,” he murmured, while placing his bottle on the ledge.

I bit my lip when his hand left my breast and started to trail down the flat plane of my belly.

“I love this one,” my breath hitched.

His hand finally found the curls between my legs, fingers sifting through the coarse hair.

“I like this,” he said, giving my curls a gentle tug.

I moaned involuntarily.

That little bite of pain made my heart stutter in my chest and start to beat harder, my breathing becoming faster.

His erect cock was bobbing on the inside of my thigh, bouncing up and down slightly in time with his movements, tapping gently against the lips of my sex with shift of his hips.

With the lights out, every one of my senses were heightened.

Every single touch and breath felt monumental.

I was so wet that if he'd tried to enter me right then with his massive cock, I would've accepted him with ease.

But that wasn't what he was doing right then.

No. He was teasing me.

Petting me.

Letting his callused hands run all over my body, back and front. Caressing my breasts, my face. Gliding them up my arms, over my neck.

"Get the soap," he ordered roughly.

His gravelly voice had gotten even rougher as his arousal started to take over, and I found that I quite liked that…what I did to him.

I placed my beer on the side of the shower when I bent over and felt around on the floor for the soap, bracing my hand against the wall in front of me to hold myself steady as I searched.

Which was a good thing when his long, thick finger shoved straight into my pussy with no warning.

I gasped, closing my eyes, as I pressed my ass back against him, completely forgetting that I was supposed to be finding the soap.

"Soap," he ordered again, smacking my ass for emphasis.

I gasped again and restarted my search for the soap, pausing when he worked not two, but three fingers into me.

"Soap," he continued, sounding barely fazed by what was happening to me.

My orgasm was just suddenly there.

One second I was thinking he needed shut up about the soap, and the next my orgasm was slamming into me with the force of a freight train.

I would've fallen forward, too, had Silas not stopped pleasuring me and gripped me by the hair and hip, hauling me back into him.

His hand slid around my hip, cupping my sex and filling me with two fingers as he said, "You didn't get the soap."

"Fuck the damn soap," I said, lifting my arm to loop around his neck.

"Tsk, tsk," he said, stopping the slow back and forth movement of his fingers. "There's something you should know about me, darlin.'"

I closed my eyes and swallowed. "W-what?"

Suddenly, I found myself whirled around, my back pressed up against the cool tile of the shower, Silas' body pressed firmly against mine, holding me in place with just the strength of his legs.

His hands were tickling up and down my sides lightly, his cock standing like a steel bar between us, so hard that it had to hurt.

"When I tell you to do something…I expect you to do it. I'm not a man like any of the others you may have known. I'm older and set in my ways, I expect things to be done the way I want them done, and all that means you need to follow my directions. Everything I do and say has a purpose, and that purpose is what's in your best interest. So from now on, in all ways, you obey me," he ordered, his mouth only inches away from mine.

I should be offended, right?

Except I wasn't. Not at all.

I was turned way the hell on.

Once again, my troubles were all but forgotten as I handed myself over to Silas on a silver fucking platter.

"Okay," I panted out breathily.

His lips pressed to mine as he mumbled against them, "Now, get the fucking soap."

Needless to say, I dropped to my knees and *got the fucking soap*.

When I stood once again, soap in hand, he guided my hand holding the bar of soap in it and pressed it against his chest.

"Wash me," he ordered.

I licked my lips and searched in the darkness for his face.

It was no use.

I could just barely make out his form, and I couldn't see his expression at all.

There was no light whatsoever in the shower, and coupled with the storm's darkness outside, it was useless to try, but I still strained to see his face.

Using both hands to work the soap into a foamy lather, I started at his shoulders, running my hands over the very tops of his very broad shoulders, down his muscular arms to his hands, working the lather over every inch of his skin along the way.

I circled each finger with my fist, working them like I would his cock.

Once I was done with his left hand, I switched the soap to my left and went to work on his right hand.

He growled when I got to his thumb, but he held still letting me do my thing.

Smiling, I dropped down to my knees in front of him and went to work on his feet.

I tapped the first one I encountered, and he accommodated me by lifting and holding it up so I could wash the bottom of his foot. I repeated the process on his other foot.

I then moved on to his leg, massaging my way up the bulky thickness of it from his ankle to his groin.

Running my soapy hands over his hips, I also encountered his rock-solid cock as the head of it bumped against the corner of my mouth while I leaned forward to wash his hips and belly.

And really now, what was a girl to do?

But when I opened my mouth to take him inside, he took hold of my hair and used it to stop me in my tracks.

"Not yet," he growled. "Finish."

I looked down as heat rushed to my face, keeping my mouth shut tight to hold the laugh in that was tempted to escape.

He didn't let go of my hair as I soaped up his other leg.

Meaning, he didn't trust me not to take his cock back into my mouth.

I had no idea why he thought I'd be unable to follow his instructions.

It wasn't like I was a girl who didn't have any self-control, even when there was a cock rubbing against her cheek and the side of her neck for two minutes straight.

When I finished his legs and got to his cock, though, he stopped me.

"Start with my balls," he ordered.

Getting my hands thoroughly wet with the water that was hitting my back, I started on his balls.

Lathering my hands up, I put the soap down by my knees and lifted both hands slowly, really not wanting to do any undue harm to Silas' balls considering I still couldn't see jack shit.

Then lightning flashed across the sky, and the sight before me was illuminated for a few short seconds, letting me know that I was mere inches away from his tightly drawn up testicles.

Lifting up a bit on my knees, I started to slowly work the soap into his balls, being extremely careful yet thorough with my efforts.

My knuckles bumped against his cock numerous times, but the hand in my hair never tightened, meaning he knew I'd done it by accident.

"Now my cock. Stay away from the head with the soap for now."

I fisted his cock with both hands, knowing that would enable me to stay away from the head by experience.

I shuttled both of my hands back and forth along the shaft of his hard cock, surprised when the hand in my hair tightened and pulled my head back.

Water splashed down my face and ran in rivulets down my body as I held my breath in order not to breathe water into my lungs.

"Stand up," he said huskily.

I did as he asked, coming to my feet and leaving the soap on the ground.

Silas pushed forward, rinsing the soap from his body quickly before he reached for the faucet.

The water was turned off from over my shoulder, and with his hand still in my hair, he guided me out of the shower and stopped me when my feet hit the towel I'd laid on the floor this morning.

Silas followed me out, stopping when just the tip of his cock prodded my ass.

Then, reluctantly, he let my hair go and wrapped a towel around me.

I clutched at it, pulling it around me tightly as the cool air hit my overheated body.

Hearing the distinct sound of foil ripping, I turned my head to follow the sound.

I don't think that Silas even bothered with a towel, because the next thing

I knew I was bent over the toilet, my hands resting on the back of the tank, with Silas filling me.

I gasped, the scream trapped in my throat, as he started to slam into me.

With nothing to hold onto, I dropped down to my elbows, rested my head on my arms where they crossed, and held the fuck on.

Silas was relentless.

And I liked it.

An orgasm that wasn't even on the horizon moments before suddenly started building with each rough thrust of his huge cock inside of me.

My entrance screamed as the widest part of his cock finally worked its way inside of me.

He filled me like never before, going even deeper in this position than he had the previous night.

I felt him everywhere as he pushed into me repeatedly, dragging the head of his cock over sensitive spots that had my eyes rolling back in my head and my toes curling up in the towel I was standing on.

Each thrust of his hips had our wet skin slapping together so loudly that even the thunder from the storm raging outside couldn't drown out the sound.

The tornado sirens were now going off, but neither one of us stopped or even slowed down for that matter.

Too lost in each other to think about the world around us.

"Come now, Sawyer," he gritted through clenched teeth, moving one of his hands from my hips circling my waist, and trailing over my belly on its way down.

When his fingers met my clit, giving me exactly what I needed, I shot straight into orbit.

I came hard, clenching and clamping down around him forcefully.

A growl was ripped from his throat when my pussy started to convulse relentlessly, and he suddenly yanked himself from my still contracting pussy.

I heard the sound of the condom being ripped from his cock, and seconds later, I felt the hot, wet splashes of his orgasm decorating my back and ass.

"I don't think I finished my beer," I said, not even remembering when or where I put it down.

He laughed and I yelped.

Mostly because I felt the bite of his teeth on my shoulder before he pulled the towel free of my grip and cleaned my ass off.

"I think it's at the bottom of the shower. We'll have to get it tomorrow," he said, tossing the towel down onto the ground and helping me stand.

I turned in his arms and wrapped my arms around his shoulder as the siren continued to wail around us.

"We should get out of this apartment," I told him.

"Hmm," he agreed, walking me to my bedroom.

I felt, what I guessed was a T-shirt, hit me in the face, followed by a pair of shorts.

Slipping them both on, I waited for him to finish.

When he did, his hand was once again in mine, and we were walking down the back entrance that led to Dallas' garage.

"Have you been here before?" I asked in surprise.

How was he able to do this without any light?

"No, but I have good night vision, and I was here for about an hour before you got here," he admitted.

That made sense.

Obviously, he didn't sit on his ass while he'd been here.

Silas wasn't the type to do that.

I had doubts that he even slept since whenever I saw him he was either standing, fucking me or had just finished fucking me.

"Ah," I said. "Do you think there's really a tornado?"

He squeezed my shoulder. "They wouldn't have turned the sirens on if they didn't have a real reason to. False alarms tend to piss off the masses."

My heart fell.

Although tornados weren't really a 'new' thing for me, they weren't something I'd had to worry about the past eight years.

However, where I lived now was an area that the weathermen referred to as 'Tornado Alley.'

There was even a whole season that was devoted to the storms that usually produce them.

When those sirens went off, we had been taught from a young age to immediately seek shelter in a windowless room.

Texas didn't have underground tornado shelters like they did in other areas along Tornado Alley.

The soil was too dense to dig through.

The shattering of glass had my head whipping around, but it was Silas' arms that circled around me, lifting me off my feet, that had my heart beating a mile a minute.

"What was that?" I gasped, wrapping my arms around his neck.

“Hail,” he answered, setting me on top of what I guessed was my brother’s workbench.

Should’ve worn shoes, I thought to myself.

“Stay there while I run and get your shoes,” he muttered as I heard his boots going back upstairs.

I stayed there on that bench, looking out of what I assumed was the broken window.

It was getting pretty bad out.

The garage around me was shaking, and I had the hysterical thought that Dallas better have insurance on it, because it wouldn’t surprise me if the whole thing blew away with me inside.

Then the horrid thoughts of whether Dallas’ prized Nova being ruined by a possible tornado would affect him more than it would if *I* was hurt.

But Silas’ return jolted me out of my bad thoughts.

“I found some rain boots, figured they would be better,” Silas said.

I thought about what rain boots he could be talking about and decided they were probably ones I hadn’t worn in over ten years.

I wasn’t sure if they’d even fit.

But when Silas easily slipped socks over my feet and then helped me get my boots on, I realized that they, surprisingly, did.

Pretty well, too.

“You have a flashlight, don’t you?” I accused.

He snorted. “Yeah, what man doesn’t?”

I thought about it. “My father and brothers don’t carry them.”

I felt him lean into me causing my unbound, t-shirt clad breasts to rub up against his leather vest.

I hummed in contentment as I snuggled into his arms.

"I like your vest."

"It's called a cut," he muttered laughingly.

"What's a cut?" I asked.

The storm was getting worse. The rain was slapping against the roof and the side of the garage in sheets, and the sound of the hail bouncing off the house in a loud succession of pops echoed through the space.

"A leather vest," he quipped.

I giggled against his chest, turning my face so it could rest against his neck.

He growled when I kissed his exposed throat, but otherwise didn't move.

"All joking aside, the cut is me. It's my club. The top rocker, the white banner, is our club name," he said.

I felt along his back as he spoke, running my fingers over the patches as he explained what each one meant.

"The bottom rocker is our club's location. We're the Benton chapter, and we have chapters all over the south," he explained. "On the front, over my heart, is my name, my club title, and the city again."

I knew he was explaining this to me to get my mind off the fact that the roof was shaking over our heads, *literally*.

"I can't believe Dallas hasn't at least come to check on me," I muttered darkly.

He tangled my hands in my hair, and I looked up at him…or where I thought he was.

"Your brother is a shit head. And I don't think he even realizes that he is. Because if he did, he wouldn't be telling your parents anything about how you were doing. My guess is that he really is worried, but he doesn't know how to handle it. So, he closes himself off, telling himself that by telling your mother how he thinks you're doing, he's helping. Which, in reality, he's not," Silas said. "Maybe it's time you had a talk with him. Let him know you don't appreciate being tattled on like a child."

I wholeheartedly agreed, and I'd already planned on doing just that.

"I was going to do that today, but then he had that huge freakin' party," I said, annoyance unmistakable in my tone. "I had to park on the street."

He lowered his mouth down to mine.

"Well, then it's a good thing he's preoccupied, because I could really fuck you right about now, on top of his car, and he'd never even know," he said tightly, lifting my body off the bench and laying me down on the car's hood.

I laughed. "You know," I said as he stripped my shorts from me, "this car is my brother's pride and joy."

"Well your brother's pride and joy is about to become our fuck stand," he muttered, and then he was on me.

CHAPTER 11

If a man says he will fix it…he will. There's no need to remind him every six months.
- Coffee Cup

Sawyer

Despite the way Silas was able to keep my mind off the storm that raged on outside, our town, as well as the surrounding towns, was hit hard.

Really hard.

I drove to work in my now *very* dented car, and I pulled into Dr. Zack's office lot to see a flurry of activity.

I parked in the back of the lot where the employees had been told to park, and walked into the office, straight into total pandemonium.

"What's going on?" I asked Joanie.

Joanie, who was standing at the front door, her back holding it open, lifted her head to me and visibly wilted.

"We're swamped. Zack asked me to send you straight to the back, but you'll have to walk around the building. There are so many people and dogs here right now that you won't be able to make it through."

Giving the crowd one last look, I hefted my bag on my shoulder once more and started to walk through the damp grass around the building.

The building itself was just plain brick. There were only three windows in the entire place, which meant Zack's office didn't get hit as hard as he probably could have.

The road to work today had been perilous.

Two of the roads had still been under water.

One had been inaccessible due to a downed power line and there had been so much debris scattered about that I'm sure I looked like a crazy person with all the swerving I had to do to get around the stuff.

I wasn't risking running it over, though.

That would've been just what I needed, to run something over, getting stuck on it or getting a flat and not making it to work on time.

"Sawyer!" Zack called. "Hurry!"

I picked up my pace, moving back through the lot toward Zack, who was in his truck.

"Hey!" I said, stopping at his open window, "what's going on?"

He shook his head as he ran a hand over his weathered and tired face.

"The tornado that hit Dixie was bad. I'm headed there now to see what assistance I can offer." He pointed toward the front. "I've already got people bringing in animals that they've found. I've called in my old partner, Bane. He's going to handle the practice and help anyone who comes in today. You wanna go with me?"

He looked so hopeful that I really couldn't tell him no.

"Yeah, sure," I said, circling around the front of the truck.

I smiled when I saw Zack's Labrador Retriever, Belly, in the front seat.

"Hey there, big girl," I cooed as I scooted her over and sat next to her.

"You're going to put her back into action?" I asked hopefully.

He nodded.

Belly was a retired police dog.

Her specialty was finding things, like one would use a Blood Hound.

Belly had been hurt two years ago during another storm similar to this one, and she'd been temporarily retired while she got back into fighting shape.

Even now she walked with a slight limp, one she sustained when the house she'd been searching caved in around her.

"If you're game, I'd like you to take Belly. I already know I'm going to be busy with a lot of triaging," Zack said as he pulled out of the parking lot, giving a wave in Joanie's direction.

"What?" I asked in surprise.

He nodded. "Yeah, I'm going to be helping with the animals coming in to the shelter. You can take Belly and start wherever the police direct you two, once it's been deemed safe though."

Holy shit.

Belly was attached to Zack's hip.

It absolutely floored me that he'd willingly give me the responsibility of handling Belly.

"Are…are you sure?" I asked with hesitantly.

Zack tossed me a grin. "Yeah, I'm sure. You're pretty awesome, girlie. You'll do just fine."

I highly doubted that.

I'd never seen anything like this level of destruction, though, and I was really nervous.

Adding responsibility for Belly to the mix made me feel positively nauseous.

The ride to Dixie, Louisiana was relatively short – less than a fifteen-minute drive – which further drove home just how bad it could've been for our little town.

How lucky we had been that the tornado hadn't formed just ten miles south.

"Okay," Zack said, pulling in to park in the bank's parking lot. "Let's go. I'll introduce you to the incident commander, and we'll go from there, okay?"

I nodded, following Zack and Belly.

My eyes, which I imagine mirrored the haunted expression I wore, were scanning all around me as I took in the destruction.

"My God," I breathed. "Oh, my God."

Trees were uprooted, large ones that I couldn't even fit my arms around.

Park benches that'd been bolted to the ground, gone. Laying as if they'd been carelessly tossed to the side, twisted into scraps of metal that no longer resembled a bench and never would again.

Signs hung haphazardly from their perches. Letters and numbers missing off of the remnants of what once were the buildings of downtown Dixie.

Only *one* of the buildings was still standing, relatively intact.

The only thing that was really *there*, were the roads.

And even those were ripped up in some places.

"Yeah, this isn't my first rodeo, but this one is pretty bad. I'd bet it was an F-3," Zack muttered, stepping over what appeared to be a car's bumper.

My stomach was in knots.

How could a town of this size ever come back from something like this?

And if I wasn't mistaken, an F-3 was at the middle of the scale, a scale that ran up to F-5. My God, I couldn't even begin to imagine how it could have been any worse.

"There's the command tent," Zack said, interrupting my contemplation.

I looked up in time to see a rather large firefighter dressed in bunker gear shouting out orders to men and women alike.

They got their orders and then immediately started on their assignments without any hesitation.

Then he turned fully around, and I was greeted with a younger version of Silas.

Sebastian, I think I'd heard Silas call him.

But I wasn't one hundred percent sure.

What was he doing here?

Then I saw Silas not too far from him with a little girl in his arms that looked to be two or three at most.

When he'd left my house this morning after the storm had passed, I'd thought it'd been rather abrupt. I never expected to see him here doing this.

He'd gotten a call before he'd left.

And I was ashamed to admit that I thought that maybe it'd been another woman.

But now I was glad to see that I was wrong.

"Sebastian!" Zack called.

Sebastian turned at the sound of his name being called, and he smiled when he saw Zack.

"Hey, Guzzy. How's it going?" Sebastian asked somewhat distractedly.

"I'm setting up in Old Miller's place. I just wanted to lend Belly and Sawyer here to you. Use 'em as you see fit," Zack said, offering Sebastian his hand.

Sebastian took it.

"Thanks," Sebastian said, returning the handshake. "I just got here myself. I'm on two different volunteer departments, but since Dixie was hit worse than the other town, I came here. And suddenly find myself in charge of everything."

He seemed like he was doing a good job, though.

Even if he didn't think he should be the one in charge.

"Alright, Sawyer. Take care of my Belly and take this," he said, passing a handheld, two-way radio to me. "Call me if you need anything."

I took the two-way radio, strapped it to my jeans and reached for Belly's leash, scared as hell and trying my damnedest to hide it.

"O-okay," I said.

Zack smiled reassuringly. "These boys will take good care of you. Promise."

I didn't need his reassurance.

Silas had taken care of me very well last night…not that I'd be telling him or anyone else about that.

I nodded firmly. "Thank you."

He smiled, hefted his bag and started walking away.

Belly gave a soft bark, making Zack turn around and smile at his friend before he turned and continued on his way.

I turned from watching Zack walk away to find both Silas and Sebastian watching me with varying degrees of surprise etched on their face.

"What?" I asked, concerned.

Silas went back to his phone call that I hadn't realized he was on, turning around without saying a word.

Sebastian, though, smiled.

"Never seen Zack give up Belly. He's usually the one to do the searching and rescuing with her," Sebastian said.

I nodded.

"I'm a little confused as to why he did it myself," I answered.

He shrugged.

"He blames himself. While he was searching the building that'd caught on fire for survivors, it'd started to shift with him and Belly in it. He stayed, and Belly ended up paying the price for that decision. He thinks he's not worthy of leading her anymore," Sebastian said, ushering me over.

I didn't know what to say to that.

"H-he thinks that I'm going to be better at that?" I asked a bit shrilly.

Sebastian's eyes met mine. "He must see something in you that makes him believe in the trust he just gave you. Don't let him down."

It sounded like a threat, and I had to fight the urge to take a step back.

"I'll need you right here. We haven't had a chance to search these houses yet. What we'll have you do is just circle the houses as best as you can. Belly should do the job from there," he said, pointing to a road on a real life map.

"Can you, you know, tell me how to get there?" I asked.

Sebastian nodded.

"Dad!" Sebastian called over his shoulder.

My eyes moved from the map and the point he wanted me to search to the man whose attention he'd wanted.

My breath caught in my throat when Silas turned, said a few words into his cell phone ending the call.

"Yeah?" He asked shortly.

Sebastian waved his hand in the universal sign of 'come here.'

Silas, annoyed, came.

My eyes fell to the girl he was holding.

The closer she came, the more my breath caught in my throat.

She looked just like him.

But when Sebastian reached forward and pulled the girl from Silas' arms, I realized that the girl belonged to Sebastian, not Silas.

My heart felt a little lighter, but I couldn't help the pang of longing that went through me at seeing the little girl in his arms.

"My papa," the girl said, reaching her arms out for Silas again.

"No, Blaise. Papa has to show this woman where to go. You can have him when he gets back," Sebastian gently chastised his little girl.

Blaise then turned her baby blues on me, and I was struck speechless by how beautiful this little girl was.

She was going to be a heartbreaker when she grew up, and the two men that were currently looking at her with such adoration were going to be busy keeping up with her.

Someone called Sebastian's name, and I was left alone with the man who'd held me all night long.

"Hey," I said nervously, twirling Belly's leash in my hands, intertwining it with my fingers.

He smiled at me.

Those beautiful eyes of his drinking me in.

"Didn't think I'd see you so early," he said as he took hold of my arm and steered me out of the command tent.

I was slapped upside the head once again by the devastation all around me.

From here, you could see the exact path the tornado had blazed through this little town.

Buildings sat untouched on either side of the path of destruction, making the devastation within that path all the more remarkable. Within the path that the tornado took, you could barely make out a single distinguishing feature of the buildings that used to be there.

Up ahead I saw a sign for the high school.

My breath caught when I saw how the tornado had traveled right through the center of the high school.

"God," I breathed. "God."

Silas' eyes turned down to me. "Yeah, it's pretty fucking bad. I've been a part of a lot of search and rescue operations due to natural disasters, but this one being so close to home is really fucking with my head," he said almost absently. "I mean, I volunteer on this fire department. A fire department that's now gone."

He pointed to something that was nothing more than a pile of rubble.

Brick, mortar and wood.

Sticking straight up the very middle of the pile was the fire pole. I was stunned that it was still standing.

"Shit," I breathed. "Where were the fire trucks?"

My question was answered moments later when we turned the corner.

The fire truck in question was currently on its tail end, resting against a building.

"Right there," he said.

I shook my head.

"How are y'all going to get that down without damaging it even more? Is it safe to be around that?" I asked worriedly, sinking my hand into Belly's scruff at the base of her neck.

She ran her wet nose along my arm in silent reassurance.

"There's a car beside it keeping it in place," he said.

"They've already checked all this?" I asked, holding my hand out to indicate the street we'd just passed.

Silas nodded. "Yeah, the fire station was the first place we came to, and everything in about a three block radius has been checked."

He waved his hand to someone, and I turned to find Trance with his own dog.

"Find anything?" Silas yelled.

Trance shook his head. "No."

Silas nodded and continued walking, still keeping a hold of my arm.

It was surprisingly comfortable, despite the way he gripped it like I was a criminal.

I doubted he even realized he was doing it.

"We've found more alive than dead. Six casualties so far. Twenty-four rescues," he said.

Six deaths.

Holy shit.

"This is where we're searching right now. The white X indicates the property has been searched. Red circles mean the property is unstable and don't go near it. Okay?" he asked.

I nodded.

“Call me if you need me,” he said. “If you find something, or Belly finds something, just holler and they’ll come running, okay?”

I nodded again, suddenly very nervous to be left alone.

“You’ll be okay,” he said. “Promise.”

Then, with a kiss to my forehead, he was strolling down the street, and I was left with a dog that looked very eager to get started.

“Alright, Belly, let’s do this,” I said, giving her a pat on the rump.

She licked my hand in response, and we got started.

***

It was forty-five minutes into my search that I found my first victim.

Or, I should say, Belly did.

She started barking like crazy at a pile of rubble, debris and dirt.

“I need help!” I yelled, walking forward until I was standing directly in front of the pile.

I didn’t know what to do, though.

So I gingerly started to pull off pieces of wood that I could reach without actually standing on the pile.

If there was a person under all that, they probably wouldn’t appreciate me standing on it to help them get out.

As suddenly as Belly had gone crazy, I was surrounded by huge, hulking men.

Some of them wore official-looking clothing, but most of them were in what I assumed they had most likely been wearing the night before.

“Back up, sweetheart,” one burly old man said softly.

I blinked and looked up at him.

He wasn't 'old,' but he wasn't young, either.

He was huge, though, so I took his direction and backed up to let the men work.

It was ten horrible minutes later that a shoe was uncovered, followed by the foot that shoe was attached to.

But that foot wasn't moving.

Fuck.

Please be alive, please be alive, I chanted in my head.

My wish wasn't granted, though.

By the time they had fully uncovered the man's body, I known that he was dead.

No doubt due to the sheer volume of debris that was lying on top of him. Crushing him.

Then my eyes narrowed in on the bottle that the man still held, even in death.

"Oh, my God," I breathed. "There's a baby in there. There's a baby!"

I hadn't meant for it to come out sounding so scared, but it did.

One of the men turned to me, the big one with brown hair styled into a mohawk. The same one who served me at Halligans and Handcuffs.

He was wearing a Benton Fire Department shirt and was looking at me like I'd grown a second head.

"He has a baby's bottle in his hand," I said desperately.

He looked down, and the explicative that was propelled out of him spurred the rest of the men around him into a frenzy.

I walked around them with Belly, heading through a small path between debris piles.

I wasn't sure how it was made, but I was going to use it.

Belly sniffed and sniffed, walking this way and that, until she came to a stop beside smaller pile of what resembled wood shavings and splinters.

She started barking.

"Over here!" I yelled, bending down to grab a piece of wood.

I was pushed back once again by the older burly guy and the Mohawk guy.

It still wasn't the baby. I could tell that the moment they pulled off what looked to be half of a wall.

It was the mother.

She had what looked to be a teddy bear clutched tightly to her chest.

And she was dead, too.

I could tell that when Mohawk Guy pressed two very large fingers against the woman's throat, just under her chin, and then shook his head.

"Shit," I hissed. "Let's go, Belly."

Two dead people in one day.

How positively horrible.

Tears clogged my throat, and it took everything I had to stop them from leaking out and running down my cheeks.

Once again we started searching the house, but found nothing.

Belly and I, reluctantly, moved on to the next house.

Or some semblance of what was once a house.

We found two more who had perished before we found our first live one.

I'd just given the signal, and this time Trance and Mohawk Guy, as well as the big burly guy, showed within seconds of my call. Immediately, they started searching, getting down to the bottom of the rubble and unearthing a police car.

The guy inside was alive.

I could see his chest moving.

"Yes," I exclaimed, practically jumping up and down.

My excitement garnered the attention of Trance, and his eyes were much more amused this time than the last time I'd seen him over by the dead mother.

"Keep going, girl," he ordered, pointing in the direction of more destruction.

I smiled brilliantly at him, giving him a pat on the forearm before escaping through yet another small parting in the debris.

Minutes quickly turned into another hour before I decided to take a little break.

Although Belly didn't look tired, I knew she was hot and most likely needed a drink.

"Come on, old girl. Let's get you something to drink," I said, petting her head lovingly.

She gave me a doggy grin, pushing her head into my hand and closing her eyes in bliss as her tongue lolled out the side.

I passed Mohawk Guy and said, "We're going to get a drink of water."

Mohawk Guy looked up and smiled. "10-4."

As I walked back to the command tent, where I assumed there would be water, I realized just how far we'd walked today.

"I guess I should've gotten you water earlier, eh?" I asked my companion.

"Dogs are resilient creatures," the burly guy said as he caught up to me.

I smiled at him.

"Oh yeah, I know. I used to work with them during my…old job," I said. "I know they're tough."

I didn't really want to ruin the mood by telling him I used to be in prison.

That was an instant mood breaker, and I probably had to work with him the rest of the day.

But the moment the command tent and Silas came into sight, the man was gone.

One second I was having a conversation with the man, and the next he was nowhere to be found.

"Weird," I said aloud.

Silas spotted me the moment I came into sight.

"Who was that with you?" He asked when I was within ten feet or so of him.

I shrugged. "A man that I've been working with all morning."

He smiled.

"It's about two in the afternoon now, Sawyer," he said chidingly, lifting his finger to run it down the bridge of my nose. "You're burned."

I shrugged. "Not the first time and won't be the last."

He shook his head slightly, wearing a little grin, as I grabbed a water bottle from the table in front of him. I picked up a bowl full of Band-Aids that had been sitting under the table, dumped them out, and filled it up with water for Belly.

Belly gulped it down quickly, and I felt even worse for neglecting her.

"Stand up," Silas ordered.

I blinked and looked up at him to find him holding a bottle of sunscreen with a good amount already squeezed out on his extended palm.

I stood, trying not to smile as he rubbed the lotion into my face.

It burned as his fingers met the already sun kissed skin, but nonetheless I stayed still until he was finished.

Then his hands started on my neck and arms.

I shivered slightly as he took his time rubbing the lotion into my skin, dipping past my shirt to run along the swells of my breasts.

I was panting when I finally looked up into Silas' eyes.

Leaning forward, my hips met the distinct bulge of his cock, and his eyes flared as we came into contact.

My mouth opened, and I started to speak when I was interrupted.

It was like a dousing from a cold bucket of water in the middle of a desert.

"Silas!" A distinctly familiar voice called. "Help me!"

I closed my eyes and looked around Silas' large body to see my mother barreling down on us with a box of food filled to the brim.

"Sawyer! What are you doing here?" My mother asked.

Silas stayed where he was while I skirted around him, stepping over Belly who'd laid full out on the grass in shade the command tent's shadow.

"Hi, Mom," I said. "I'm here helping Dr. Zack."

She smiled.

"Awesome. It's good to see you out here," she smiled, blissfully unaware of what she'd just interrupted.

"Reba," Silas said as he turned around.

He had a clipboard he'd picked up off the table held in front of his erection, and I turned my face down so my mother wouldn't see my satisfied smile.

I felt a pinch on my ass and whirled around to see Silas glaring down at me.

My head whipped around to stare at my mother, but she was so busy pulling food out from the box that she never even noticed our little interaction.

I widened my eyes at Silas, who only smiled and walked to the table.

"Whatcha got?" Silas asked, pulling out a couple of Styrofoam boxes.

"Barbeque," she smiled. "I got your favorite!"

His favorite?

And why, if they were only neighbors, did she know his favorite?

I didn't know his favorite *anything*, and I'd had sex with him multiple times!

I knew how he liked his cock sucked, though.

Which I guess was better than knowing he preferred chopped brisket to sliced brisket.

"I also got you pickles like you like," she continued. "I brought you a Coca Cola but also brought a couple more bottles of cold water just in case."

Silas took the package she handed him and tossed me a weird look.

One that oddly appeared almost calculating.

I wasn't sure if he was watching me to gauge my reaction to my mother, or if he was watching me to make sure I didn't say anything in front of her.

"I'm sorry, baby. But I didn't know you would be here," my mother continued. "I only brought Sebastian, Silas, and Blaise something to eat."

So she knew them all on a first name basis.

Well now, that was interesting.

"That's okay, I'm not hungry," I lied.

I'm starving.

I hadn't realized that it was two. I'd missed lunch and I skipped breakfast because I wanted to do other things this morning.

Things that involved Silas' massive cock and my vagina.

Which was better than breakfast any day.

"You'll have some of mine," Silas ordered.

I gave him a look which clearly said, '*You can shove that food up your ass.*'

He gave me one right back that said, '*If you don't eat some of my food, I'll spank you in front of your mother.*'

Clearly that wasn't an option, so I reluctantly sat down.

He handed me one of his sandwiches, and I reluctantly took it.

It was massive, and I really couldn't see how he'd get one in his stomach, let alone two, but who was I to judge?

I could eat an entire bag of potato chips in one single sitting.

Something I'd only just discovered that I could do the day after I'd gotten out of prison.

Then my mind sobered, and unsurprisingly, I wasn't very hungry any more.

I'd done a good job these past few days forgetting about the reality that was my life.

Silas was a good distraction.

Actually, he was a great distraction.

I hadn't had to drink myself to sleep for a good four days straight, thanks to Silas' and his skills.

"So how have you been, honey? You haven't stopped by lately. I've been worried about you," my mother said, picking up a small container of coleslaw and digging into it with a plastic fork.

"I've been fine, thanks," I said. "How's work?"

My mother worked as a float nurse at the hospital in Shreveport.

She'd been a nurse there for nearly thirty years.

She and my dad met there in fact.

My dad had been hit by a drunk driver, and he'd been in the hospital with a broken femur.

My mother had been his nurse during his hospital stay, and the rest, as they say, is history.

"It's good," my mother said distractedly.

"How's dad?" I asked, trying to get her eyes off Silas.

My brows furrowed.

My mother was staring at Silas with worry.

For some unknown reason, I wanted to step in front of Silas to block my mother's eyes from him.

It was jealousy.

I was jealous!

Of my mother!

My mother obviously had some sort of relationship with Silas, the man *I* was sleeping with, and it was beginning to really rankle and unnerve me to know that she clearly knew him better than I did.

"He's fine," she said, finally looking at me. "He's busy at work." She turned away from me once again. "How's your daughter, Silas? Is she doing well?"

Ok, so she also knew his whole family.

Wonderful.

"She's good. Her husband got into a little trouble a week ago during a SWAT op. But he's fine. She's worrying over him like any good woman would," Silas said around bites of his sandwich.

I really didn't have much of an appetite any more, and I couldn't handle watching this familiar, comfortable interaction between Silas and my mother any longer.

I put the sandwich down, minus the four bites I'd taken, placing it on to Silas' plate.

"I gotta use the restroom," I lied. "Be back."

Belly got up when I did, and I was so grateful I could have kissed her.

Maybe she could feel my anger and confusion over the situation, this clearly unmistakable friendship that my mother and Silas somehow shared.

I didn't understand whatever it was that was going on between them, and I wasn't happy about it at all.

This meant I didn't plan on coming back after I finished supposedly using the bathroom.

Silas and my mother didn't stop talking as Belly and I left, and something about that enraged me.

They acted like they had a relationship!

And it wasn't normal.

My dad was a territorial man. A *very* territorial man.

When I was sixteen, my mother had innocently smiled at another man, and my father had flipped way the freak out.

So given that fact, a fact that my mother was very well aware of about my father, what in the ever lovin' hell was going on between her and Silas?

I walked down the street to the high school, remembering seeing volunteers disappear and reappear out of the gym doors, a gym that was completely separate from the falling down building surrounding it.

That's where I assumed the restrooms everyone was using were located.

I was right.

According to the man sitting on the brick wall outside, I'd made the right call.

"Bathroom?" I asked him.

He nodded. "Walk in and take a left. It'll take you right where you need to go. Just follow the line."

Great. Just what I needed right then, a line.

But alas, that was the way it was, so just like a good girl, I went to stand in line waiting for my turn.

"All yours," the woman that had been in front of me said.

We'd been chatting while we waited about how crazy the weather had been since the first of the year.

Something I hadn't witnessed for myself until about a month ago.

The weathermen predicted this unusual weather pattern would continue for at least another ten days.

I didn't think I'd seen the sun shining in well over a week, yet I'd still managed to get sun burned, even through the clouds.

Once I was done in the bathroom, I picked up Belly's leash from where I'd hooked it onto the stall's door and headed over to the sink.

There wasn't any soap left, and I grimaced as I used water only.

"Gross," I muttered as I walked out, wiping my hands on my shorts seeing as there were no paper towels either.

I smiled in mutual commiseration at the women waiting in the line and continued on my way, Belly at my side.

Wiping all other thoughts of my mother and Silas from my mind, I got right back into the thick of things, thoughts focused solely on finding more people.

Hopefully – preferably – alive.

And Silas could suck it.

CHAPTER 12

I may look calm, but in my head we've already made use of the table. The wall. And the bed, three times.
- Sawyer's secret thoughts

Sawyer

Sixteen hours later, I was fairly certain that I couldn't feel my toes.

My legs hurt so bad that I honestly thought I was going to die as soon as my back hit the bed.

And that wasn't even the worst of it.

Silas was mad at me.

Me!

What the hell had I done to him?

When he'd spent more time speaking with my mother during that fifteen minutes of barbeque, I realized something.

My mom and Silas had some sort of relationship.

And not only did it piss me off, since my mother was married, but it pissed me off because Silas was now with *me*, and he hadn't said a word to me about him having a relationship with my mother.

"Who was the man you were talking to this morning?" Silas asked again.

Apparently, I'd spent too much time with the old guy for his comfort.

I had a thing for *him*, not every old guy on the planet.

Not that Silas was old, or that he looked old, but Silas didn't see it that way.

"I already told you I don't know his name," I said with annoyance. "He helped me lift crap off of people. He said goodbye this evening. That was it. We didn't exchange names or anything."

"With a hug?" He half snarled under his breath.

Was he jealous?

I shrugged. "I don't know. To tell you the truth, the last twenty-four hours are kind of a blur."

So on top of having sex with Silas throughout the night, I spent a very long, hot and physically exhausting day, as well as the whole night and into the early morning hours, on my feet, handling Belly, as we searched through the aftermath of the tornado for victims and survivors.

I was lucky to be sitting upright now and not slumped over, face in my pancakes.

Silas might have had something to say to that, but Zack interrupted us with his exclamation of excitement.

"Lookie here, girlie! You made the front page," Zack laughed, tossing the paper down in front of me.

I smiled as I looked at it.

It was of Belly and me walking around the grounds of the high school.

It'd only been taken about eight hours ago. I was surprised they'd gotten it into the paper so fast.

"Look, this is the guy I was telling you helped me get that old woman out," I said, pushing the paper down toward Silas.

Silas caught it and brought the picture up to look at it better.

I smiled and turned back to Zack, who was sitting in the booth in front of me.

We were at a diner eating breakfast.

It had been well over twenty-four hours since I'd last slept, and despite the tiredness I understandably felt, I was still invigorated.

I actually felt alive for the first time in eight long years.

Doing something important, helping people in need, had made me feel like I was a half decent person. It was the closest I'd felt to my pre-accident self since the moment of impact.

"Motherfucker," Silas growled. "Goddamn motherfucking son of a *bitch*!"

I blinked at his use of so much profanity.

"Silas, what's wrong?" I asked, turning to find him standing, anger flowing off of him in waves that were nearly visible.

My question bought us the attention of everybody at the surrounding tables, including the members of his club.

"I gotta go," I heard him say, and then, without another word to me, he turned and practically prowled straight out of the diner's front door.

"What the heck was that all about?" Zack asked.

I picked up the newspaper that he'd been so intently staring at, almost as if it were a ball of venomous snakes, and looked at the picture once again.

Was it the man?

Was he the reason Silas had gotten so upset?

The man had seemed sweet to me.

He'd helped me nearly all day long.

What the hell?

***

I woke to a body sliding into bed behind me.

Silas.

Silas was here.

My bleary eyes cracked slightly open, and I turned to look at the alarm clock.

I'd been sleeping for nine straight hours, but it felt like I'd only been asleep for one.

I could barely keep my eyes open as Silas worked one of his arms underneath my head and wrapped the other around my waist to pull me into his chest.

"What's going on?" I asked him sleepily, punctuating my question with a yawn.

"Shhh," he said. "We'll talk about it when we get up."

I took him at his word and let my eyes drift back shut.

But I didn't immediately fall back to sleep.

Pressed into Silas' chest, I could feel the tension in Silas' shoulders, in his arm that was locked tightly, almost stiffly, around me.

I could feel the pounding of his heart on my back, too.

Fighting the pull of sleep, I opened my eyes and frowned down at him.

There wasn't a lot of light in the room, just what was coming from the alarm clock and the display of DVD player.

"What's wrong, Silas?" I asked again.

This time he didn't try to deny me.

Instead, he tried to distract me.

His mouth found mine, and I sensed his desperation.

"I can't do it again. I can't," he said between kisses.

"Silas," I said as best as I could with his mouth against mine, getting worried now.

But his hands, those skillful, beautiful, busy hands of his started to work their way down my body.

One stopped at my nipple, plucking it lightly.

The other went down between my legs while his talented mouth trailed across my cheek, down my neck and over my chest to ravage my breasts.

I could sense his worry in the way he shoved his hips between my legs, kneeing them apart as he fell in between them.

But his mouth, which hadn't stopped working, suddenly reversed its journey to return to my mouth.

He somehow managed to pull his cock out, open a condom and smooth it down his length, and then he was right there, shoving his way in to me.

He cupped my face tenderly when his mouth met mine, his tongue stroking along my lips as they parted.

I gasped into his mouth at his body's abrupt entry into mine, lifting my hips to meet each thrust of his cock.

My heels dug into the bed as I tried in vain to get closer to him, but not succeeding at all.

"Goddammit," he growled, the vibration of his voice rattling his chest.

I placed my hand over the back of his head.

The other looped around his neck as I held on tightly.

But just as quickly, he pulled out of me and flipped me over to my stomach.

The suddenness of it caused me to be disoriented for a long moment, but the same couldn't be said for Silas.

He shoved himself roughly back inside of me, so deeply that he bottomed out.

My eyes crossed as pain flashed through me, followed quickly by ecstasy.

He was out of control, and I found that I liked it.

This Silas was different from *in control* Silas.

I felt more with this Silas.

I could tell his emotions were walking a thin line between desperation and lust.

He was trying to outrun some demon that I had no clue about.

The only thing I could do was hold on for the ride.

Something I did by curling my fingers into the sheets.

"Touch your pussy," he ordered.

Well, more like growled.

It was so sexy.

Closing my eyes and dropping down so my cheek was pressed against the mattress, I snaked a hand between my legs and touched my clit.

But I continued down until I could feel him slamming in and out of me.

Feel the stretching that my pussy did for his big cock.

I felt the wetness there, gathering around my entrance, and used it to lube up my fingers.

Gliding them back to my clit, I started to work it frantically.

I had a feeling that if I didn't get myself there quickly, he'd be going without me.

My suspicions were proven correct when, moments later, he hissed as his cock started to jerk inside of me.

I moaned when he pulled out unexpectedly, yanking the condom off with a sharp *snap*. He drove three fingers into me as I continued to work my clit, helping me to chase the orgasm that was nearly upon me. And help it did.

I felt the hot spurts of his seed hitting my ass and my back and coupled with the feeling of his calloused hand moving over my skin, what I was sure would be an epic orgasm was tightening in my belly.

The taboo feeling of it all – picturing him working himself to orgasm behind me and the way he rubbed his cum into my skin – really turned me on. Silas' hand stopped its movement across my back, and I moaned into my pillow as he continued to work his fingers in and out of me.

All of these sensations collided together shooting me straight into fucking orbit as I came harder than I ever have before, harder than I even knew a person could!

My eyes closed as they rolled back in their sockets, and my pussy clenched tightly around his fingers.

I bit into the pillow to hold back a scream would have woke the neighbors but instead I managed to muffle into a moan, all while Silas continued to pump his thick fingers into me prolonging my orgasm.

My stomach clenched so hard that I had to have pulled a muscle, but there wasn't a damn thing I could do about it until my orgasm began to slowly recede.

My breathing came out in ragged gasps as I collapsed onto my belly. Blood pounded in my ears and little bursts of light flashed behind my closed lids. I had had no idea something like I'd just experienced was even possible!

Silas' fingers stayed planted inside of me as he lay down at my side, pressing his lips against my temple. It was several long minutes before my breathing began to calm and the aftershocks stopped convulsing through me.

"Although that was fucking fantastic," I told him, panting slightly. "I still want to know what garnered that reaction."

He was silent for so long that I was positive he wouldn't answer me, but he surprised the hell out of me when he started to explain.

"That man that was beside you all day, the one that gave you a fucking hug. That man was the man that ruined my life. He destroyed me and everything I'd ever hoped I could be. And he did it with a fucking smile on his face," Silas said emotionlessly.

I started to sit up, but Silas shoved his fingers harder inside of me.

"Stay there," he ordered darkly.

Given his tone, I felt it prudent to listen to him.

"Who was he?" I asked. "Why's he so bad?"

"I gotta start from the beginning if you're going to understand," he said softly. "And it's not pretty."

"Tell me," I urged, trying my hardest not to grind down on him.

He held his fingers perfectly still, but the entire thing was distracting as hell.

"When I was eighteen, I was recruited out of the military by the CIA," he said without preamble.

I froze.

He was in the fucking CIA?

Wasn't that for people...*not* like him?

Silas was pretty high profile kind of guy. Weren't CIA agents supposed to be ghost-like people that no one ever saw?

When I didn't say anything, mostly because I couldn't stop my mind from whirling in surprise, he continued.

"They recruited me away from the military, the moment I finished basic training. I was a crack shot with a bad attitude. Joined the Marines, but I had a hard on for ignoring anything type of authority figure. I was on the verge of being kicked out, probably just a meeting with my commanding officer away from it, when I was approached by someone. His name was Rotund Rosenthal," he continued.

My head was spinning trying to process everything he was telling me.

He was recruited for the CIA at eighteen? For real?

An eighteen year old had no clue what they wanted to do with their life.

Let alone to be thrown into that kind of a situation.

"Okay, but if that's the case, where does that guy from today fit in?" I asked.

"The summer I met Sam's mother, Leslie, was when I first began my infiltration into a MC that was known for chain-raping women, filming it and selling the videos. They also had a lucrative stable," Silas said, but I interrupted him.

"What's a stable?" I asked.

He laughed slightly.

"A stable of prostitutes. They also did some coke dealing on the side. The first time I saw Leslie was the day that they normally did the grabs. She'd been in the sights of one of my 'brothers' when I claimed her. I didn't know what else to do. Goddamn mission and all that shit didn't care about a few casualties. They were looking at the bigger picture. So, I did what I had to do, only they wanted to film me taking her the first time as my initiation into the club. That was my test. I passed with flying colors," he snarled.

"You…you raped her?" I asked, my breath again coming out in pants.

When I tried to dislodge him from my body and get up to my knees, he stopped me.

"There's a reason I have you like this," he growled, removing his fingers and flipping me to my stomach.

I rolled, breathlessly, and gasped when he straddled my hips, sitting down on me to keep me in place.

"Listen to it all before you go all half-cocked," he ordered.

I snapped my mouth shut and glared.

"I didn't have a choice. It was either I do that, or the entire fucking club raped her. I didn't have a choice!" He yelled. "And I didn't rape her, I seduced her. And then fell in love with her while I was at it. She had no clue why she was there. She thought she was there for a fucking party."

I didn't say anything.

Maybe he didn't have a choice, but it was still wrong.

"That's the day Sam was conceived. I kept Leslie separate from the club. Fell so head over heels in love with her that I could barely breathe. However, the club didn't do monogamy, and I wasn't expected to either. Not wanting them to hurt my 'citizen wife', as they called her, I found Lettie, Sebastian and Shiloh's mother. I had an 'ol lady, that was aware of what went down in the club to an extent, and then I had Leslie, my real wife in the eyes of God and the government."

"Why are you telling me this?" I gasped, tears starting to leak down my cheeks.

"Because you need to understand," he said, bending down to press his lips against my face. "Because I think I'm falling for you when I promised myself I'd never do this ever again. Because it hurts too fucking bad."

My heart started to flutter, and I couldn't resist kissing him back.

But I couldn't help feeling it was wrong, what he'd done.

That it was wrong of me to want to be with him.

"I stayed in the CIA. They felt it was imperative for me to stay in the club, so I did that too. It was my assignment, *my job*, not a choice. Made a name for myself, but also kept the CIA informed on what I was hearing. By the time Sam was three, I'd made so many enemies, it wasn't safe for me to leave The Company or the club, which was well on the road to becoming completely legal. The club became my home. But Shovel…Shovel was a thorn in my side from the very beginning, and he made it a point, on a daily basis, to watch me. Study me."

I nodded, waiting for him to continue.

"He didn't like how fast I rose within the club. Hated that he no longer made the money that he used to make before I came along. Blamed me for everything that'd changed since I'd arrived," he said. "Which was true. I'd changed the club, made it mine. Changed every single thing about it that was illegal, and made it a place that I was proud of."

I blinked, stunned.

He'd done that all at such a young age.

"My kids continued to be in danger, though. Years, I had to deal with Shovel's shit. He just wouldn't leave it alone. Then he hurt my boy, knocked him down with a right hook to the face. Which I didn't take kindly to, especially when Sam's face split open like an orange on Shovel's bike spokes. After beating the absolute shit out of him, he continued to dig at me. Just kept picking and picking and picking until I had no other choice but to get rid of him," Silas said roughly.

His eyes met mine, and I knew what he'd had to do had hurt him.

"I was done following orders that were sent from The Agency at that point. It felt like I'd given my whole life to them and got nothing but heartache in return. So I retired from the CIA and started living my life as the club's president. Those men were mine, and I'd do with them what I damn well pleased. The club was very important to me, but my kids, my family were more so. Shovel was the last boy left from the old club days who wanted everything to go back to the way it was. We weren't making the same money we had been, but it also wasn't anything to sneeze at either. He was pissed at everything I represented. It was the worst mistake of his life, taking his anger for me out on Sam. So I made a call. The last one."

I rubbed my hands up and down his thighs, urging him to continue without saying a word.

"The CIA put together a plan that would tie him up in a huge bust. They wanted the information he had, though, so he wasn't to be killed. And he wasn't. He went down for life. I checked up on him every week since he was put away, but the week you arrived, he was released on bail without my knowledge. And I know he's here. He wants revenge against me and what I took from him," he grumbled, looking at his hands.

"What about your kids…your ex-wife…ex-girlfriend. Will he try to hurt them?" I asked softly.

It burned to think about him protecting them, to have his attention on another woman, but I couldn't live with myself if I didn't bring it up and something were to happen to them.

"I've got a few men working on it. They have teams on them, but it's not them he wants. He wants me. And he won't settle for anything less," he said, his hands smoothing up and down my bare back.

"Shovel…he's nasty. He knows your hopes…your fears. He knows how to get into your head. He can see what will scare you the most. For me…all those years ago…it was my kids. Kids that I hadn't realized he even knew how much I cared about since I'd taken such great pains to ignore and alienate from my life," Silas rumbled.

"So maybe he knows more than he did all those years ago, and maybe you should really start watching your kids…letting them know what's going on," I offered.

He closed his eyes. "Yeah, I need to do that. The boys are smart fuckers. They'll see the security detail after a while."

"You need to call them tomorrow, tell them what's going on. They need to know," I urged once again.

He smiled down at me sadly, and my heart started to hurt.

"They'll just hate me more," he said.

I looked into his eyes, and pulled him down by my hand wrapped around his neck.

"But they won't be dead, and from what you just told me, you can't really do much more harm," I whispered. "And besides you'll have me."

"Do I?" He asked, rolling me over to my back.

I blinked. "Do you what?"

"Have you?"

I nodded. "I'm still here, aren't I?"

He smiled sadly.

"Only because I wouldn't let you go," he countered.

I kissed his lips softly. "Well, I'm not yelling or screaming. That's gotta count for something."

"You could just be buying time. Waiting until I fall asleep to make your exit," he said.

My hands went down to his cock that was laying against my belly, and even flaccid, it was a force to be reckoned with.

It grew in my hands as I slowly stroked him up and down.

"Yeah," I said. "But I like you too much to leave. Just know that if you ever get into a circumstance where you have to do anything similar to that to me, I'll tear down heaven and earth to have you at my side. I won't tolerate cheating under any circumstance, even if it's supposedly to protect me. Understand?"

He smiled, a brilliant one that made my heart throb in my chest.

"Yeah, I gotcha."

"Good."

"Good," he whispered against my lips.

Then he was sliding those three fingers back inside of me, and I forgot to ask him the lingering questions about my mother and their relationship that were still floating around my head.

Guess I'd ask him tomorrow.

CHAPTER 13

Bikers don't go gray. They turn chrome.
- Biker Patch

Silas

"Thanks, man. I appreciate it," I said to the warden of the Huntsville Penitentiary. I wanted to get some information over the phone before I made arrangements to visit the prison.

"You're welcome. I'll get her in here in about ten minutes," Warden Walker said. "She's got to come over from the women's side, which works well because this is where we hold the parole hearings. You worked a miracle getting her out of there when you did. She's going to be ecstatic."

Warden Walker and I went way back.

He'd been the Warden for the Huntsville State Penitentiary since he was a young man of thirty years old. And now at age sixty, I knew him about as well as I knew most men.

He was my informant on the comings and goings of a few men I'd locked up during my time with the CIA.

"Hello?" A timid woman's voice answered a few moments later.

"Ruthann Comalsky?" I asked, confirming I had the right person.

She hesitated.

"My name's Silas Mackenzie. I'm seeing Sawyer Berry," I said, hoping it would get the intended effect.

"You're kidding me," she breathed. "Is she okay?"

I smiled at the true compassion and worry in Ruthann's voice.

The genuine longing to know how her friend was doing.

I'd looked into Ruthann, too.

I knew she was also inside for something stupid that didn't warrant hard time.

It was good that she and Sawyer had been paired together.

Both of them were truly decent people, and it was a good thing to have someone you could trust at your back in there.

Ruthann had been shafted just like Sawyer had, and I was seeing to it that she got out *now*.

Sawyer could use the shoulder to lean on in her life.

"She's good, very good," I said. "But she's been having dreams…ones that concern me. And I want to know some names."

I could tell I'd surprised her.

"Are you a cop?" She asked softly.

"Yeah, kind of," I answered evasively.

She didn't need to know what exactly I was. She only needed to know that I was getting her out, and that I wanted the names of the men that had made Sawyer suffer for eight years.

I, of course, could guess.

But it would be easier for Ruthann to tell me.

"Does she know what you're doing?" She asked softly.

I smiled.

"No."

"Good."

My smile grew wider.

"Names?"

"Donner, Bryant, Holloway and Jones. Those were the four that were her main torturers," she whispered.

"Thanks, darlin,'" I said. "I'll see you soon."

"What?"

I didn't answer.

Instead, I hung up and started out of my office, heading towards the main room of the clubhouse.

I wasn't surprised to find a few of my men

"Come for a ride with me, I need some help…and a witness," I ordered the two men at my side.

Kettle and Torren looked up, surprised.

I'd just entered the clubhouse, and I was fucking pissed.

And surprisingly not about Shovel, but about two other people.

"Where are we going?" They asked as they followed me outside without a question.

"Huntsville, Texas," I answered.

"What?" Kettle asked.

"Why?" Torren asked.

Torren was a good man, as was Kettle, but I had a feeling if I told them they wouldn't be as calm as I needed them to be when we got there.

Having four hours to stew about something wasn't a good thing, and in this situation it would be a really, *really bad* thing.

I was afraid if I didn't have someone along, I wouldn't be able to prevent myself from doing something I'd regret later.

And I was really worked up.

After letting go of everything I had on my chest to Sawyer last night, she'd fallen asleep in my arms.

And it had been perfect.

Absolutely and utterly perfect.

I'd not had a night where I'd slept the entire night through for ages, but last night, I did.

Sawyer was quickly becoming a very important piece of my life, and I was really contemplating bringing us into the light.

Especially after how she'd reacted to her mother bringing me lunch two days before.

Sawyer wasn't stupid, that much I knew.

She knew there'd been something between us, she just didn't know what.

And although it'd only been mostly innocent, two lonely people spending time with each other mostly because of proximity and convenience, I knew it wouldn't be a small matter to Sawyer.

It'd be huge.

And I needed to talk to her about that.

I'd intended to talk to her about it this morning.

But then Sawyer had cried out in her sleep, startling me out of my contentedness so dramatically that I'd jackknifed right up in bed.

Then she'd started moaning about some guard named Officer Donner, and I knew that I had to take care of this for her.

Not just for her, though, but for me, too.

Something inside me didn't sit right, knowing that she was abused in that jail.

And I'd learned all that I needed to know from her former cell mate, Ruthann Comalsky, as of twenty minutes ago.

***

"What are we doing here?" Torren asked as he took in the prison.

I got off my bike.

"I've been seeing someone," I said, hoping they wouldn't get into *who* just yet.

But, of course, it was Torren who was the ever so curious one.

"Who?" He asked quickly, a smile tugging at the corner of his lips.

Rolling my eyes, I didn't answer.

It wouldn't be long before they figured it out anyway, I just didn't want to be available for questioning when they did.

Because I knew they would offer their opinions, whether good or bad.

And right now I was already pissed, I didn't want to have to defend my choices to them, getting more upset in the process.

When I didn't answer, they went on to the next question.

"If you won't answer that, then how about you tell us what we're doing here," Torren asked.

Sadly, I couldn't answer that, either, without telling them.

So I just sucked it up and said, "Sawyer Berry was sexually assaulted for eight years while she was here. I want to speak to a few of the guards."

They both blinked.

"So she wasn't just a passing fuck for you?" Torren asked carefully.

I nodded. "No, she most certainly is not."

"She's the one?" Torren asked.

I shrugged, this time not answering with a yes or a no.

They must've realized that it was a sensitive subject right then, and they let it go.

"Well then, by all means, let's go talk to the fuckers," Torren said.

I smiled.

That was the good thing about having a club at your back.

They were a band of my brothers, and no age gap between us would change that.

They knew me just like I knew them.

And they realized that if I was protecting Sawyer, treating her like my own, then they'd treat her like family as well.

They'd protect her just as I would.

"Right on, brother," Kettle agreed, propping his helmet on his handlebars.

I followed suit and made my way to the front doors, where Walker was waiting for us with the door open.

"You made good time," Walker observed.

I nodded. "Roads were clear."

He raised his chin at Kettle and Torren, waving us in to follow behind him.

"Warden?" A male guard raised his brow, gesturing to us.

Walker shook him off. “No, they’re feds.”

Well…*not technically.*

The guard nodded and went back to his post at the front door, eyes scanning the wall of computers in front of him.

“I’ve got to say,” Walker said as we walked down a narrow hallway. “When you called I was surprised to hear from you. Haven’t seen, nor heard, from you in over five years.”

No, he hadn’t.

I tried not to wear out my welcome lest he think I’m only there because I want or need something.

Which I guess was technically true, I just didn’t want to burn a bridge that I might need in the future.

“My girl, she just got out of the Women’s side, and I’ve heard some disturbing things about what’s happening over there. Not from her directly, but from outside sources,” I explained. “I just wanted to look through your surveillance tapes, confirm my suspicions before I go about explaining any further.”

Walker nodded. “Well, I looked at the dates you requested myself during the four hours you took to get here, and let’s just say that I’m not at all happy with what I saw.”

My brows lowered as he came to a stop at a security panel.

I watched as he punched in number after number before opening the door.

I, of course, memorized the number instantly.

I had a photographic memory, and it came in very handy at times like this.

“It’s not what I saw, per se, but what I didn’t see,” he muttered, making sure the door was closed behind the four of us.

My brows furrowed. "And what didn't you see?" I asked impatiently, tired of hearing him hedge and haw over what he needed to say.

"Nothing. The camera feeds had something over them from the time of seven in the evening until eight in the evening. And you can't see who did it either, because of the angles," he answered, looking up at me now just as we made it to another door.

This one was made up of only steel bars and required an actual key from Walker's pocket to open it.

I couldn't help but see how easy it'd be to overpower the warden.

Although I counted him as a friend, I felt a little more than annoyed that he wasn't taking more care to protect himself.

Me or my boys could've gotten the key off of him in thirty seconds flat with no one being the wiser.

"So you're saying that you didn't notice that the cameras went off at nearly the same time every night?" I confirmed.

He shook his head. "No. Not every night. More like every three days," he corrected.

"So…like one specific guard's shift, correct?" I asked.

His eyes widened slightly, but he nodded instead of lying.

Police officers had a code.

Protect your own.

And it looked like the warden and his guards had a similar saying they did their job by.

Needless to say, he answered me, even though I could tell it was bothering him to do so.

"I have four guards on that cell block that work that shift. One of them is in charge of the cameras, and the other three rotate positions on the same cell block," he answered. "I've already called Jody Daniels, the guard in charge on the women's side, to bring them in. They should be arriving within the hour."

I was glad that the men's side was the one that handled all the legal stuff.

The courtroom was on the male side, while they shared an infirmary between the two.

A fifteen-foot-high brick fence spanned the separation between the two sides, with security guards on both sides being able to monitor the walk between them.

Neither one of them had access to the other prison's tapes, though.

Warden Walker was bigger than just a 'warden.'

He was also a retired special forces officer that was in charge of both units. He kept such a strong leash on both units that I was truly surprised that this entire thing went by unnoticed to him.

"Speak of the devil," Walker muttered, going to his door and opening it.

I didn't look up at the door, instead keeping my eyes on the video monitors on Walker's wall.

There was a woman there. Possibly around thirty-five or forty.

She had blonde hair tucked up into a tight bun on the back of her head. Her eyes were hard, shoulders stiff.

She looked pissed off, and she hadn't even heard what we had to say yet, because then she'd really be pissed.

"Thanks for coming, Jody," Walker said, holding out his hand.

She took it, but her eyes went to the three of us standing behind Walker.

"What can I do for you? You know today's a busy day for us. We have an inmate that wasn't scheduled for release for another two months being released, and I wanted to look into why," Jody said, crossing her arms in a defensive move.

I smiled inwardly.

Good luck with that. I covered my tracks well.

Ruthann was getting out whether Miss Jody liked it or not.

She was nervous.

"It's been reported by a prisoner that she's been sexually assaulted. On the days she claimed it happened, I've looked back over the security feeds during those times, and they're nonexistent. Something was placed in front of the camera, and the video is a blank piece of paper for exactly an hour," Walker said.

I watched Jody's face during Walker's explanation, and I knew immediately she had no part in the assaults.

She was horrified.

"That's why you had me call the four guards in on B shift?" She asked, horror evident in her voice.

Walker nodded. "Yes, that's exactly why."

"Motherfucker," she breathed. "Goddamn *motherfucker*."

Walker's office phone chimed, and I watched him as he picked it up, frowned, then said, "Show the first one to the conference room. One at a time, please. Wait till the other leaves before you let the next one in," Walker instructed before hanging up and crossing his arms.

"If you all will follow me, I'll take you to the conference room and then we can get started with the questioning."

Four hours later, I watched as the four guards on the shift responsible for making Sawyer's life hell, were loaded into the back of separate police cruisers.

They were being taken to the police station where they would then be questioned further.

I'd planned on a different course of action when I'd arrived, but with so many witnesses, I realized that I'd never be able to get away with what I really wanted to do.

"Take it easy, Silas. I hope next time we speak it's under better circumstances," Walker said as he shook my hand one final time.

After he disappeared back inside, it left just the three of us standing there, *waiting*.

Kettle, Torren, and I were waiting outside the huge brick wall for Ruthie to be released.

"So what'd this girl do to get in there?" Kettle asked to pass the time.

"She killed her husband," I answered.

There were a few moments of stunned silence while they digested that.

"And why are you trying to get her out early? Just because she's your girl's friend?" Torren asked.

There was no accusation in his tone, only curiosity.

They knew there was more to it than that, so they patiently waited for me to explain.

I took a bite of the sandwich I'd had Torren run up to the corner deli to get, chewed, and then explained.

"According to one of the conversations I had with Sawyer, Ruthann was beaten, nearly to death, by her husband when the cops finally showed to intervene. He was arrested, but arraigned less than two hours later, only to come back for her. She was able to get away once again, but the cops weren't able to do anything from there until his trial. Trial date comes and the husband is let off with an ankle monitor and a slap on the wrist telling him to stay away from his wife. Ruthie was in jail because her husband tried to beat her to death, and instead of taking it lying down, she shot him while he was taking a piss."

"Well fuck," Torren said.

I nodded. "Fuck indeed."

***

Sawyer's eyes narrowed on me as I pulled up to the back of Berry's house.

She was pissed, that I could tell.

Then again, having a woman on the back of my bike that wasn't her had to look bad.

"Take your helmet off before my woman goes postal on your ass," I ordered Ruthie.

Ruthie immediately complied, pulling the helmet that Sawyer usually used, off her head and shaking out her wild mane of red, curly hair.

Instantly, Sawyer went from ragingly pissed off to stunned.

Then she started to cry.

Her hand rose up to her mouth, and she covered it as a cry escaped her lips.

I pulled to a stop finally and shut the bike off.

With both feet on the ground, I smiled at Sawyer and held out my hand for Ruthie.

Ruthie used it to step free of the bike, then immediately started running full tilt toward Sawyer.

Sawyer caught Ruthie, and both women went down to their knees as they wailed and cried.

"Looks like you did well," Kettle surmised.

"Looks like you are going to get some good hea…" I gave Kettle a glare that could wither his balls to raisins.

Needless to say, he shut up.

I got off my bike and walked up to the two women, stopping beside them to look down at them.

Sawyer was babbling about how happy she was to see Ruthie.

“Ruthie,” Sawyer wailed. “I’m so glad you’re here! How’d you get out? I thought you had two more months!”

Ruthie clung tighter to Sawyer. “Your man is what happened. He worked some magic with the Warden. They were able to move up my release to today. And you should see how crazy that place is right now after he got rid of four guards. They had to go into lockdown for an hour because they were questioning every single guard there about their involvement. It made the five o’clock news!”

Sawyer’s eyes widened, then she turned her face up to my accusingly.

“What’d you do?” She hissed.

When I didn’t answer in enough time, she stood up and crowded in close to me.

“Tell me,” she growled.

I had to contain my smile.

She was like a little housecat with her ferociousness that bordered on suicidal.

It was refreshing to have someone stand up to me.

Normally, they backed off before they could get too close.

“It took some doing, but I started doing some research after hearing you cry about this in your sleep a few weeks ago. Then the night before last, when you were asleep in my arms, you spoke. I got two names out of that, and from there I was able to talk to your friend and get the rest,” I explained.

“Had you asked,” Sawyer hissed at me, poking me in the chest with one long finger. “I would’ve told you that I was never raped.”

I narrowed my eyes at her.

“So you weren’t raped…were you ever touched inappropriately? Was something done to you that you didn’t want to happen?” I asked carefully.

She snapped her mouth shut, moving her face from me to Ruthie.

“I handled it…we handled it,” she finally decided on.

My brows rose.

“And what about all those other women? So y’all protected yourselves…good. But what about the other women who don’t have what y’all had with each other? Where did that leave them?” I countered.

Her head dropped, and her shoulders dropped instantly in defeat.

“I don’t like this,” she whispered. “I’m going to have to go to a court hearing now and tell them what happened.”

I moved so my hand could cup her face.

“Because it’s the right thing to do. And it’ll make you feel better when they’re gone. And because you don’t want me to kill them and go to jail if you don’t,” I whispered to her.

Her eyes widened.

“You wouldn’t,” she challenged skeptically.

I smiled.

I would, and she knew it.

Not that I’d go to jail.

I had too many connections and knew too much for the charges to stick if I were caught, which wouldn't ever happen.

I was too good to get caught.

"I think you know the answer to that," I said, placing my lips against hers softly. "I'm going to leave you here to catch up with your friend. I'll see you in the morning."

She pressed her lips against mine and wrapped her hands around my shoulders.

"Thank you, Silas," she said urgently. "Thank you so much."

"What are you doing with my sister?" Dallas bellowed from behind us.

Fuck!

CHAPTER 14

Real women ride men who ride Harley's.
- Fact of Life

Sawyer

"I asked you a fucking question, you cradle robbing son of a bitch!" Dallas continued.

"Jesus, Dallas, chill the fuck out!" I yelled a little too loudly.

Dallas and Bristol were at the back steps of their house, watching the five of us, taking us in and sizing us up.

Well, Bristol was.

Dallas was upset over something that was quite ridiculous.

"That's your brother?" Ruthie whispered from behind me.

I looked at her over my shoulder.

"Yeah, that's one of them, anyway. The oldest of the four of them," I told her.

I'd yet to see the other three. They were all in the Army and each one was currently deployed.

Cole, Brody and Johnson were all the most badass badasses that I knew, and I was so damn proud of them that I could barely see straight.

I just wished I could have seen them in the past eight years.

Hand written mail just didn't cut it sometimes.

Dallas, though, was making up for their lack of being there.

In spades.

"I asked you a fuckin' question, old fuckin' man!" Dallas continued to scream.

My eyes rolled over to Silas to see his eyes smiling, but his mouth set in a thin line.

"I guess we're not a secret anymore," I whispered. "Maybe we shouldn't tell him that we've used his car as a 'fuck stand.'"

He snorted and aimed his eyes down at me.

"You're not helping," he growled.

I shrugged. "I was always good at really fucking shit up,"

"Obviously," Ruthie said.

Bristol finally broke from her husband, an official looking document in her hand.

"Um, this just came for you. I had to sign for it. It's from the state," she said, handing it to me.

I frowned, brows furrowing, and took it from her.

"What is it?" I asked worriedly.

The last time something official had been delivered, it was at the hands of two police officers saying I was being arrested for the death of those four people.

Scared as hell to open it, I clutched it to my chest and looked at Silas worriedly.

"It's okay. Open it," he urged.

My brows rose. “What is it?”

He smiled. “Just open it.”

So I opened it, with my brother fuming at my front, and Silas and Ruthie at my back, giving me silent encouragement.

And what I saw the minute my eyes met the paper astounded me.

“What…how…why…” my brain wasn’t working.

I couldn’t get my thoughts together.

“The charges against you have been dropped, and restitution has been delivered to you from the state,” Ruthie said in awe as she read over my shoulder. “$25,000 is all they’re going to give you for them being wrong? What the fuck is that supposed to be?”

“I don’t understand what’s going on. Why would I be proved innocent? I killed four people!” I burst out, surprising everybody.

“I don’t understand,” Dallas said, reluctantly adding his two cents into the conversation.

“How about we all take this inside, and I can explain. It wasn’t supposed to happen until next week,” Silas said. “I was going to ease everybody into this before it blew up in y’all’s faces.”

Everyone followed, even the two big guys.

Torren and Kettle, a.k.a. Mohawk Guy.

Dallas entered first, being sure to toss ugly looks over his shoulder at Silas the entire way.

We both ignored him.

“When did you do this?” I asked him, holding back from the others.

He shrugged nonchalantly. “That was who I was on the phone with the day you showed up to help with the tornado aftermath. I’d been working on that all for nearly a month, trying to figure out just what the hell happened."

I looked at him. "I killed them, that's what happened."

He took me by the hand and led me through Dallas' house as if he owned the place.

Must be a skill, though, because he did the same in my apartment.

"Sit down and let me explain this, okay?" He asked.

Reluctantly, I did so, sitting down in the chair that was facing the room as a whole.

I loved this house.

It was the same house that I'd grown up in when I was a young child.

My parents had turned over the payments for the house to Dallas about a year after I'd been incarcerated. They had moved what was left of the family to the lake house.

Something that'd burned since I'd expressed interest in taking over payments since they'd hinted at wanting to move out to the lake as soon as we were all out of the house. It was easier to make one house payment, so they had moved sooner.

And it'd burned when my mother had told me she'd given the house to Dallas and Bristol.

Burned deep and became a wound that would never heal.

The whole entire house was an open floor plan. The dining room, kitchen, living room and entry way were all part of a single, massive room.

There were four bedrooms, three of which we'd had to share between five kids.

"Alright, cradle robber. We're all here," Dallas growled deep in his throat.

Instinctively I grabbed for the nearest object, which happened to be a throw pillow, and launched it at him.

It smacked him in the face, and he turned his glare on me.

"We're not allowed to throw stuff in the house," Dallas said sarcastically, pulling the pillow into his chest.

I rolled my eyes. "Says who?"

"My wife," he shot back.

My brows rose. "And since when does your wife have any control over me?"

His eyes narrowed. "You're in her house, so you need to have more respect."

I was sure that my eyebrows were even with my hair-line at that moment in time.

"I've lived in this house longer than she has. So if anybody has claim over the happenings, it's me. I'm the eldest, after all," I countered.

"Yeah, but mom gave it to us, not you. I'm the one making the payments on it, not you. That's where you're wrong," he hissed. "This isn't your house anymore. And hasn't been since you killed those people."

Dallas realized what he said when it left his mouth, but the damage had already been done.

I turned my tear filled eyes to my Silas and said, "If you could tell us, that'd be great."

Silas' eyes were not on me, though.

They were on Dallas.

He was acting like an ass, and Silas noticed.

Hell, everyone in the room noticed.

Ruthie was sitting on the side of my armchair now, and sometime during the spat between me and my brother, Kettle and Torren had migrated to stand directly behind me, giving me their silent support.

I wasn't sure how I'd won over these two men, but I was thankful.

I could use all the help I could get right then.

"Silas," I said again.

Reluctantly, he turned his head to me, then squared his shoulders.

"The boy that was driving the car with the Neeson's in it, his father, Rydel Jones, was understandably upset, and he paid off everyone involved to make sure that you went to prison for the maximum amount of time that you could," Silas said without hesitation. "It took a while, but I realized the boy's father was involved heavily with the government. He knew the right people, and he made sure he could fix it to where you went to prison based on evidence that wasn't actually viable. You, although technically had some hint of alcohol in your system, had nowhere near enough to be considered legally 'drunk.' Although it's still technically 'manslaughter,' it's not something you should've been imprisoned for. And once I followed up with a few of those involved, I started to see a trend. I followed the money trail, something that Jones didn't do a very good job of hiding."

"But how?" I asked, stunned. "What now?"

"Nothing now. A judge has already reviewed the case and ruled in your favor. That's what this is," he said, tapping the paper in my hand. "Although $25,000 isn't nearly enough. I'll be making a call to the club's lawyer. We'll get this taken care of quickly."

"So what… I still killed them. It doesn't seem right to me," I said softly.

Silas' hand touched my chin, and I looked up as he urged me to do.

"That was an accident. Something that could've happened to anybody in this room. I can name off fifteen people right now that drink a beer with dinner every time they go out to eat. Then they drive home. If it's done in moderation, like you'd done that night, then it really would've been an accident if something happened similar to what happened to you. He pulled out in front of you. Not to mention it was raining, and they didn't have their lights on," he informed me. "Ask yourself this, could you have done anything differently?"

I thought back to that night.

It'd been very dark.

The storm was raging around us, and there wasn't a single streetlight where we the accident happened.

The only thing I was able to go by were the truck's headlights, and with the amount of rain coming down, there was only about a ten-foot section of road in front of me illuminated.

And the Bronco had come out of nowhere.

One second I'd been yelling at Bristol and the jackass to put on their seatbelts, and the next I was looking at the hood of a truck pulling out in front of me.

"I don't know," I said. "It really wasn't..."

I shook my head, unable to articulate what I wanted to say.

Silas dropped down to his knees in front of me, and it felt like every single person in the room disappeared.

"I swear to you," he said. "That you didn't mean to do what you did. You know it, and I know it. Hell, everyone in this room knows it. I spoke with the chief of police about this, went over what had happened, and he agrees." He leaned forward. "The lead detective that was on your case is dead. The judge retired. Your lawyer's dead. Now does that seem like a coincidence to you?"

I blinked. "My lawyer died of a heart attack."

He shook his head. “Your lawyer died of a suspected heart attack. There was no autopsy performed on him, so they don’t know what exactly he died from, and there are medications out there that can stop the heart and make it look like a heart attack.”

“So then…what? Do I have someone out there that’s going to try to kill me now that I know? What about the rest of the people in this room?” I asked worriedly.

“As of right now, there should be a man serving a warrant,” Silas said. “Rydel Jones should be in police custody.”

My eyes were wide.

How had he accomplished all of this without me knowing?

He grinned.

“Ex CIA, darlin,’” he whispered so only I could hear. “Just trust me. He’s going down.”

Then I started to cry.

“Can I go get my nursing license? Can I finish that? I was almost halfway through!” I whispered fiercely.

To think of all those years wasted.

Where would I be right now had I been able to finish?

I only had another year.

He nodded. “You should be able to. I’m not really sure how any of that will work out, or even when it’ll all be finished by. But yeah, you are being pardoned, your record will be expunged, you’ll no longer have any criminal record at all.”

I looked at him and knew, had this not awful thing not happened to me, I wouldn’t be sitting where I was right then.

I wouldn’t have this wonderful man in front of me.

He may seem harsh and hard to everyone else, since I'd heard no less than twenty people say that, but he was a big ol' marshmallow with me.

He had an ooey gooey center that only I could see.

"I lo…thank you, Silas," I said. "Thank you so much."

His eyes flared at my near slip of tongue, and I thought I detected a note of panic in his eyes before they cleared.

"You're welcome, Sawyer. I'd do anything for you," he said roughly. "Anything you need, I'll give to you if it's within my power."

***

Hours later found Ruthie and I at a diner in town.

And none other than Isaac and his new wife two booths in front of us.

"That's my ex that I thought stood by me through it all," I whispered, leaning forward so only she could hear. "But I found out the day I got out that he was about to get married and had a kid on the way. He has been openly cheating on me since I went in."

"Seems like you bounced back well," Ruthie's eyes sparkled. "And with an older man at that! Jesus, is he sexy as hell or what?!"

I smiled.

Silas *was* sexy as hell.

"I know, God, how did I get so lucky?" I whispered conspiratorially. "And I never even saw him coming! It was just one second he was there, and I couldn't stop thinking about him. I saw him everywhere I turned!"

What he didn't know, is that he half saved me.

I was well on the way to being depressed.

And Silas had been there to rip me off that path with such ease that it was scary.

"So what's his story?"

"You're never going to believe this, but I think he had some sort of relationship with my mother," I whispered. "And I haven't had a chance to talk to either one of them about it. Although I guess I can now. Dallas won't keep his trap shut about the two of us. My mother and father will know by morning, I'm sure."

Ruthie's mouth dropped open.

"So you think they were like…what…fucking? He didn't seem the type to cheat."

I refrained from saying that he *was* the type.

That he'd done it in the past.

Then she'd think I was crazy for still being with him.

Ruthie hated cheaters.

Her now dead husband had been a cheater.

And she had an irrational annoyance with them.

She contributed her husband's desire to beat her to the fact that she'd confronted him about his cheating.

So I decided to steer clear of that topic.

"I don't know," I answered honestly. "I have to talk to him about it. There hasn't been time to ask. And I don't want to ask my mother, because that's just awkward. What if they did share a relationship of some sort?"

She shrugged.

But before she could say anything else, a man's throat clearing had me looking up.

At Isaac.

Oh, yay!

"Yeah?" I asked with a raised brow.

"I thought I'd check to see how you were doing," he said, eyes smiling at me.

I blinked.

"How I'm doing?" I asked, confirming what he'd said.

He nodded.

"Yeah, I'm sorry I didn't get to meet you. I didn't have much choice," he said, pointing with his thumb at the woman behind him.

Ruthie snorted into her drink before taking another sip, trying gallantly not to get into the middle of what she knew was about to become a huge fight.

"Well, Isaac, I guess I'm doing alright considering," I said smoothly.

He blinked.

"Considering what?" He asked.

It was my turn to blink.

"Are you really that stupid, Isaac?" I asked slowly.

He frowned. "What are you talking about? I didn't do anything to you."

"Let me start from the beginning then," I said, holding up one finger. "You forced me to go to a party eight years ago that I didn't want to go to, and, as a result, I killed four people." I held up a second finger. "Then you lead me on for eight years. Telling me you'll be waiting for me when I get out. Yet, the day I get out, you don't show up, and my best friend tells me that you're getting married – to the woman you knocked up."

His eyes narrowed. "A guy has needs, Sawyer."

I laughed humorlessly.

"Oh yeah, a guy has needs. Sure, I understand. How about you just on and leave with the girl who met your needs, and leave me to eat my burger in peace, hmm?" I asked snidely.

His eyes narrowed. "I don't know why you're being such a bitch."

Patience has never been Ruthie's strong suit, and I was waiting for her to make her move; I intercepted it before she could.

"Ahh," I reprimanded Ruthie, taking my cup of coffee from her hands and placing it back on the table. "It's not worth it. And I'm over him anyway."

Ruthie turned annoyed eyes to me.

"Well, he definitely could use a talking to," she hissed. "Leave already."

Isaac gave the two of us one more long look, before he turned on his heel and walked back over to the woman that was staring daggers at me.

I waved back at her, amused that she thought she could intimidate me.

It'd take a lot more than a glare, bitch, to make that happen, I thought humorlessly. *I've got a black belt in prison yard tactics. I could have her on the ground before she even had a chance to lift that finger she was pointing at me.*

"That was fun," Ruthie said as the waitress placed a chocolate milkshake down in front of her.

Ruthie pounced on it like a starving dog.

"God," she breathed. "I forgot how great this shit was."

I could entirely relate.

You just seemed to have a greater appreciation of the simple things in life after having them withheld from you for any length of time.

For instance, going to the bathroom or taking a shower.

A day hasn't gone by in the last month that I haven't said a silent prayer of thanks over the fact that I now had a door I could shut while I was using the restroom.

You could never really understand the humiliation of having to do number two in front of a guard unless you'd had no choice.

Ruthie and I had done damn near everything in front of the other.

There wasn't one thing she could do right now that would shock or surprise me.

"Your Bristol didn't look very happy with me," Ruthie said once she'd downed nearly half of the chocolate shake.

I'd noticed that.

"I think she's a tad jealous," I told her. "It's like she didn't think I made any friends or anything had changed since the day I'd gone inside. She picked right back up where we'd left off the day that I was released as if not a single day had gone by. It's almost as if she's scared to broach the topic."

"She still blames herself," Ruthie finally said, finishing the last of her shake.

How she'd been able to down something like that – so thick and cold – in under three minutes, I didn't know.

But it sure was fun to watch her do it.

"I think she does and she doesn't. I think she feels guilty for living her life when I couldn't live mine. She's also worried that I'll get mad at the fact that she and my brother married," I told her.

"Are you sure she won't mind me staying with you?" She asked worriedly.

I shook my head.

"No, she won't mind. Then again, that place where they're living is technically mine. Something that Bristol informed me of when she picked me up," I explained, bringing my glass of water up to my lips.

"I don't fuckin' care if you're not serving breakfast anymore. If you don't give me some of your biscuits, I'll literally have a new asshole made for me by my extremely pregnant wife. Seriously, just two is fine. Please!" A man's annoyed voice pleaded.

"We don't have any more. I'm sorry, sir," the old woman behind the counter said, not sounding sorry in the least.

Ruthie and I looked up to find a dark haired man with even darker eyes looking at the waitress with a frown on his face.

"We took the last ones," Ruthie said, pointing down at the biscuits we'd just been given.

I looked down at the succulent morsels, and my stomach growled.

We'd gotten to the diner about ten minutes before they'd stopped serving breakfast, and we'd never gotten any jelly, so we'd yet to eat them.

But seeing the pleading look in the man's eyes, I stood from the table and made my way to him with the biscuits in my arms.

The real reason I'd even contemplated giving him the biscuits was because of the leather vest, or what Silas like to call a 'cut,' on his back.

He was a Dixie Warden.

And the name on his vest declared him to be 'Cleo.'

I vaguely recognized him as someone I'd seen at the clubhouse Silas had dragged me to last week, and I knew what I had to do.

"'Scuse me," I said.

The man's dark eyes turned to me, then dropped to the biscuits in my hand.

"You can have them," I said.

His eyes narrowed.

"Why?"

I barely contained the urge to snort.

"Because you're wearing that," I said, pointing to the cut but not touching it.

I'd gotten a lesson in that, too.

Apparently a brother's 'colors' were sacred.

No one was supposed to touch them unless they were intimately involved with the man wearing them, such as a significant other or an 'old lady', as Silas had called it.

"What's your name?" He asked, eyes narrowing.

I smiled.

"Sawyer Berry."

Recognition flared in his eyes. "You're Silas'."

I cocked my head. "How do you know that?"

He grinned. "The whole fucking city knows. When Silas wants something known, he makes it known. Plus, I saw you at the clubhouse last week. Thanks for the biscuits."

Then he took the biscuits from my hand, and I was left standing there stunned.

It'd only been a few hours since my brother had found out about us.

Now, supposedly the whole town knew? *Holy shit!*

CHAPTER 15

I don't have a reason to be politically correct anymore. There's no one left I want to impress.
-Silas

Silas

"Are you sure I should be here?" Sawyer whispered worriedly.

I gave her a look.

"Why shouldn't you be here?" I asked, laughter evident in my voice.

I was taking her to a club party for the first time, and she was nervous.

So nervous that she had a death grip on my hand.

I stopped just before we made it to the door, pulling her to the left of it, and pinning her against the wall next to it with my body.

"What's the deal, honey?" I asked, tucking a stray lock of her hair behind her head.

"What if they all know me…what I did?" She whispered, her eyes haunted.

I placed my hand against her smooth skin, rubbing the apple of her cheek with my thumb.

"So what if they do? Do you think they're all saints, that no one in there's ever done anything wrong?" I asked her.

She closed her eyes, and a tear slipped out of the corner of her eye.

"I just want them to like me," she explained.

I nodded. "And they will. It's hard not to like you, darlin.' You're a good person; don't let anyone else tell you differently."

She face planted into my chest, and I laughed.

"Come on," I said, lifting her face away from my chest and setting her back a little further. "Let's go inside so you can meet my family."

She nodded, rearranged her emotions, and tilted her head back.

Chin up, shoulders back, she walked with me inside the clubhouse and gasped.

"Wow, this is like an indoor theater," she whispered. "Is that what you intended?"

I looked around at the clubhouse.

It was a glorified warehouse with a ton of recliners, couches and chairs spaced sporadically around the room.

There was a bar in the very back of the room and just beyond the bar were a slew of bedrooms the club members could use, as well as my office and Sebastian's.

"Not at first, no. But each member has their own chair or couch, and as we grew in size, the room just kept collecting more and more chairs until that's all there were in here. The big screen in front came out of necessity," I explained. "Mostly because Dixie broke the last one when he was trying to play the Wii."

She looked at me, then a smile turned up the corner of her lips.

"Which one is Dixie?" She asked.

I looked around until I finally spotted Dixie sitting at the corner of the bar talking to Trance.

"He's over there," I said, pointing in the direction.

She followed my finger and smiled.

"He looks like Santa Claus," she whispered.

***

Sawyer

"That's what I thought, too!" A woman's voice broke into our conversation from behind us.

I turned to find myself staring at a blonde woman dressed in a paramedic t-shirt and jeans.

She wore a leather vest, much like the ones worn by the men, only hers had a rocker claiming her as *Property of Shiva.*

What the hell?

"You know who Santa Claus is?" I asked, a smile in my voice.

She winked. "His real name is Dixie Normus."

"As in, his dick's enormous?" I confirmed.

The woman grinned. "The one and only. My name's Baylee."

I shook her hand as Silas said, "This is Sebastian's wife."

"Ahh," I nodded, letting her hand go. "I've heard a lot about you."

"Only good things, I hope. Silas, mind if I steal her?" Baylee asked.

Silas shrugged and looked down at me. "You don't have to go if you don't want to. Although they'll just talk about you behind your back if you don't."

I blinked. "I, um… Well, I guess if you put it that way…"

Baylee snorted and took a hold of my hand, looping her arm through the crook of mine, and heading off with a slight wave over her shoulder at Silas.

"Take care of my girl, Baylee," Silas rumbled.

I tossed a blushing smile over my shoulder at him, and he winked.

A jolt of desire shot down my spine, but it was just as soon forgotten when I turned back around to see Baylee leading me to a table of women who were all staring at me expectantly.

"Ladies," Baylee announced loudly. "I'd like to introduce you to the bear tamer, Ms. Sawyer Berry."

There was a gaggle of 'ooooh's and 'ahhh's' as they took me in.

"So you're the one who has put Silas in such a good mood lately…I've never seen him this way," a woman with long black hair and tattoos said cheekily.

I blushed as her words sunk in. "Yeah, I guess that's me."

There was a woman that looked to be the tattooed woman's twin who spoke next. "My name is Viddy, and this is my twin sister, Adeline. She's married to Kettle, the one with the Mohawk. I'm married to Trance."

She would've continued, but I interrupted with, "The one with the dogs!"

The table laughed collectively.

"I was going to say the hot one with the weird eyes," Viddy laughed. "But the one with the dogs is probably better."

"From left to right," Baylee said. "This is Tru, Rue, Channing, Adeline and Viddy."

I waved at them all.

"Nice to meet you all," I said, taking a seat when Baylee pulled one out for me.

"So what do you do, Sawyer?" The one Baylee had introduced to me as Tru, asked.

I smiled. "I work at Deguzman Veterinary and Associates. I'm a technician there."

"Hey, that's where we take our dogs!" Viddy exclaimed.

I nodded. "That's how I knew you belonged to the one with the dogs."

She laughed. "Well that sure does make an awful lot of sense."

"Where'd you meet Silas?" The one named Rue asked.

I turned to her and said, "I met him at Halligans and Handcuffs."

And so the evening begun.

They asked questions, and I answered them.

I didn't drink like the majority of them did, though.

My eyes were taking in my surroundings, wondering what the big deal about a 'biker party' was when I finally said, "I thought biker parties were supposed to be wild and out of control."

Adeline snorted. "It probably would've been three years ago before Baylee came along. Now it's all about family and friends. They don't get too wild unless the other chapters come around."

"Other chapters?" I asked, taking a small sip of my Dr. Pepper.

Baylee was the one who answered.

"The Club has different 'chapters,'" she said, forming her fingers into air quotes. "They're all members of the same club, the Dixie Wardens, just based in different states. All the chapters have the same name, though. They all come around once or twice a year for the big parties. This year it's our turn to host, too. Last year, it was the Alabama chapter's turn, so we all went down there for a week."

I nodded in understanding. "That's cool. Kinda like one big extended family."

They all nodded their heads in agreement. "Yeah, those parties get pretty wild just because of the sheer number of people here."

"That," Viddy said, "And the fact that they don't have the same limits that our guys do. Our chapter is made up of men who are all public servants of some kind, which means they don't generally do anything obviously illegal, unless things get really out of hand and it's unavoidable. Most of the time, though, Silas is pretty good at keeping all our boys under control."

My brows rose. "Silas doesn't ever get out of control."

Every single one of them laughed.

"I don't think any of us has ever seen him have more than two beers at most. He doesn't yell. Curse. Fight. Posture. He's an all-around good man who just wants his club to have fun, while keeping their shit together as they do it," Baylee admitted. "And he's so set in his ways. I've never once seen him in anything but jeans, a t-shirt, boots and his cut. When there's a pool party at one of our houses, he's always there, wearing the same thing. Sometimes I wonder if he even sleeps in those clothes."

It was my turn to laugh.

I'd seen the man naked.

And I knew he wore jeans only when he was at home relaxing.

Although I did notice when people came over, he always slipped on his boots and a t-shirt.

I'd never seen him drunk, but I'd seen him close.

And he laughed all the time with me.

Was it me who did that for him?

Because, if so, I kind of liked that. I liked the thought that I did the same for him as he did for me.

I was one very happy woman, and I wanted him to be happy, too.

“So he’s not so uptight around you?” Viddy asked hopefully before bringing her margarita up to her lips.

I nodded. “No. Actually he’s pretty laid back.”

“Glad to hear you think so, darlin’,” Silas’ voice said with amusement from behind me.

I turned my head upside down so I could look at him standing over the back of my chair.

He had both of his strong hands resting on either side of my shoulders, and he was looking down at me with a smile on his face.

“I was only telling the truth,” I informed him.

He winked and leaned down until his mouth touched my own.

“The boys want to go for a ride. You up for it?” He asked.

“That’s not fair!” Rue yelled. “I can’t ride!”

It was then she stood up and gestured to her belly, and I was surprised to see she’d been hiding a pretty sizable baby bump underneath the table.

I would’ve never even realized it had she not stood up.

“Cleo went to get the truck,” he answered her. “Apparently you’re going to the doctor early tomorrow anyway. And he said he had to be at work at five in the morning.”

Rue pursed her lips. “He’s such a liar. He just wants to get me home. Do you realize how hard it was to get him to let me come out here?” She grumbled, annoyance clear in her voice.

I snorted and stood. “I’m just going to use the bathroom,” I whispered to him. “And then, yes,” I said, pressing my lips against his, “I’d love to go for a ride with you.”

He caught the back of my head and forced my mouth down on his once more. "Good."

***

I closed my eyes and let my mind wander.

My face was pressed against the leather of Silas' cut.

My hands were gently tracing the waistband of his jeans where it met the skin of his taught belly.

My inner thighs and crotch were pressed snugly to his backside.

The rumble of the engine was soothing, even though it was loud.

My ears had gotten used to the sound of the bike, it's growling repetition lulling me into a peaceful and happy place.

Silas leaned into a bend in the road, and my body leaned with his. I was kind of amazed at how close to the road we tilted on the bike as he maneuvered us through the turn.

Silas handled his machine expertly.

It was powerful and beautiful all at the same time.

I loved the way the tension seemed to leach out of him the longer we were on the bike.

The more we rode, the more relaxed I became because *he* became more relaxed.

His friends rode around us, one on each side, two in front and two in back.

The women were much the same as I was, although they were probably more used to the way their ass went to sleep after a while than I was.

In fact, I was so relaxed as we drove down yet another back road that I almost missed it.

Almost.

I happened to glance over to look at Baylee, and I immediately noticed that she was as white as a sheet and her eyes were starting to roll back in her head.

I grabbed a hold of Silas' hair to get his attention, then I pointed in the direction of Baylee.

Silas' response was immediate, surprising me with his quick reaction.

Instantly, he maneuvered the bike to the side, crowding closer to Sebastian's bike.

My heart was pounding in my chest as I did the only thing I could think of to do as we traveled at fifty miles an hour down the open road with nothing surrounding us.

I reached out and caught her, shoving her back up against Sebastian in an effort to keep her where she was supposed to be. Silas kept his motorcycle steady next to theirs, while we both slowed down, allowing me to keep a hold on her as I held her in place on the back of Sebastian's bike.

Sebastian was also trying his hardest to hold her to him while slowing his bike one handed, and I knew she wasn't going to make it.

She was going to fall.

She was going to be ripped to shreds by the pavement before my eyes.

Oh, God. Please no.

But a miracle happened.

We somehow managed to stop.

And, by the grace of God, she stayed in place on the back of Sebastian's bike.

Once the bike finally came to a full stop, I gasped out a breath like I'd just run a fifty-mile marathon.

I was half off the bike, the only thing holding me back was Silas' grip on the back of my jeans and my grip on his cut around the base of his neck.

My thighs were screaming, though, and my mind raced with concern as I quickly got off the bike.

Kettle beat me to it, though, seeming to come from nowhere with Adeline right on his heels.

They easily moved Baylee off the bike, and it was then that I saw the amount of blood that was pouring out of her.

I could see a wound on her neck, but I couldn't tell what caused it, what the hell had happened to her.

"What's going on?" I asked worriedly.

The next thirty minutes were a blur.

Ambulances came.

Cops showed.

One ambulance left with Sebastian and a still unconscious Baylee.

And the cop in front of us kept saying words 'arrested' and 'obstruction of justice' since we didn't know what happened.

"Seriously, man," Silas finally said. "I have no clue what happened. We were enjoying a ride, and my woman practically rips my head off to let me know that something's going on. We pull over, and she was like that. She has a disease, though – Von Willebrand's. It's a bleeding disorder. Anything could've happened to her, and it'd be more serious just because of that."

I'd actually heard Baylee say something about having that disease tonight.

It made it so that she could barely function during her periods since the blood flow leaned towards the extreme rather than normal.

She'd also told me about when she'd delivered her daughter, Blaise, and how she'd almost lost her life because they couldn't get the bleeding under control.

"That's true, she told me about this tonight. I looked over and her eyes were rolling back in her head. I was lucky I saw it when I did, or she would've been hurt much worse," I whispered.

Silas' hands tightened on mine. "We really would like to get to the hospital to check on her, if you don't mind."

The officer narrowed his eyes. "We'll be in contact," he said, flipping his book shut with a snap and turning on his heel to leave.

"Dick," Silas muttered under his breath.

I squeezed his hand tighter.

"Be nice," I whispered.

He snorted. "Let's get to the hospital."

We walked to the bikes where the others waited, one of the prospects having been dropped off to take Sebastian's bike back to his place.

And all I could think about was how bad it could've been.

How she could've died. How she could even be dead right now.

Did I attract death? Was it me?

Questions that I couldn't answer right now filled my mind. I pushed them out to reevaluate later.

Because, seriously, I had a sickening feeling that this wasn't so simple. Something had happened.

I just knew somehow that the worst was yet to come.

***

"Hey," I said, looking nervously from Sebastian to Baylee.

Sebastian was sitting on the edge of Baylee's bed, her hand engulfed in his.

"My hero," Baylee croaked.

I laughed. "You're looking better."

Sebastian stood up, and I watched him stalk towards me.

He didn't stop in front of me, though.

No, he only stopped to put his massive arms around me and pick me straight up off my feet.

"Thank you," he whispered gruffly.

I patted his arm awkwardly as I tried to breathe with difficulty given the tight grip Sebastian had on me.

"It's okay," I whispered. "She's fine. Look at her."

Sebastian dropped me to my feet almost jarringly and turned to take in his wife who was watching the encounter with a smile on her face.

"What?" She asked after a while.

"Ummm, I was just telling him that Silas wanted a word with him in the hallway," I said.

Sebastian gave my shoulder a squeeze and walked over to his wife, giving her a soft kiss on the lips.

"I'll be back in a minute," he rumbled against her lips.

I blushed and averted my eyes, looking out the hospital room's window instead of at the sight before me as I waited for them to finish.

"You can look now," Baylee said with amusement.

I looked up to find the room empty, and the door closing softly behind me.

I blushed once again.

"Sorry," I said, dumping my bag onto the chair at the side of her bed.

She smiled and held out her hand.

I took it.

"Thanks," Baylee whispered. "It must've been a rock or something. It's happened before, and I didn't realize I was bleeding at all then, either."

"Holy shit," I breathed. "I kind of guessed you had a bad deal with this disease, but this was insane. You're so freakin' lucky, Baylee!"

She was, too!

Had I not seen her, she would've fallen right off the back of Sebastian's bike!

"Thanks to you," she said softly.

I patted her hand.

"Just don't make me have to do that again, it scared the snot out of me," I admitted.

"Baylee," a man's voice said from the doorway. "I swear to God, I can't take my eyes off of you anymore without you getting into some kind of trouble."

I blinked and turned to the blond giant wearing a SWAT shirt and black pants.

My mouth dropped open.

He was gorgeous!

Like, unbelievably so!

"Sawyer Berry, my brother, Luke Shithead Roberts," Baylee said dryly.

I snorted, and then covered my mouth when the giant's eyes turned to me.

"You her?" He asked.

"Am I her, what?" I wondered aloud.

"The girl that saved my sister," Luke said like I was dumb for even asking.

I shrugged, not saying anything.

"Let me know if you ever need anything and I'm there. This little turd means the world to me," Luke said. "Your man said he wanted you."

I blinked. "My man?"

My brain was fried, because I should've known he meant Silas.

I just hadn't heard him referred to as 'my man' before.

"Silas…you know, the old dude with the beard that wears the president patch on his vest?" He teased.

I blinked. "Oh, yeah."

He snorted. "Said he'd be waiting for you out front."

Nodding, I leaned down and gave Baylee another hug.

"Take care of yourself," I whispered. "Let me know if you need anything."

Baylee squeezed me extra tight and said, "Thank you, again, Sawyer."

I nodded and patted her hand. "I'll send the next visitor in."

"Tell whoever it is to bring me a coke!" She ordered as I got to the door.

I gave her a thumb's up and walked down the hall to the waiting room where the rest of the group was camped out.

My eyes went to the first person I saw, which happened to be Adeline.

"She wants whomever goes in next to bring her a coke," I said to her.

Adeline smiled. "I'll take that as my cue to go get her something, thanks."

Nodding, I walked to the door waving at all of them.

"I'll see y'all later," I said.

The women waved back, but the men all got up and hugged me, one by one, leaving me stunned.

"You're one of us now," Trance said.

"Thank you," Kettle was next.

"You're welcome," I said, blushing furiously once again.

I was pretty sure I'd done that no less than ten times tonight.

If not more.

"You're a good kid," the one with the slashed throat said, whose name escaped me.

"Thanks," I whispered, backing up until my back hit the elevator doors.

"Take care of yourself," the final one said, I think his name was Torren.

But I'd learned so many names tonight, that I wasn't quite sure.

So I said a vague, "See you later," to the group as a whole and disappeared into the elevator.

When the door's closed, I breathed a sigh of relief.

Not because I was glad to go, but because I was glad to not have their thanks anymore.

I'd done what anybody would've done…right?

Apparently, though, that wasn't the case for the Dixie Wardens.

Tonight I'd earned my right to be at Silas' side, and I just didn't realize it yet.

CHAPTER 16

There's a special place in hell for men that fuck with women. And you'll be meeting that dark little corner of the universe as fast as my bare hands can get you there.
-Silas' secret thoughts

Silas

I wanted to kill someone.

Preferably with my bare hands.

As I sat in the darkness listening to Sawyer have yet another nightmare, I was torn.

It'd been a week since I'd gone down to Huntsville and watched as the guards that'd tortured Sawyer for years get arrested.

And I'd told her last night that all four of them had been let out on bail.

Then six hours later, as she slept, she started to have nightmares.

I'd woken her from them three times already, but the moment her eyes closed once again, and she drifted back to sleep, she was right back in the throes of her nightmare.

Now it was three in the morning, and we both had to be up in less than three hours, and I was wondering if I should just wake her up completely.

The scream of terror that was ripped from her throat solidified my decision as I wrapped my hand around the outside of Sawyer's hip, letting my hand play along her ass.

"Sawyer," I said, shaking her slightly.

"*Noooo,*" she moaned. "Please. Don't."

The sound of her pain tore through me like a hot fire poker right to the gut.

Leaning down so I could gather her completely into my arms I said, "Sawyer, wake up!"

Sawyer jolted awake, shaking uncontrollably in my arms.

"What…what's wrong?" She asked shakily.

"You tell me, darlin,'" I said. "You're not ever going to get it out if you don't talk about it. Tell me what they did to you."

I could feel Sawyer's eyelashes fluttering on my chest as she opened and closed them rapidly.

Then I felt the telltale trail of tears sliding down my bare chest, and I pulled her to me a little tighter.

"Tell me," I urged.

"If it wasn't for Ruthie, I'd be a very different woman right now," she started.

Instead of saying anything, I just ran my hand through her hair. Stroking it lightly in encouragement, urging her to continue.

"I was paired with Ruthie right off the bat," she whispered. "Thank God. Ruthie had gotten there about two weeks before me, and she'd already had to suffer at those men's hands. I never really heard what exactly was done to her, because she didn't want to talk about it, but I figure they went a lot further with her than they did with me."

The hand that was propping my head up clenched in a tight fist as she got to what I really wanted to hear.

"The first time they cornered me was in the laundry area. I was in charge of folding the towels." She swallowed, her tiny hand sliding up the outside of my abdominals, playing along the ridges and valleys of my chest. "I was bent over the basket, reaching for the last towel, when one of the guards came up behind me and pinned me to the basket. My pants were around my ankles before I even realized what was happening. When his hands touched me there, Ruthie came up and started to scream, drawing the attention of the entire laundry area, as well as the guards not in the laundry area."

My eyes clenched shut tightly as I tried to reign in my fury.

"From then on, Ruthie and I had each other's back. We never left one another alone, and the guards weren't brave enough to do us both at the same time. So we basically had to stay with each other twenty-four seven," she continued. "But there were the times where we were separated. Sometimes she'd be assigned to a different job for the day. When I started working with the dogs, she wasn't allowed to do the same. That's when it started up again. Not for me, but for Ruthie. I didn't even realize anything was happening until about a month before I was let out. And I feel like a total and complete heel for not noticing it sooner."

I brushed my lips across her head before I said, "She was protecting you and letting you do what you love. You're good with those dogs."

She was, too.

I was impressed.

She could easily rivaled Trance with her ability to train dogs.

Trance's skills, however, were focused on training dogs for police procedures.

Sawyer's abilities were geared more toward training them to be service dogs.

Like Belly.

Belly was trained to find people in the aftermath of a storm or a natural disaster.

Sawyer was a savant with dogs, an absolute natural, and I bet she'd start to get serious about dog training once the trials of the guards made it through the courts and everything related to her own charges had been settled.

"Anyway, it's not really me you should be worried about. It's Ruthie. I only had them touch me. She…I don't know. They did more to her, but I don't know exactly what because she won't say. I hope one day she entrusts that information to someone," Sawyer said tiredly.

"I want you to talk to a lawyer. I want you to get more from the state than the twenty-five thousand they say they'll give you." I said suddenly.

It was something that'd been weighing on my mind since I'd read the letter Sawyer had received.

"I don't know. I don't really want to start something. I just want it all to be over with," she explained.

I shook my head.

"Twenty-five thousand dollars isn't enough. They owe you a hell of a lot more. A nurse's salary just for one year is at least twice that. And from what I figure, you should at least get fifty grand times eight years. But what I think you should really do is sue the state for assault. None of this would've happened had you not gone down in the first place. You have to believe in your government. If they made a mistake like this, they need to rectify it a little better than just an 'oh here's twenty-five grand. Go buy yourself a nice half a car. Sorry about falsely imprisoning you for eight years,'" I said.

I could tell she wanted to roll her eyes.

But I was right.

Had she been a nurse for eight years, she'd probably have a house, a nice car, and a lot more to her name than just an old beat up junker car and a garage apartment.

"I'll get the club's lawyer on the line in the morning. In the meantime, how about I do a little distracting," I said, running my bearded chin up and down the column of her throat.

She giggled and turned her face away, but that only caused her breasts to press further into me.

"Stop," she laughed, twisting in my arms.

I rolled until she was on top, straddling my thighs.

"Silas," she said breathlessly, leaning down until her face was even with my own.

The faint glow from the nightlight that had flicked on with our movements illuminated her shapely body and had my blood pumping and my heart pounding in anticipation.

I'd placed the nightlight there so Sawyer could make her way to and from the bathroom at night without tripping over any of the furniture.

Never in a million years had I envisioned the sight before me, but thanks to that nightlight, it was a vision I wouldn't soon be forgetting

My dick, now hard, strained behind my underwear and pulsed in time with the *thump-thump-thumping* of my racing heart.

"What?" I replied, lifting myself up to grind into her.

She pressed her lips softly against mine, then pulled back long enough to say, "Make love to me," before she was pressing them back against mine, tangling her tongue with mine.

If a woman had said that to me a month and a half ago, I would've balked.

But in that moment, with the woman I considered mine, I didn't hesitate. Not one bit.

Running my hands up her sides, I caught the tails of my shirt that she'd commandeered for the night, and quickly pulled it up and over her head.

She separated her mouth from mine, hunching her shoulders, causing her breasts to hang down over my face.

"Are you trying to suffocate me with these things?" I asked teasingly as I let the shirt go and immediately latched onto both breasts.

I pinched and flicked her nipples as I reached into the bedside table, pulling out a condom and ripping it open.

Placing my palm flat on her belly, I pushed her back slightly until she fell flat on her back.

I followed her as I lowered the band of my underwear, allowing my cock to pop free.

I ground the bare length of it into the wetness of her vagina, wishing like hell I could just slip inside of her without a barrier for once.

Alas, since she wasn't on birth control from what I could tell, I slipped the annoyance down over the length of my shaft and lined up the head of my condom-clad cock at the entrance to her pussy.

Slowly easing inside, I filled her until she gasped.

"Silas," she breathed.

I leaned down to allow my chest hair to play along her turgid nipples, grinding my cock into her core and relishing the tightness of her.

She was the tightest pussy I'd ever had, and I couldn't get enough of it.

Reaching down, I gathered both of her knees into my hands and pressed them up over her shoulders as I slowly started to pump in and out of her.

This positon allowed me to get deep inside of her, exactly where I liked to be.

My hips pumped back and forth in to her as her wetness eased my way.

The head of my cock was bumping against her cervix with each plunge.

"You feel so good," I said roughly against her lips.

She sighed, and her hot little tongue licked the seam of my lips, causing my hips to jerk.

She gasped at the deepness and clutched my ass with both hands as she urged me on faster.

I obliged as I gave her my length, harder and harder.

My hips slapped against her ass with hard thrusts, making that distinct *smack-smack-smacking* sound as our bodies collided.

My balls slapped against her ass with each thrust, and when I felt her hand move down to gather her wetness before trailing back up to her clit, I knew I was fighting a losing battle.

My eyes squeezed tightly shut as I used every ounce of my strength to hold off my impending orgasm.

When her orgasm finally hit, I was panting.

My eyes crossed as her pussy clamped down on my cock with the start of her orgasm, and I groaned in relief as I finally let go.

Hard, hot pulses of my come filled the tip of the condom.

I wished like hell I was filling her to the brim, but that would be for another day.

"Jesus," Sawyer breathed long moments later. "I prefer that to having nightmares."

I laughed. "I'll remember that."

Pulling out of her tight heat, I carefully pulled the condom from my cock and tied it in a knot before placing it in the trash can beside the bed.

Then I pulled her into my arms and rolled until she was lying directly on top of me.

“Go to sleep, darlin’,” I ordered.

She smiled and rolled her head to kiss my chest, right above my nipple.

“Alright, Silas,” she agreed, settling a little deeper onto me.

My eyes closed, and I finally let out a breath I hadn’t been aware I was holding the moment the words slipped free of her mouth.

“I love you, Silas.”

She was asleep in the next breath, so she didn’t hear my reply.

“I love you, too, darlin’.”

***

“What is this place?” She asked.

I lifted my leg from the bike and held out my hand to her, which she took almost immediately.

“Life Flight,” I said. “I own it.”

“You…you own this?” She asked, looking in awe at the huge helicopter that was sitting on the front lawn, taking up the helipad and the majority of the front lot.

“Yeah, I own it. I bought it about a year or so ago,” I told her, leading the way to the front door.

It was set up much like a fire station would be.

“Life Flight employs ten people. Four flight medics, four flight nurses and two office dispatchers. Each medic works with a nurse, so there’s always one of each on every flight. The dispatchers work opposing shifts, and we use an answering service that specializes in medical office procedures to cover the phones during non-business hours,” I explained as we made our way inside the main room.

I wasn't surprised to find Cleo kicked back on the couch and his partner in the closest recliner.

There was a lot of down time being a flight medic.

Although, it was inevitable that when it did get busy, you were hit with a ton of shit all at once. Our calls usually came in back-to-back-to-back.

"Biscuit Girl!" Cleo yelled, surprising the ever-loving shit out of me.

I blinked, then turned to Sawyer with raised brows.

"What the hell is he calling you that for?" I asked.

Sawyer smiled. "I gave him my biscuits for his wife one day when he came into the diner. They'd just stopped serving breakfast, and we'd gotten the last batch."

I nodded in understanding.

The Pub Diner was a pretty happening place during breakfast hours.

Most of the time, the line was out the door just to get into the place for breakfast.

Cleo had been lucky that Sawyer was willing to give those biscuits up.

I'd personally had them, and *I* sure as hell wouldn't have done that.

"Yeah, thanks to her, my wife didn't try to kill me that day. Sawyer's a hero in my book," Cleo said emphatically.

Rolling my eyes, I took hold of Sawyer's hand and led her into my office, shutting the door behind us.

I didn't even notice Sawyer's wide eyes until she asked, "Do you not know how to file?"

I looked at my desk and the mountains of paper collecting dust on every available surface.

"I do my best, but I seriously need a secretary," I told her, dropping down in my chair and punching the power button on my computer. "Why don't you make yourself useful?"

She laughed, which was what I'd intended for her to do.

She hadn't been the same since last night, which was why I'd kept her with me today.

Today was Sunday, so Zack's office was closed, and she was off.

Which meant she would've been home all day stewing on things she couldn't change, which was why she was here with me instead and not at home alone.

"I guess I could try to help you out," she said as she came up behind me, threading her arms around my neck.

I patted her hand. "Gotta get this payroll done, then we can christen another office," I teased.

She snorted and pressed her lips against my neck.

"Let me know when we can get to that," she whispered.

I turned my face up towards hers as I guided her lips to mine by way of my hand in her ponytail.

"Be good, and I'll see what I can do," I told her.

She giggled against my lips, and I found that I quite liked that sound.

"I can do that," she whispered. "I can be very, *very* good."

Yes, she absolutely could.

Within the hour and a half I'd been working, she filed not just one of my paperwork piles, but all of them. She even started cleaning up my office when she was done.

And yes, we christened the office.

Twice.

CHAPTER 17

What's better than a man in uniform? A biker in leather.
- Fact of Life

Sawyer

The next morning dawned rainy, yet again.

I could really go for some sunshine right about now.

The clouds and rain paired with the blinds on Silas' windows reminded me too much of being caged in…and Silas' bad attitude wasn't helping my mood.

"Hey," Silas said, interrupting my thoughts. "Do you think you can do something for me?"

I blinked. "Sure, what?"

He handed me a letter.

"I have a brother in the Navy. He's deployed right now. Do you think you can go get him these things, and a few extras, so we can send a care package over to him?" Silas asked.

I nodded. "Sure. I was heading over to Target anyway."

I'd of course heard him talking about the man in the Navy.

Sterling, I think he'd said his name way.

He was a SEAL from what I'd heard through passing conversation.

"What else should I get him?" I asked. "And do you want me to go ahead and send it out today?"

He looked up distractedly from something he was reading.

It looked like a case file or something, but I'd learned not to butt into his business.

The last time I'd looked at one of his manila folders, I'd seen the gruesome carnage of a teenager that'd been hacked up with…something.

I didn't want to know what was in those files, and I'd resigned myself to not even thinking about them.

I still wasn't quite sure what exactly it was that he *did* for a living.

I knew he was a CIA operative at one point, but he didn't really go anywhere aside from the firehouse, the Dixie Warden's clubhouse, Halligans and Handcuffs and the Life Flight office.

"Get him some candy that won't melt," he offered.

"Silas?" I asked.

He looked up. "Yeah?"

His beautiful blue eyes were intoxicating.

"What is it that you do for a living?" I finally asked.

He grinned. "I'm a crime analyst. I freelance, which means I do it on my own, and I'm paid as a subcontractor for my expert opinions and analysis. I usually get my cases from the CIA and the FBI. I look for trends in criminal activity across the country, and I track them using the software program I developed. It's a central source of criminal information for all branches of law enforcement. I track the details of crimes, so that when another similar crime occurs, we can determine if the similarities are just coincidences or the crime is actually related to other crimes. This is helpful to law enforcement in deciding if a crime is the work of a serial criminal, a copycat or an unrelated coincidence.

My mouth dropped open, and I could do nothing but stare at him.

"You're shitting me."

He shook his head. "No. What do you think I did?"

"I don't know. I didn't realize you did something so specific. But you always have these," I said, indicating to the file folder with a long finger. "I guess I just thought you were still kind of in the CIA, but just didn't get any calls."

He grinned. "All you had to do was ask."

I rolled my eyes. "I'll remember that next time."

Walking over to him after picking up my purse, I pressed my lips against his.

"I have to go see my parents after work today. I saw my mom leaving this morning when I went to get the paper. She's pissed, I better head it off before it gets too complicated."

He winked and pressed his lips against mine again.

"You know your mom and me…we never had anything. It was just two lonely people spending time with each other," he told me, holding his big hand at the back of my head so I couldn't back away.

I blinked. "Actually, no, I didn't know that. I've wondered, though."

He shook his head, and a smile ticked up the corner of his mouth. "There you go again. Darlin', all you gotta do is *ask me* whatever it is that you wanna know."

I shrugged. "Oops."

Placing another kiss on my mouth, he gave me a slap on the ass and said, "Go on, before you're late."

I looked down at my watch.

Shit.

I was going to be late if I didn't go now.

"Okay, I'll call you around lunchtime to see if you want anything," I said.

With one last kiss on the lips, I walked out the front door of Silas' place.

I was taking Silas' truck because he hated my car, so I bypassed mine and went straight to his pretty black Dodge Ram.

Not that I was complaining. I loved his truck.

And I loved that he wanted me safe, which was why I hadn't driven my car in well over a week.

Hell, all of my stuff was even in his truck.

You know, those little things that everyone leaves in their vehicles?

Phone charger. Chap Stick.

Tampons.

I looked in my rearview mirror to see the familiar silhouette of a motorcycle behind me.

That wasn't new.

I'd had them following me around for a while now, courtesy of Silas.

He thought that Shovel would try to come after me, and who was I to argue? I didn't know the man, so I had to trust that Silas knew what he was talking about.

And deal with the fact that a man followed me everywhere I went twenty-four seven.

Turning my eyes back to the road, I swung the huge beast into Target's parking lot and parked at the back of the lot.

I wasn't used to parking this big boy yet.

My phone rang as I slid out of the truck, landing on my feet lightly.

“Hello?” I answered, pressing the lock button on the key fob as I started to walk towards the front of the building.

“Hey, I’m going to be late for lunch. I have a job interview,” Ruthie said excitedly.

I squealed. “How exciting! Where?”

“Halligans and Handcuffs,” she answered. “I’m pretty sure it’s a pity job given to me by your man, but I’ll take just about anything at this point.”

I laughed. “Trust me. If Silas didn’t think you were qualified, you wouldn’t be getting the interview. He may like you, but he likes his businesses better.”

“Businesses?” Ruthie asked.

I nodded, coming to a stop at the side of the building so I didn’t have everyone and their brother listening to my conversation.

“Yeah, apparently he owns Halligans and Handcuffs, as well as Life Flight,” I told her. “Although I just figured it out a couple of days ago when he took me with him to the office and forced me to file paperwork while he did something on the computer.”

Ruthie laughed. “Forced you to file paperwork? I’m sure he did that.”

I laughed. “Okay, well I did it willingly. Regardless, I just found out about the place, though.”

“Well, you’ve only known him for like two months. What did you want to do, know his whole life story in that short of a time period?” She asked laughingly.

I sighed. “I gotta make a run for it into the Target. But I’ll call you back later today and let you know how the meeting with the parents went!”

Something I so wasn’t looking forward to.

At all.

"Later, chicka. Good luck," she said.

I laughed as I pressed the 'end call' button and dumped the phone into my bag.

Making a mental list in my head of things I needed to get, I quickly started for the front door, stopping when I reached the very corner of the awning in the front.

Which was why I saw my dad, who hadn't seen me.

He was with a woman…a woman that was not my mother.

And I couldn't tell you why I stopped and listened to their conversation instead of saying hello like I usually would have.

Instead, I moved until I could just barely see my father's back, but I could hear everything he was saying to the pretty blonde-haired woman in front of him.

"I'm sorry, Judy. I didn't mean to string you along. I never would've done that intentionally. It's just that my ex-wife and I decided to give it a second go, and I've wanted that since we'd divorced six years ago. I'm so sorry I hurt you," my father said, touching the woman in front of him on the arm.

My heart sank.

"If you loved her, why'd you leave her?" This Judy chick hissed at my father.

I stopped behind the huge red pillar at the front of the Target and waited to hear his reply.

"After my daughter went to prison, my wife and I took a break. My wife decided that the break needed to be permanent when she and I had a difference of opinion where our daughter was concerned," he admitted.

It all finally made sense.

Were my parents ever going to tell me this?

Or was I supposed to go on blissfully unaware?

Getting back to the truck wasn't very hard.

I just pulled my hood high over my head, tucked my bag back into the crook of my arm and walked slowly back to Silas' truck.

The moment I was inside, I pulled my phone out and called Silas.

He was the first one I thought to talk to, and that no longer made me nervous.

Because I loved Silas.

Even if he hid stuff from me.

"Did you know?" I asked, tears coursing down my cheeks.

"Know what, baby?" Silas asked worriedly.

"About my parents," I answered.

"What about them?"

"That they were divorced," I cried.

I could tell he paused in what he was doing. "Yeah, I knew."

My eyes closed. "Why didn't you tell me? Why did I have to find out because I listened in on a conversation between my father and his ex-girlfriend in front of Target?"

He cleared his throat and said, "Because it's not my job. They're your parents, baby. It wasn't my place."

"God," I breathed. "They divorced because of me."

"They divorced because they were both hardheaded and wanted to divorce. Talk to them. I have no answers as to what they were thinking when they did that," Silas said. "But if you talk to them, then you'll get the answers you need. I'm sorry you found out that way, baby."

Oh, I'd be getting answers all right.

A lot of them.

***

My gut was churning as I made my way up my parents' front walk six hours later.

I looked longingly over my shoulder at Silas' place, then waved at the man on the motorcycle that was parked under the tree across the yard.

He waved back, and I walked into my parent's house without knocking.

I found my mother at the kitchen sink, and my father sitting at the kitchen table reading the paper.

They both turned in surprise when they saw me.

"Hey baby," my mother said. "Are you hungry?"

"No." I shook my head. "I'm not."

I hadn't meant for my voice to sound so forlorn, but I couldn't help it.

I hadn't been able to stop thinking about the fact that my parents had divorced.

"What's wrong, baby?" My dad asked as he stood up.

I looked at my dad as he walked across the room towards me.

He was a big, burly man with a pot-belly that confirmed his love his of beer and cake.

But he was still so handsome with his brown hair and his honey brown eyes.

He had a killer smile that was still the same as the day he married my mom.

"I…I overheard you today at Target," I said, eyes on him and his reaction.

He froze and looked over his shoulder at my mother.

Had he told her what he'd done?

That question was answered moments later when my mother said, "You saw him with Judy."

I nodded. "Yeah."

She sighed and turned the water off, grabbing the towel beside the sink and drying her hands as she went to the table.

"Come sit," she said, patting the seat. "Seems we have quite a bit to talk about."

I could tell she wanted to talk about the whole Silas situation, too.

She'd been calling me since the night I'd found out about my prison sentence being for naught.

My brother had a big mouth and had probably told my mom the instant we'd left.

"How about we just get it all out on the table," my father said without preamble. "Your mother and I divorced because we couldn't get over the fact of how much we'd failed you. She wanted to keep fighting, but I forced her to stop the only way I knew how. By divorcing her."

I blinked. "What?"

He nodded. "Without both of our incomes, she couldn't keep it up, and she was forced to stop beating the dead horse."

My mother's eyes filled with tears.

My father's head dropped. "We couldn't afford anything else."

I blinked. "I don't understand."

"Your mother and I always believed that you were innocent of the crime they'd accused you of, but we had no way to stop what was happening.

We'd used our entire life savings, and all of the money in our 401Ks. Every penny we had, we used, and we just couldn't do it anymore. It was already a struggle before, but after that, with the lawyer's fees, we couldn't do it and stay afloat." My father's voice cracked, "You'll never know how truly horrible it was to do that to you…to your mother. But we just couldn't do it anymore."

I closed my eyes.

"I'm so sorry," I whispered with devastation evident in my voice. "I'm so, so sorry."

My father's arms wrapped around me, as he said "It wasn't your fault, and from what your brother's told us, we really were right about it not being your fault. We love you, baby girl. And every cent and heartache was worth it. I only wish I would've let your mother try harder so you wouldn't have had to spend eight years of your life in there."

All this time I'd been avoiding them, and they'd sacrificed so much!

"I'm such a bad person," I whispered brokenly as I clutched my father's chest.

I felt my mother's warm body at my back as she pressed her lips against my forehead. "It's not your fault, honey bun. We both know you had no control over what happened."

"I've been horrible to you since I've gotten back. I've been so ensconced in my mind that I haven't been thinking about how it felt for you," I whispered, wiping my tears on my father's shirt.

My mother sifted her hand through my hair like she used to do when I was upset as a child.

"We understand, baby girl. We understand everything. *Everything*. We promise," she explained.

I had a feeling we were no longer talking about just the way I'd treated them anymore.

I pulled away from my dad and turned to my mom, taking a deep breath.

"I love him," I told her.

She smiled. "He's easy to love. I'm just glad he loves you back."

I blinked.

"How do you know that?" I asked.

"Because he's come over and spoken with us about his intentions," my father said at my back.

I gasped. "He what?"

My father nodded. "The day that your brother told us about you and him, he came over here and let us know personally. Then he let us know where everything stood with the charges, and how he was trying to convince you to get a lawyer to seek more restitution."

I blinked.

Which was all I seemed capable of doing.

"Which we wholeheartedly agree with. We believe that you should be compensated for all the money you spent in legal fees, as well as your school loans," my mother added.

I grimaced.

I'd forgotten about those.

But it didn't surprise me that I would have to pay those back still.

Wonderful, yet another thing I had to worry about paying.

Shit.

"Okay," I said finally. "I'll think about it."

My mother smiled.

"Good. Now, are you ready to have some pie, or should I wait a couple minutes before slicing it? It just got out of the oven," she smiled, clearly hoping to entice me.

Really, there was no other option, so I had some pie.

And thought about ways that I could get my parents married again, since it was apparent they were living in sin.

CHAPTER 18

The best things in life are the things that have the greatest consequences. Like cake. Calories are a bitch.
- Fact of life

Sawyer

The drive to Kilgore, Texas wasn't a long one.

What made it feel long, however, was the way Silas was acting.

I had my hands wrapped around his waist, but it could've been a tree for all I knew.

Silas was pissed at me, because I insisted that his children needed to know about Shovel being released from prison.

It had been two weeks since I'd found out that the charges against me were dropped.

My records were in the process of being expunged, and I was in contact with the Club's lawyer who would be helping me with the restitution case against the state.

That'd been Silas' idea and not mine.

I really just wanted it all to go away.

Yesterday.

The man responsible for it all had been arrested.

And just like eight years ago, the entire town's attention was once again on me.

And I freakin' hated it.

It reminded me over and over again about how it felt to have all their scrutiny eight years ago, when the wounds of killing those four people were still fresh.

Not to mention that I'd finally bugged him enough about telling his family that the Shovel guy he'd worried about was still around. He might even be closer than they realized.

He didn't want to worry his kids unnecessarily, but after a lot of convincing done on my part, he'd finally relented. He didn't have to be happy about it, though.

And, apparently, he thought it'd be a good idea to tell his kids about this at his grandchild's baptism.

I walked next to Silas, staring up in awe at the building in front of me.

The church was massive. It was old and beautiful and just so… grand.

"Are you sure it's OK that I'm here?" I asked Silas nervously.

Silas nodded. "Yeah, I think it's time for you to meet all of my kids. It's not ever going to get any easier, and it's time to just rip the band aid off and get it done."

I didn't agree.

From what he'd told me, his kids were all around my age.

I was younger than the eldest two, his sons. His daughter was my age exactly, her birthday only two months after mine.

"Which granddaughter is getting baptized?" I asked once again.

He'd told me earlier, but I couldn't remember her name.

They all started with a 'P.'

"Phoebe," he said again, not batting an eye at my forgetfulness.

He seemed almost preoccupied, as if he didn't want to be here at all.

What I couldn't understand was…why?

These were his grandkids for Christ's sake.

Then I found out about ten minutes later when we tracked down his first-born son, Sam.

He was tall like Silas, built a lot like his dad.

He had black hair, though, compared to Silas' salt and pepper.

Each had beards, but Sam's was a little shorter than Silas'.

The moment Sam saw Silas, his demeanor changed.

No longer open like it'd been when he was talking to an older woman in front of him, but completely closed off and unwelcoming.

Silas walked up with me, and I had the urge to wrap Silas into my arms and stop him before he got too close to Sam.

But Silas was fearless, and he walked right up to Sam without any hesitation whatsoever in his step.

But Silas' eyes went to the woman first as he stopped directly in front of them.

"Leslie," Silas said, nodding his head slightly. "How are you doing?"

Oh, *shit!*

This was his ex-wife.

The woman that I couldn't seem to stop comparing myself to.

Ever since the night he'd told me what had happened with his ex, I have been slightly self-conscious.

I knew that Silas cared about Leslie.

Deeply.

He'd been head over heels in love with her.

Was he still?

Looking at Silas' face, I couldn't tell. It was unreadable.

He did that when he didn't want his emotions examined.

He was good at it, too.

It was something that drove me up the freakin' wall.

It was hard to gauge Silas at times because of his ability to literally shut down every single emotion that he was feeling.

Other people showed their anger with their words or their demeanor.

You wouldn't realize Silas was even mad until he threw the first punch.

"Silas," Leslie said, nodding her head at him. "I'll see you later, son."

Silas watched her as she walked away, and then turned back to his son when he could no longer see her.

"Sam, I need to talk to you for a minute," Silas rumbled softly.

His son, Sam, looked up at him and glared.

"I don't have time," he answered immediately, not even giving his father a chance to explain *why* he needed it.

I gritted my teeth at the accusation in the man's tone.

Seriously, who doesn't have time for their own parent?

It'd taken a lot of convincing on my part to even get Silas to tell Sam.

"It won't take but a minute. I need you to gather James and Sebastian, too," Silas continued as if Sam hadn't said a word.

"Fuck," the man hissed. "I'll meet you out back in ten."

Then he walked past us, not even acknowledging me at all.

"That was fun," I said humorlessly.

Silas looked down at me and winked.

"I know," he said. "Take a seat here, and I'll be back as soon as I can."

I sat on the bench at the back of the rapidly filling church and looked down at my hands in contemplation.

I'd met Sebastian, of course.

He'd been by many times with his kids and wife to see Silas.

The other two, Shiloh and Sam, I'd yet to meet.

And from what I'd seen so far, I wasn't impressed.

It wasn't two minutes later that two women walked up.

One had long, curly blonde hair, while the other had a short bob of brown hair.

I knew who they both were instantly from the pictures in Silas' house.

Sam's wife, Cheyenne, and Silas' daughter, Shiloh.

Shiloh was married to the blonde man I could see across the room watching the three of us.

"Hi," I said softly as they sat.

The two of them smiled.

The blonde more than the brunette, though.

"Hey," Cheyenne said. "How's it going? I'm glad you could make it."

I blinked. "Uhh, thanks."

I came because Silas looked nervous as hell, and I didn't want him to go somewhere he wasn't welcome by himself.

"We didn't know that you were coming…or that you were dating my dad…until just about two minutes ago. Needless to say, we're a little surprised. You're pretty young," Shiloh said, sitting back and crossing her arms, not holding any punches.

She was a beautiful woman, but it didn't surprise me.

Silas wouldn't have ugly kids.

Not with how gorgeous he was.

And after seeing his ex-wife, it was no wonder that Shiloh was so beautiful.

"I'm thirty in about a week," I informed her. Thirty wasn't young. Not by a long shot.

Shiloh raised a brow. "You do know that my dad's fifty-four, right?"

I blinked, then nodded. "Yeah, I know that."

"And you're still with him?" Shiloh asked incredulity.

"Um, yes?" I asked, a question in my tone.

What was the big deal about me still being with him?

I *loved* him.

The fact that he had twenty-four years on me didn't change that fact.

"So…what are your intentions?" Cheyenne asked.

I looked over at her and smiled. "You know, my father just told me that Silas told him his intentions yesterday. Then to have his daughter-in-law ask me the same question only a day later is kinda funny."

Cheyenne smiled slightly. "Yeah, I can see how it would be. But you still didn't answer my question."

Shrugging I said, "I love him."

Shiloh's eyes narrowed, but surprisingly, she didn't say anything negative to my admission.

“You better be good to him,” she whispered.

Thankfully, Silas returned twenty minutes later, because I was nearly over the two women sitting in the seat beside me.

“What happened to your beard?” His daughter asked sharply.

Silas sat.

Then Shiloh’s eyes turned to me accusingly.

What was wrong with his beard?

“Shaved it off,” he said without explanation.

Shiloh blinked. “What do you mean, you shaved it off? You’ve had that beard for years, and then all of a sudden you start dating *her*, and it’s gone?”

I blinked.

“Umm, he was like this when I met him,” I supplied helpfully.

Shiloh turned her glare on me.

“I didn’t ask you,” she hissed.

I snapped my mouth shut and turned my face to the side.

Wow. Just wow.

Should I even be here?

“I think I’ll run to the ladies room,” I said, getting up quickly.

I wasn’t sure when the ceremony was supposed to start, but I figured now was the time to go.

Maybe if they had some alone time together they could work out whatever was going on between them.

The two women, nor Silas, complained as I slipped out of the pew, and I was thankful.

Jesus.

I was really starting to doubt my sanity.

And poor Silas.

No wonder the man was lonely.

His own family didn't even like him!

Which was crazy to me, because he was a man of honor. A huge heart and willing to lend a hand to anyone who needed it.

Shaking my head, I moved purposefully down the aisle of the quickly filling church and headed straight to the bathroom.

I didn't really have to use it, but I might as well.

I might even go on a walk around the grounds. Possibly hitch a ride back to Benton.

Surely Silas could take care of himself, right?

I hurried through the bathroom ritual, washing my hands and inspecting my makeup.

It looked pretty good, even after riding a motorcycle here for over an hour.

By the time I made it back into the church ten minutes later the ceremony had already started, so I closed the door quietly behind me and took a seat in the very back.

Cheyenne and Sam were at the front, holding a young girl of four or five between them.

She was wearing all white, and her eyes were wide as she stared at the preacher in front of her.

My mind wandered as the ceremony continued, and before I knew it, everyone around me was standing as they said a final prayer over Pru…or was it Piper?

Hell, I didn't know.

Was it okay to think 'hell' in church?

Lord knew I didn't need any more black marks on my soul.

I was fairly sure God looked down upon people like me.

I looked at the huge wooden cross hanging in the front of the church above the pulpit, and thought about where my life had taken me in the last two months.

I'd been scared beyond belief the day I was released.

Scared that I was going to be alone forever, homeless and jobless.

Now, I was practically living with a man, the man that I'd fallen in love with, but hadn't formally told yet.

I was at a job I loved, working with animals that I loved even more.

And I had my two best friends at my side. One of whom was happily married to my twin brother.

My parents were happy – and together – once again.

The only thing that was missing from my life were my three other brothers, and they would all be home soon according to the letters I'd received from them.

And then there were those criminal charges.

The ones that were just recently dropped.

I seriously couldn't ask for anything more.

Oh, I take that back, I did want more. I wanted to marry Silas.

I wanted kids…kids that I knew would probably never happen.

I wanted a house to call my own, one that Silas and I built together.

I wanted a nice car that I bought myself. I wanted to wake up every morning beside the love of my life.

And I wanted Silas to be that man.

I wanted everything.

"Hey," someone interrupted my thoughts.

I blinked and turned to find Sebastian standing at my side.

"Yeah?" I asked.

He nodded across the room. "Dad asked me to get you."

I smiled. "Okay. Where does he want me?"

Sebastian grinned. "My guess would be next to him in some form or fashion."

Nodding, I walked next to the big man that was entirely too nice looking for his own good.

Although, in my honest opinion, he had nothing on Silas.

That beautiful salt and pepper hair. Those big bulky arms. Tight clipped beard. Luscious lips. Strong, sexy stomach. And those eyes.

He really had it going on, and I still couldn't figure out what he saw in me.

Especially with him standing in the sun like that, a bright smile on his face.

He took my breath away.

Once I reached Silas' side, he held his hand out to me, and my heart skipped a beat.

Sebastian disappeared, and it was just the two of us under the bright noon sun.

“Where’d you disappear to?” He rumbled, eyes full of concern.

I would’ve answered him, but a rude voice cut into our conversation like nails on a chalkboard.

“You’re an asshole, and I hope your face rots off,” a woman hissed at Silas.

I blinked.

Well, that was harsh!

But seriously, the whole damn day had been full of everyone treating Silas like shit!

First his son, and now this woman.

What the fuck was going on?

“I don’t understand,” I said. “What’s she talking about?” I asked softly, looking up at Silas.

Silas’ head hung like he had the weight of the world on his shoulders.

“That,” he said, keeping his head down. “Is my ex. And it looks like she was just talking to my ex-wife.”

I knew the ex-wife.

The ‘ex’ was new, though.

I also couldn’t figure out what she was doing there.

“I take it they don’t get along,” I surmised.

He laughed humorlessly. “No, I don’t think they do. And it’s understandable.”

Yeah, from the explanation he’d given me about the two of them, it was understandable.

I'd probably hate him a little bit, too.

It'd help if Silas explained what had happened and why he'd acted like that, but he didn't.

He thought he was doing them a favor by not saying anything to them or informing them of why.

"What is the ex- girlfriend doing here?" I asked.

Silas shook his head. "Not a clue. But I try not to have much of anything to do with her if I can help it."

I had nothing to say to that.

From what Silas had told me of his ex, she did have a reason to warrant her snotty behavior.

And I couldn't say that I wouldn't do the same exact same thing had I been in that situation.

I would like to think that I was a better person than that, but right now Silas was my world.

I could even imagine having kids with him, something that would bind us even tighter together.

I'd be lost if I found out he'd cheated on me with his *wife* on the side…one I hadn't realized he even had.

Wanting to change the subject, I asked, "How did the talk with Sam and James go?"

His mouth clenched and the strong muscles of his jaw started to work.

"Not good. They're justifiably pissed," he answered. "Don't like that I've had men on them without their knowledge."

I wondered if I should've said anything to that, but he sighed.

"I needed to tell them, it's just hard to give my own kid more ammunition against me," Silas finally admitted. "And I'm sorry that I took it out on you that I didn't want to tell them. Getting mad at you was easier than telling them that Shovel is back in the picture."

I blinked.

I never even thought that it was hard for him.

I just thought he didn't think that his sons needed to know.

It'd never crossed my mind that he was scared to hear what his son would say.

"You want to dance?" I suddenly blurted.

He looked down at me. "In the sun?"

"There's music," I said defensively.

He laughed. "I'll dance with you, honey. Just not here."

I smiled. "Where then?"

His face got close to mine, so close that I could practically taste his lips on my own.

"When we get home. Promise."

Home.

I liked the way he said that, almost as if he'd moved me in permanently.

"Sounds good," I breathed, closing the distance until our mouths touched.

"Ewww," a young kid squealed. "Papa's kissing a girl!"

I looked over to see a blonde headed rug rat watching us with disgust on her face.

"Pru, darlin.' It's not very nice to scream," Silas reprimanded his eldest granddaughter gently.

The girl grinned, and I couldn't help but smile.

"Looks like you have your hand full with this one," I teased.

He grinned. "Wait till you meet the rest of them."

***

"Aren't you the chick who killed those four people because you were drinking and driving?" Sam asked.

I sensed no condemnation in his tone, but it didn't hurt any less.

He might as well have shoved a hot fire poker into my spinal column, because that was practically the effect he had on me.

"Yes," I said softly. "I was the one who killed those four people."

Sam blinked, surprised that I'd answered him truthfully, I guess.

"Hmm," he said, not knowing what to say to that.

"Didn't you go to prison for twelve years?" Shiloh asked.

I shook my head. "Eight."

"Leave her alone," Sebastian ordered, sitting down. "Dad's going to be pissed if you hurt her."

I smiled at Sebastian.

He was such a good guy.

"We were just asking her a few questions," Shiloh defended herself.

Would it be rude to get up and leave?

Silas had asked me to wait at the table I was sitting at, yet I didn't really want to be here right now.

"How are you allowed to be drinking? Shouldn't you, you know, abstain?" Shiloh continued.

I closed my eyes.

Maybe I should be.

But then again, if I didn't drink I wouldn't be able to handle the two spoiled rotten children of Silas' right then.

"I need to use the restroom," I said softly.

I stood and walked carefully away from them, trying my hardest not to run.

I was surprised to find Silas on my way there, and instead of letting me go to the bathroom, he caught my hand and led me outside.

"Let's go," he urged.

I blinked. "You're not going to say goodbye?"

"Why would I?" He asked. "It's not like they're going to miss me or anything."

My heart ached for him.

"Let's go home," I confirmed, walking with him to his bike and ignoring my bladder's reaction at not getting to use the facilities.

Once we got to his bike, he gestured to someone in the shadows, one of his men I guessed, and mounted the bike.

Offering me his hand, I mounted behind him and wrapped my hands around his waist as he started it up with a throaty roar.

My skin tingled as I felt the muscles in his stomach clench as he slowly started to accelerate forward.

I sighed in bliss as I closed my eyes and relished the alone time. My brain was a mess.

I looked over when another roar caught my attention, and smiled when I saw Sebastian and his wife, Baylee, directly beside us.

Well, not completely alone.

But I guess, at this moment in time, that having Sebastian next to us wasn't that bad after all.

Silas could use the support.

And I'd be offering that until he didn't want it anymore.

Because Silas needed a friend.

He needed someone to always have his back and have no other loyalties but to him and him alone.

That's what a man like Silas needed in a woman.

Support.

Love.

Acceptance.

And lucky for him, I had all of that for him…and more.

CHAPTER 19

I miss you sex is always worth the wait.
- Truth

Sawyer

"What are you doing?" I asked aloud as I followed Silas.

His head wasn't there today, and I was worried about him.

I'd been worried about him for a while now.

He wasn't the same man that I'd met in the beginning, and I feared that everything was weighing him down. My problems. His problems. Everyone in the club's problems.

And what was worse was that he'd been acting different since we'd gotten back from the baptism yesterday.

I couldn't figure out why he'd completely disregarded everything I'd said.

It was as if he was hurting or something, and I was determined to get down to the bottom of it.

So when he said he had to go, taking out a six-pack of beer out of his fridge on the way, I followed him. He has taken some alone time since we have been together. We aren't together all the time, but this seemed different than his usual.

And I didn't follow him very well. And not easily, might I add.

Mostly because he was on a bike compared to my car.

He could slide through traffic like a slippery eel.

I, on the other hand, drove so slowly that I could barely keep up with him.

When we hit the highway forty-five minutes later, it got easier.

I stayed at least ten car lengths behind him at all times, because I knew he'd make me in a heartbeat if I didn't.

The only reason I saw where he was going was that I could see him turn at least three intersections away.

So I followed him as best as I could, eyes scanning my surroundings.

Finally, I caught a glimpse of him turning into what I thought was a cemetery, but I couldn't quite tell since it was so far away.

But my suspicions were confirmed a few minutes later when I pulled up behind his bike.

Silas was nowhere to be seen, though.

So I got out and started walking, saddened by the hundreds of graves that were in the graveyard.

It was an old one.

Some of the headstones I passed on the way there were from the 1800's.

I'd walked perhaps a thousand yards or so, just topping the tip of a hill, when I saw him.

He was sitting on a camping seat, one of the ones that had three poles and folded out into a triangle.

He had a beer in his hand and his back to me.

So I saw the cut clearly on his back, the huge scary, wraith like woman with her weirdly colored eyes staring at me hauntingly.

Beyond curious, but knowing he wanted to be alone, I turned on my heels and left, giving him the privacy I knew he wanted.

Well…not privacy…just not me.

And that didn't hurt as much as I thought it would.

But I did make a phone call.

"Hello?" The man on the other end of the line answered.

"Hey," I said. "This is Sawyer."

"I know," the man said impatiently.

I looked at the phone to make sure I'd called who I thought I'd called, and was surprised to find that I did.

"Umm," I said, hesitating now that he'd answered so tersely. "Your dad's at a cemetery drinking a beer with a tombstone. Should I be worried?"

There was silence on the other end for a very long time before Sebastian finally cleared his throat.

"Which cemetery?" He asked finally.

I looked up at the sign I was standing under and said, "Bayou Road."

His swift inhalation was audible over the phone line, and I started to worry.

"Should I go check on him?" I asked anxiously.

"No. Leave him alone. We'll be there."

I didn't get a chance to ask who 'we' was, because he'd hung up on me before I could say anything otherwise.

It was another twenty minutes of me sitting on the hood of my car, staring up at the streetlight that was trying to decide if it wanted to turn on or not, when I heard them.

It sounded like hundreds of motorcycles, but was more like ten.

I sat up and looked behind me to where I could hear the noise coming from, and smiled when I saw six men.

They pulled up behind me, each of them wearing much the same as I'd seen Silas put on before leaving the house.

"Hey," Sebastian said.

"Hey," I replied back.

He gave me a long look. "What are you doing here?"

I blinked. "I, uhhh….followed him."

"You followed him?"

That came from the big man.

Kettle this time.

"He's not going to just let you follow him," Trance said.

I shrugged. "Maybe he didn't see me."

The blonde one, Loki, with the scary scar across his throat snorted, bringing my attention to him.

Him I didn't know as well yet, but I could tell he was laughing at me.

"What?" I asked.

He smiled, showing off a row of straight, white teeth.

"Nothing. Just find it funny that you think he didn't know you were following him," the man explained.

I shrugged. "Well, he hasn't said anything, and I've been here for forty minutes now. I would think I'd at least get a glare or a 'fuck off' from him had he known I was here."

That earned me a couple of hard stares, but it was that of his son that caught me by surprise.

"Why do I feel like I'm not getting the entire truth from you?" He asked. "Where'd you pick him up at if you were following him?"

I couldn't very well say 'your father's house' to him. I wasn't sure who knew that I was staying at Silas' house. They knew we were in a "relationship" of sorts, but not that I was living with him.

Not that there was much of a relationship.

We fucked.

That was about the gist of it.

"Well, I gotta go. See y'all later," I said, scooting off the hood and rounding the car.

I dropped into the seat and was happy that they moved out of my way without me having to tell them to.

Waving at the six of them, I pulled back onto the dirt road, did a three point turn, and started back the same way I came, my shadow of prospects following in my wake.

I was happy that Silas wouldn't be alone.

I only wished we had the type of relationship where we could talk about what was going on with each other, because I'd love to know that he was okay.

***

Silas

"Your girls' are doing great," I told Tunnel. "Your little one is starting school soon. Only daycare, but school nonetheless."

I took another sip of my beer, aware of the eyes that were on me from the top of the hill.

She hadn't been very inconspicuous as she followed me.

She was good, yes. But not trained. And not good enough to fool my seasoned eyes.

But she stayed far away, and for that I was thankful.

This was the time I used to chill out.

I tried to come out here every Friday night, rain or shine, and share a beer with Tunnel Morrison, the man that I couldn't prevent from dying.

That marked eight brothers that I'd lost since I'd come in as the president of The Dixie Wardens MC, and this one hurt ten times more than all the rest.

Tunnel had been young.

Too young.

And he'd left a wife and small child behind.

Although it'd been a little over two years since it'd happened, it still felt just as raw now as it did then.

Mostly because it was my fault.

I should've done something…figured out that little shit head of a girl had had a hand in it all.

But I hadn't…and it'd cost me.

It'd cost me a very good friend and a hole in my heart.

It hurt every single time to see Tunnel's wife and kid without him.

To see how badly they were struggling.

When I'd started to come here, it'd been because I needed the solace and peace that this certain piece of history gave me.

To have a beer with a friend.

But then I'd kept coming.

And nobody knew.

Well, nobody had known.

Now, that silly woman who didn't know how to leave well enough alone had followed me, and I knew it was only a matter of time before the rest of them caught on.

Hearing the telltale scream of Sawyer's car starting up, and the belts screeching all the way down the road, I finally took a deep breath, thankful that she'd left me to my demons.

I had a lot of fuckin' demons.

So many that it was hard to breathe sometimes.

Sawyer was slowly helping me defeat them.

One by one, until I could breathe deeply once again…and sleep all the way through the night.

Grass crunching had me turning around to see Kettle, Sebastian, Loki, Trance, Torren, and Cleo walking towards me. I heard them pull up, but I wasn't sure that they would come down here with me.

I sighed in annoyance.

"You know, I've been doing this for months now, and one call from my woman has all of y'all running out here like you have a right to be here…and drinking my beer. Perfect."

The men took their seats on the grass beside me, each taking a beer from my cooler without asking.

"If we'd known there was a party, we would've been here to join you," Cleo muttered darkly.

I glanced over at the silent man, surprised he was the first to say anything.

Cleo was an observer.

He waited until he had all the facts before he acted and usually was one of the last to butt his nose into where he didn't belong.

"If I'd wanted y'all to join me, I would've called y'all," I told them honestly.

I wasn't one to beat around the bush. I told it like it was, always had, and always would.

"So…she's your woman?" My nosy bastard of a son asked.

I looked at him sitting directly across from Tunnel's grave, and nodded. "Yeah, she's mine."

"You gonna marry her…make babies with her? You realize she's only thirty right? She's gonna want kids," he said defensively.

And not in my defense either. In Sawyer's.

"I'm going to marry her, yes. But I'm not so sure about the kid part. I'm an old man, after all," I admitted. "But that's something she and I will discuss."

"Sam and Shiloh were pretty shitty to her last night," Sebastian said.

The others stayed quiet as I digested that.

"What'd they say…and do?" I asked.

"Just being their usual shitty selves. Putting their noses in where they don't belong. Asking her questions about the past that upset her," Sebastian informed me.

My hand clenched around my beer.

"I'll talk to them," I said. "Inform them that they're about to have a new stepmother that's younger than them."

They all laughed. "You gonna make her your old lady?" Torren asked cheekily.

I raised the beer to my lips. "Sure am."

"After you catch Shovel?" Sebastian asked.

"Yeah, on the off chance that he finds out about her, he'll think she doesn't mean as much to me since she doesn't have my name covering her back. Or, at least, that's my hope," I said.

"We've been looking for him high and low for the last four weeks. You can't put your life on hold while you attempt to find him," Kettle said.

Kettle sounded sad for a moment there, and I looked over at him to gauge his words.

Kettle had lost his child when he was deployed and he hadn't been the same man until he married his woman, Adeline.

Adeline had changed Kettle for the better, giving him a new lease on life in the process.

"I know," I said. "I just need a few more weeks."

"Why just a few more weeks?" Trance asked curiously.

I smiled.

"Because I have a plan," I informed them.

"And does your plan have anything to do with the dog you just bought from me?" Trance continued.

I grinned. "No, that was all for Sawyer. She liked him and hasn't really stopped talking about getting one of her own someday."

"Ahh," Trance said. "Well, I can drop yours off when I drop Cleo's police academy drop out off tomorrow. It sure is nice knowing he is going to a good home."

"What do you mean, mine?" Cleo barked.

The group started to laugh at the note of panic on Cleo's face.

"I've already got a dog!"

"Yeah, and according to your wife, you're about to have one more!"

CHAPTER 20

If you let me kiss you, I'll take your breath away.
- Silas to Sawyer

Sawyer

"Wow, this is a big party," Ruthie said at my side.

I nodded and took her hand, pulling her with me.

Today was the day that one of the club's members came home from the war.

He was a Navy SEAL and had been deployed in Iraq for nearly a year.

Today would be his first day back, and the club had gone all out trying to show him how excited they were for him to be home.

I'd never met him.

But I'd sent him a care package.

Heck, I'd bought the man underwear.

"Have you been to one of these before?" She whispered, her hand tightening on mine.

"Once," I told her. "But this one is bigger because of all the other chapters coming in. They're having it at a warehouse for Christ's sake. Do you think I've been to one of these?"

She laughed. "Dually noted."

"What my problem is, is that I called that man of mine over an hour ago to tell him I was coming out here, and would be here at exactly this time…so where is he?"

Hard, strong arms wrapped around my waist, and suddenly I was tossed over a shoulder like I was a sack of grain.

"I'm right here, little girl. Right where I said I'd be," Silas teased, jolting me up and down slightly.

I turned my glare on Ruthie when she started to giggle like a savage, her hand still in my own.

"Shut your face," I hissed at her.

She snorted. "That didn't work the first day I met you and definitely doesn't work now. So try something else."

I flipped her off after letting go of her hand before Silas started to walk inside the building.

"Where are we?" I asked Silas' ass.

His large hand smoothed up and down the back of my thigh, getting perilously close to the goods, but stopped just when it started to get interesting and set me down on my feet.

"You're the one who drove out here," Silas said dryly.

I waved my hand in the air as if to clear it.

"I mean, I know where we're located. What I wanted to know was what is this place?" I clarified.

Ruthie stood behind me as we took in the massive space.

"And why is there a boxing ring in the middle of it?" I wondered aloud.

Silas placed me on my feet.

"This is where we usually have our fight nights," Silas said, taking my hand and leading me through the crowd of people.

Everyone was in varying degrees of dress.

There were, of course, the sluts…or tag-a-long's as Silas liked to call them. They were the women that hung around the club and hoped to get something…maybe a quick thrill or even just the excitement of partying with a bunch of bikers.

Then there were the people like me, mostly old ladies by the looks of the property patches on their backs. They were wearing jeans and t-shirts, mostly. One or two had a dress on.

Then there were the men…the bikers.

There were bikers here a plenty.

It was a virtual sea of black leather covering the shoulders of men in varying ages and sizes.

"You have a fight night?" I asked, a little surprised that I hadn't heard about it yet, and I'd been with Silas for well over two months now.

"Yeah," Silas said. "We've not had one in a while. The weather's been fucking with everything lately. Every time one is scheduled to happen, it starts to rain. And the warehouse isn't all that waterproof, not to mention that the parking is grass. I don't want eight million people stuck out here in their cars. That would blow."

I snorted.

Ever so honest, was my Silas.

"It's raining right now…" I told him the obvious.

He squeezed my hand slightly.

"Yeah, but this has been planned for a year now. Not like I can just up and change it. We just have to have about eight million buckets catching all the water. Luckily, we have prospects to empty them and replace them when needed," he said, pointing out one such prospect doing that very thing. "And the party is gonna go on nearly the entire night.

Hopefully the rain dries up and they can get out when the time comes."

"Who is that?" Ruthie gasped from my side.

I followed the direction of her gaze to a man I'd never met before, but then again, that wasn't surprising when there were about five hundred people here, and I only knew about fifty of them.

"That's my brother, Sterling," Silas said with a smile in his voice. "He's the reason we're celebrating tonight. Made it home in one piece from another tour."

I blinked.

"That," I said, pointing at the man who was absolutely stunning. "Is Sterling?"

I'd bought underwear for that man!

"Come on, I'll introduce you," he said, pulling me behind him, skirting a bucket every now and then as he went.

We came to a stop in front of a crowd, but Silas' booming voice made them part.

"Move," Silas ordered two men.

They weren't dressed in their biker cuts, which was why I assumed that Silas spoke to them like that.

The man we'd come over there to meet looked up at Silas' barked order and grinned.

His gaze followed Silas' arm down until he found me and smiled widely before moving to Ruthie's hand in mine.

She squeezed my hand tightly once his eyes hit hers, and I barely smothered a smile as I watched him watch her.

Finally his eyes moved back, and Silas stepped forward.

“Sterling, this is my woman, Sawyer. Sawyer, Sterling. Sterling, Ruthie; Ruthie, Sterling.”

Simple, yet effective, and so Silas.

Sterling was gorgeous.

Tall with muscular arms leading up to wide, broad shoulders. Deep green eyes and a messy mop of dirty-blonde hair tumbling over his eyes and capping a face that was the very definition of ruggedly handsome.

His beard was pretty wicked, too.

The man standing before me grinned as he took two huge steps towards me and then scooped me up into a bear hug.

“Thanks for the underwear,” he said as he valiantly tried to squeeze the air from my lungs with the ferociousness of his hug. “I really needed them. They’re now my favorites due to the fact that they don’t chafe.”

I laughed, patting his back awkwardly since I was pinned down by his arms.

“You’re welcome. Nobody likes to chafe,” I laughed.

He set me down on my feet, and I turned to Ruthie.

“This is my best friend, Ruthie.” I looked over at Ruthie, who was wearing a wide-eyed expression.

Sterling’s eyes were all for my friend, too.

I couldn’t help but smile.

Ruthie was beautiful.

Like incredibly so.

She was about five foot two inches of perfect wrapped in a beautiful bow of happiness and sunshine.

She had curly hair that was styled perfectly.

She had worn a bit of eyeshadow, but it was the smoked eyeliner rimming her green eyes that made them pop like emeralds.

And I'll be damned if her smoky, sparkling emerald eyes weren't just as focused on the man staring her down.

He didn't move; neither did she.

For so long that I started to worry, but then Sterling smiled and offered his hand.

Ruthie took forever to take it, and I felt like it was something pivotal in her healing.

"Well," I said, turning to look at Silas. "What's next?"

"Silas is going to fight Stone," Sterling chirped at my side.

I blinked, turning to see Sterling looking at some man across the room and leaning up against one of the bars.

"What? But, but… why?" I asked stammered worriedly.

My hand clutched Silas' who looked down at me in amusement.

"Because it's tradition. The presidents of the chapters fight to see who gets to host the next year's event," Sterling said. "Stone is the winner on his bracket. Silas the winner on his."

I blinked.

"So you lost last year?" I asked.

He shook his head. "No. Last year a tornado took out the Alabama chapter's clubhouse, so we went there for a week and helped them fix it up."

"He won last year. Was supposed to be here," Sterling offered helpfully.

I nodded. "Gotcha."

Turning to Silas I said, "When is this fight taking place? And what kind of fight is it?"

"Boxing, mostly. And in about fifteen minutes," he answered, picking up a beer off a waitress' tray and bringing it to his lips.

"Shouldn't you be refueling your body with a Gatorade or something, instead of a beer?" I asked.

He winked at me. "Honey, I'm too old for those electrolyte drinks. Now I'm drinking because my liver would probably revolt if I didn't."

"Dad doesn't know how to back off," a tight-lipped voice said from our side.

I smiled at Sebastian and moved to hug him.

"How's Baylee doing?" I asked.

He smiled and hugged me back before letting me go and pointing in the direction of the bar where Baylee's arms were waving in front of her as she spoke animatedly with some woman I'd never seen.

She had red hair that came down to her waist and a ready smile.

When I turned back to Silas, his gaze was on something across the room.

"Silas," I said. "When are they going to start cooking?"

"A couple of minutes, I guess," he shrugged.

"What's wrong?" I asked him again.

He shrugged again.

Something *was* wrong.

I just didn't know *what*.

Something had changed in the last few minutes, and I wanted to know what.

Smiling down at my shoes, I suddenly took his hand and started pulling him along with me to his office, leaving Ruthie to speak with Sterling.

"Take me to your office," I ordered.

He went, but I could tell it was reluctantly.

The moment we got inside, I pushed him back until I could close the door.

I flicked on the light, then dropped down to my knees in front of him.

"Sawyer," Silas growled.

I looked up at him to see his face still set in stone.

He didn't want to talk?

Well I wouldn't make him.

"This isn't the time," he growled once again.

I ignored him.

Reaching for his belt buckle, I quickly undid it.

The metal buckle clanged loudly as I quickly removed the belt from the loops and tossed it somewhere behind me.

I saw his hand move to his back and heard him grunt as he caught what I assumed was the gun he kept at the small of his back.

Whoops.

Regardless, I started working on his pants, roughly yanking the zipper down.

"Shit," he hissed.

Then I yanked his underwear and jeans right down to his knees.

His soft cock fell free from its confines, and I licked my lips as I marveled at how big it was even in its softened state.

A challenge?

Looking up, I smiled at Silas.

He glared.

"What's wrong, Silas?" I asked, leaning forward to trail my tongue along the head of his cock.

The moment my tongue met his skin, his cock jerked.

Keeping contact with his eyes, I leaned forward and sucked his entire cock into my mouth.

I'd never felt it when it was soft.

Well, I'd felt it, as it was unusual for me to cup his package on occasion as I would walk past him or even sometimes when the mood just came over me. What can I say? I love his cock.

I'd just never had it in my mouth while soft.

This was the first time I'd ever been able to get his entire cock in my mouth, and I savored the feeling.

Except he still wasn't getting hard.

Was he reciting the ABC's or something to keep from getting hard?

"What? Should we get you some Viagra or something?" I teased, cupping his balls. "You're too old to get it up?"

I felt like I'd just taken my life in my hands as I said it.

Nervous as hell, I finally looked up into his burning eyes.

"You wanna know what's wrong?" He asked, gently cupping my face.

I nodded, albeit reluctantly since he now had a firm grip in my hair that was hurting already, and he wasn't even doing any tugging.

"My problem, honey, is that you were talking to a man. Touching him.

Hugging him. Allowing him to put his hands on you," he said softly. "You're mine. Not his. He doesn't get to have you like that."

I laughed. "Silas, you're name isn't tattooed on me. You have no right to say who I can and can't hug. I promise you I won't be fucking anyone else, but there are occasions when I want to hug other people of the male and female variety."

"Suck my cock," he said, tugging my hair until my face was resting against his still flaccid cock.

I opened my mouth but instead of sticking his cock in my mouth, he placed his balls there.

"The thing about me," he said. "Is that I have complete control over my mind and body. I'm not a little boy to be trifled with. If I want to fuck you, I'll allow myself to get hard. If I don't want to fuck you, it won't happen. Now, run your tongue around my balls."

When I didn't comply fast enough, he yanked my hair and I moaned.

God, I was such a whore.

This shouldn't be turning me on, this domineering side of him.

But it was, and I was fucking *dripping*.

I could tell my panties were soaked.

And the next thing would be my jeans, and I really didn't want that to happen.

I still had to walk through a gaggle of bikers and their women. And I didn't think for a second that they wouldn't notice.

"I said lick," he growled, pulling on my hair again.

His other hand was holding his cock out of my face, allowing him to watch my eyes and mouth.

I could see his cock hardening out of the corner of my eye, but my gaze stayed on Silas'.

His were hard and unbending.

My eyes narrowed, and in an act of defiance I sucked.

He hissed and yanked back hard on my hair.

"Bitch," he growled.

Removing his balls from my mouth, he replaced it with his cock.

His now *hard* cock.

Really hard.

I choked on it the moment he got four inches into my mouth.

I wasn't an expert at giving blow jobs.

Turns out I had a hell of a gag reflex.

Something Silas had been battling for a while now.

This time, though, he didn't care that he was making me gag.

He was forcing his hard cock into my mouth, causing my eyes to water.

I was surprised that I really liked this side of him.

How he was forcing me to take him.

It was almost like he was forcing me to enjoy it, too.

He'd always been so careful with me, afraid that it'd scare me off.

And I'd wanted more from him, but I had no clue how to tell him that I wanted more, I wasn't even sure what exactly the more was that I wanted.

Apparently, Silas knew, though, because he was giving it to me right then.

"Suck me," he said.

Keeping my eyes on him, I started to suck.

I wasn't sure how hard to suck, though.

Hard? Soft?

Soft like I would suck on a Popsicle, or hard like a vacuum?

I went with medium…like I would work a straw while drinking a milkshake.

Which apparently was the right choice because he growled his approval.

"Good girl," he said, pushing his cock in and out of my mouth now, using my hair as leverage.

I hummed.

His grip tightened.

After a few long moments of this, I suddenly found myself picked up then face down on his desk.

"The door," I said, hearing the song change as he ripped my jeans down over my ass.

I looked up at the door nervously, trying to recall whether I'd locked it or not.

But that was quickly forgotten when the drawer beside my hips opened and I heard the distinct crinkle of a condom wrapper. The sight of him sliding it down his hard length wiped all thoughts of whether or not the door was locked right out of my mind.

My shirt was quickly shoved up over my shoulders and was now pooling around my neck. I felt his cock brush against me as it lined up with my entrance right before he slammed inside.

"You didn't care about the door earlier when you were trying to use your mouth on me to get me to talk. Don't worry about it now, either," he ordered, pushing his length in and out of me so forcefully that I was fairly sure my hips would be bruised in the morning where they were connecting with the edge of the desk.

My head fell forward until my forehead was resting against the large calendar on his desk that had Silas' manly scrawl scratched all over it.

My breasts were rubbing deliciously against the edge of the calendar, making my nipples pebble and harden with each thrust.

"Fuck," I hissed, feeling my orgasm start to build.

Silas growled.

Then the door opened.

I looked up into the startled face of some woman I'd never met before in my life, mouth open as my orgasm crashed through me.

My eyes closed of their own volition, and I vaguely heard Silas' snap at the woman, but I was too engrossed in the way my orgasm was poured over me like warm, melted butter to care about anyone else.

My hands clenched the edge of the desk, and my toes curled in my ballet flats.

My head turned so I could breathe, and my stomach muscles started to burn.

Silas grunted loudly behind me, and his thrusts became even rougher until he stilled.

His cock started to pulse and jump inside of me, and the hands on my hips clenching them so roughly that I knew I'd be sporting bruises there.

I was coming down off a high from an orgasm that nearly converted my religion to anything that worshipped Silas Mackenzie as a God, so I didn't really care that I'd looked like a trauma victim at that moment in time.

“Told you,” I said after long moments.

“Told me what, darlin’?” He asked.

My eyes were heavy as I said, “That we should’ve locked that door.”

He laughed as he pulled out of me, and I stayed where I was draped over the top of his desk.

“You know,” he said. “I already have a hard enough time thinking about you when I’m working. Now all I’ll be able to think about is you bent over the desk.”

I laughed and stood, my vagina deliciously sore from Silas’ rough use.

“I can’t say that that bothers me,” I admitted, bending down to pull my pants back up and over my bare flesh.

He watched me as he threaded the belt back through the loops of his jeans, then reached for the gun that’d been next to my face the entire time we’d been doing the dirty.

He placed it back at the small of his back, then tightened the belt down.

“You’re gonna have to not hug men until I can get my ring on your finger,” he ordered.

My mouth dropped opened.

“And when will that be?” I asked a tad hysterically.

I wasn’t even getting into the fact that one of the men I hugged was his son.

His married son. And the other man had just returned from deployment.

He winked. “When I want it to be.”

With that, he left out the door, only looking back at me to offer me a grin.

Shit head.

Wondering if he expected me to follow, I did so, albeit a lot more slowly than he'd left.

When I made it into the main room he was talking to Sterling and Sebastian.

His eyes followed my movement through the crowd, and I glared at him, causing a smile to quirk up the corner of his lips.

"What's that look for?" Ruthie asked as took a seat in the seat next to her.

"Silas annoys me," I told her.

The other women at the table froze.

"What?" I asked them.

"Nothing," Viddy said. "It's just that Silas' is so nice to everyone, even if he is a little scary. I can't see how he'd annoy you."

I rolled my eyes.

The women of The Dixie Wardens MC thought Silas walked on water.

He didn't.

CHAPTER 21

He's got the pole, I've got the bobbers!
-T-shirt

Sawyer

"Yo," a man yelled over the loud speaker. "Time to fight!"

I pursed my lips and turned to find everyone crowding around the ring where Silas and the man named Stone were warming up.

Silas handed his beer over the ropes to a woman standing there, and I suddenly had the irrational urge to go yank it out of her hands.

She didn't deserve to hold his beer!

"Whoa, tiger. What's got you so riled up?" Viddy asked.

"That woman standing next to the ring, the one who just took Silas' beer. Who is she?" I asked.

Viddy's eyes turned in that direction, but it was Adeline who answered me.

"That's Tattie. She's a…'hanger on,' I guess you'd say," Adeline answered.

"Hmm," I said. "Has she slept with Silas?"

The table quieted. "Umm, we don't know. Silas is very discreet about his relationships. I couldn't tell you if he has or hasn't."

"Hmmm," I said, getting out of my seat and walking towards the ring without another word to them.

I wasn't used to being irrational.

The only man I'd ever dated I really didn't care about all that much.

Hell, Isaac had slept with, and impregnated, another woman while we were supposed to be together, and I hadn't reacted with so much as a 'fuck you.'

But Silas handing his beer over to some chick dressed in a strapless dress and hooker shoes made me practically homicidal.

Pushing through the crowd now, I came to a stop when I reached the very edge of the ring, and reached up until I caught a hold of the rope.

Tattie eyed me with a malevolent look, and I couldn't help the smirk I shot her when Silas saw me and immediately held up his hand to the man he was standing in front of, Stone.

"Yeah?" He asked, walking over to me.

I ran my hand down his shirt.

"You're not going to take your shirt off like Stone did?" I teased.

He looked down at his shirt, then over at Stone, before turning back to me.

"I don't want to distract him with my finely honed physique."

I laughed.

It was one that bubbled up from the bottom of my belly and made my abs hurt.

God, I loved this man and his sense of humor.

"The Dixie Girls are calling you straight laced. They think you don't know how to let go and loosen up," I said, circling my finger around the collar of his shirt.

He winked, then, making my mouth go completely dry, he stepped back and ripped his shirt from his shoulders.

One good yank at the back of his collar had the entire thing folding over his arms and pooling at the base of his hands.

I sighed when I got a good look at his chest.

So muscular and mouthwatering.

"Here, hold this for me," he ordered me. "And step down so you don't get hurt."

I reached out for the shirt and brought it into my chest, leaning far over the ropes to offer him my lips.

"Good luck," I said right before he kissed me.

I moaned in his mouth when it got a little heavy, and he pulled away, leaving us both gasping.

"Thanks," he muttered, turning back around to face Stone.

Grimacing, I stepped down and stood next to Tattie, ignoring the scowl she was throwing my direction.

Plus, my eyes were glued to the man in front of me in his sexy jeans that looked to be about a year past the time he should've thrown them away.

He had a gun holstered at his back, and I wondered why he hadn't taken it off.

It was likely he never took it off. Or at least he didn't when I was around.

He slept with it under his pillow at night and kept it on until we went to bed or he took a shower. But it was never more than an arm span away. I even felt it while I leaned against him when we were on the bike.

I admired his back like I always did.

He had Roman numeral dates on his shoulder blade, three of them, which I guessed were his kids' birthdays.

He had a skull tattoo on his bicep, and a US flag just underneath that.

And he was sexy.

Oh, so sexy.

"You know he gets bored easily, right?" Titty…or whatever her name was, said.

I ignored her and kept my eyes on Silas as the man in the middle of the ring with the referee shirt held up his hand and started to speak.

"No hair pulling, scratching, guns, knives, ball grabbing, or bitch slapping allowed. Ready?" The referee called out.

Both men nodded, grinning, and all I could do was snort.

Ball grabbing or bitch slapping?

I mean, they really had to spell that out in the rules?

At the nods of both men, the referee held his hand up and said, "Start."

I blinked when Silas' fist shot out and connected immediately with Stone's face.

"Ohhh," I said, putting my hands over my mouth as my stomach knotted.

That had to hurt.

And it wasn't over, because Stone returned the favor two seconds later.

Then they proceeded to beat the ever-loving shit out of each other.

***

"Does that hurt?" I whispered, wincing when he hissed a breath in through clenched teeth.

"No, not at all. I don't know what would give you that idea," he said sarcastically.

"You're gonna need stitches," Rue said from beside me.

"And possibly a new face," Baylee quipped from my other side.

"I don't know about that," Kettle drawled. "I'm pretty sure he's happy right where he's at."

I laughed.

"Yeah, I'm sure he is," I said, leaning into him.

His hands went around my waist and he pulled me in close.

"So I have a question to ask you," he asked.

I leaned in, aware that the women at my sides hadn't moved and were now leaning in, too.

"Yeah," I asked with a laugh.

"So…what are you doing…for the next fifty years?" He asked nonchalantly.

I inhaled swiftly, but his twinkling eyes made me suspicious of what he was going to ask next.

"N-nothing," I said. "W-why?"

He didn't spare the women at my sides a glance as he kept his gaze on me, his swollen eyes looking like they were going to hurt for the next couple of days.

But his eyes were all for me as he said, "Because I want you to be my woman. In front of my family and friends, my club, I want you to know that I love you, and I want you to be mine forever."

I was crying and I didn't even realize it.

Crying hard, too.

He leaned forward until my face was in his hands, and his baby blue's were staring into mine.

"You got anything to say?" He asked after a while.

I shook my head.

"No," I whispered.

"Not even a yes?" He confirmed.

"Yes."

"Yes what?"

"Yes, I have something else to say."

"Well?" He asked, sounding like he was starting to run out of patience.

"Are you asking me to marry you…or just be with you forever?"

He grinned and pressed his split lip against mine.

"Little bit of both."

"Then yes."

"Yes to which?"

I laughed.

"Yes to both."

Cheers, whistles, applause and hoots erupted behind me, and I turned to find every single one of the Dixie Wardens MC, Benton Chapter, thundering their approval.

I laughed through my tears as I threw my hands around Silas' neck.

It wasn't long before the two women at my side did the same, and we gave Silas one big woman sandwich.

"I love you too," I whispered into his ear.

He growled and rubbed his bearded face against the sensitive skin on the inside of my neck.

"Good," he rasped. "Because that's kind of a requirement."

"Bossy man."

"You know you like it," he whispered into my ear.

I shivered when those words penetrated my brain.

Yet, I couldn't disagree. Not even a little bit.

I did like it!

CHAPTER 22

I love food. But I hate my fat pants. The dilemma is real.
-Fact of Life

Sawyer

I woke up to a ring on my finger and a leather vest similar to Silas' in my size lying next to me.

On the back of it was a rocker stating I was the 'Property of Silas.'

I was freakin' ecstatic.

Although it wasn't the most romantic of gestures, I knew he'd really meant it.

He'd had the vest made.

He'd gotten me a ring.

He wanted it all, and I was so happy I could burst.

There were about a million and one things that went bad from the night I'd decided to go out with my friends, and I couldn't name one single thing that I looked forward to after I was sentenced to prison.

Now, though, I had my whole life ahead of me.

If someone had told me I had Silas waiting at the end of the tunnel as my prize for making it out, I would've never believed it.

Why?

Because people like Silas just didn't exist.

They weren't real.

Or at least that's what I'd thought.

But Silas *was* real. And he was really mine, and mine alone.

And he was everything I'd never even dared to dream for.

Getting up, naked as the day I was born, I slipped on the vest and smiled at how soft the leather felt against my skin.

And it fit me perfectly.

Buttoning the three buttons at the front, I walked to the dresser drawer that I'd commandeered from Silas, and slipped on a pair of panties.

They were hot pink and said '*Pink!*' across the back.

They were from high school, of course, but they still fit.

And I wasn't picky right then.

Practically skipping out of Silas' bedroom, I walked through the house with a stupid smile on my face.

"Silas!" I yelled as I skipped around the corner.

And I ran into the kitchen skidding to an immediate stop at the sight of the entire room filled with Dixie Wardens.

"Shit," I hissed, turning tail and running back out of the room.

I could hear the laughter following me as I dashed back into the bedroom and slammed the door shut behind me.

I went straight into the bathroom and turned the water on, warming up the shower.

Shucking the vest, I hung it up lovingly on the door and smoothed my hand down it, all the while my face flamed at all those men seeing me in nothing but my panties and a vest that barely covered my breasts.

"Shit," I laughed. "That man needs to warn me when people are coming into the house!"

I hadn't heard them at all, either.

And Silas' place wasn't so that large I wouldn't have been able to hear them unless they were intentionally being quiet.

"Silly man not warning a woman when…eek!" I screamed when I turned around and saw Silas staring at me with an amused expression on his face.

"You were saying," he drawled.

I laughed, placing my hand over my chest where my pounding heart was trying to beat its way out of my chest.

His eyes went down to my bare chest, and I saw his pupils dilate as he started to move forward.

I put my hand up to stop him, but he ignored it, walking around my hand and crowding right up against me so that my back met the shower door with a soft thud.

"We can't," I tried, knowing that there were about five men in the kitchen that were probably very aware of what was going on in here.

"You're going to come out there, wearing what you were wearing, and expect me not to touch you?" He asked, pushing his hardness into me with his body.

My back was chilled from the cold glass my bare back was pressed against, causing my nipples to pebble in reaction.

And Silas didn't miss it as he brought both hands up and gently cupped each one in his hands.

My lips parted on a soft pant as I watched his eyes move up from my breasts to connect with mine.

"So no complaints?" He asked. "You said yes?"

I groaned as he pinched both nipples.

"I wasn't aware that you'd asked me a question," I panted out.

His reply to my comment was to pinch the very tips of my nipples as he pulled slightly down, causing me to follow his movement and press my body even further into his.

"Silas!" I gasped.

"You were saying?" He urged, letting go of my nipples and gliding his hands down my body until they rested against my hips.

I shook my head. "I can't reply until you ask."

He growled. "Is that right?"

I nodded. "That's right."

And then he dropped to his knees in front of me, pulling my panties down to my ankles.

"I don't think I heard you right," he continued.

I watched him as he leaned forward and pressed a chaste kisses against each of my hips before looking up at me, watching as his hands slid up from my calves all the way to the apex of my thighs.

I bit my lip as I looked down at him and watched as he slowly leaned forward and pressed a kiss at the top of my pubic bone, right above the lips of my sex.

His beard tickled my clit as his thumbs traveled down and in, spreading me apart for his tongue to tickle the little bundle of nerves.

I gasped and instinctively spread my thighs for him, and he took full advantage by shoving two thick fingers inside of me and curling them towards my front.

"Fuck!" I hissed, hips jumping as he slowly tapped his fingers against that sensitive spot inside of me.

The steam from the shower was starting to fill the small room, and I could see the silhouette of my body in the mirror when words rising through the steam on the glass began to appear.

Thanks for the show.

"Silas," I said, pulling his head away from me. "Did you write that?"

He pulled away, his lips glistening in my juices, looking over his shoulder to where my eyes were pointed, and he completely froze.

His muscles locked tight, as he suddenly exploded away from me, gathering a towel from the rack beside the shower and wrapped it around me.

"Get dressed," he growled, walking to the door and yanking it open.

The tone of his voice told me that this clearly wasn't just one of Silas' moods, and I hurried to do as he instructed.

This was serious, his whole demeanor told me so, and I wouldn't be screwing around.

I rushed into the bedroom and got dressed. Quickly.

And it was good thing I did, too, because within two minutes of him leaving the bedroom he was walking right back into the room with some type of electronic box in his hand, all of the men that had been in the kitchen following behind him.

I sat down warily on the bed, scooting to the middle and crossing my legs in front of me as I pulled my knees up tightly to my chest.

Wrapping my arms around my legs, I watched as each man methodically searched the room, moving things around and generally making a colossal mess in their quest to find whatever it was that they were looking for.

"In here," I heard Kettle yell.

I blinked and watched as Silas moved to the closet, which was between the bathroom and the bedroom.

"Motherfucker! Goddamn motherfucker was in my house!" Silas growled low.

I looked down at my hands, remembering all the things I'd done in this room with Silas.

When had whatever he'd found gotten there?

Was it there since the beginning? Only since last night?

Where'd it face?

"Looks pretty new," Trance said, inspecting what looked to be the smallest camera in the world. "Ran off a battery, too. Has a memory card in here. Looks to be one of those ones that he'd have to come to the house to check the footage."

I was relieved at hearing that news, it was definitely better than the alternative of it being a live streaming device allowing the person who placed it there to check in anytime they wanted to.

Now my hope was that it'd been put in very recently and hadn't yet been checked.

Which was a realistic hope, given the fact that I knew for certain that the maid cleaned the bathroom mirror when she was here last.

"You know," I said, interrupting the intense conversation that was going on in front of me. "The maid came last Tuesday, and I know for a fact that she cleaned the bathroom mirror. The note that *I* left on the bathroom mirror is gone. Remember Silas?"

His eyes went far away for a minute while he thought back to the note.

I'd left in a hurry that morning with him in the middle of the lake fishing from his boat.

So I ran around inside the house like a chicken with my head cut off looking for a piece of paper to tell him that my phone was dead and I had to go into work to get the charger for it. In my haste to leave, I'd written him a note on the bathroom mirror knowing he'd see it.

It'd been there for two days until the maid had come and cleaned the house, since apparently Silas didn't even own a bottle of glass cleaner.

I remember being embarrassed at the thought of her reading what I'd said: *I'm going to the office to get my charger. Your ass looks sexy in your boat.*

I hadn't even been able to see him from where I'd been.

But I knew it to be a fact, so I'd written it to him knowing it'd make him smile.

"That was Tuesday," Silas said, eyes again going far away as he looked at the camera in his hand. "Today is Sunday."

I nodded but didn't say anything.

Then Silas hauled back and threw the camera across the room, shattering it as it smashed against the wall.

Pieces of glass and plastic littered the floor, and I closed my eyes, knowing that Silas was worrying.

Worried Silas equaled bad mood Silas.

Something I'd come to recognize since we'd met and started dating.

"Can you just…get her out of here for a little bit? Take the boat," Silas said roughly, pulling his hands up to sift through his hair.

Sebastian nodded and pulled away, walking to the closet and pulling out a pair of shoes.

He tossed them on the bed and I slipped them on to my feet, watching Silas's chest heave as he drew in breath after breath.

Never once did his eyes turn to me, and I knew the best thing I could do right then was leave.

Standing up, I moved in between big bulky men that were taking up the space of our bedroom and stopped in front of my man.

"So, do I get to call you my old man?" I whispered, pressing my lips against his strong jaw.

He finally looked down at me, and his muscles immediately softened.

"Yeah, you do," he said simply.

"I love you."

His eyes closed.

"I love you too, which is why it pisses me the fuck off that I have to get you out of here while we figure this out," he growled.

I hugged him around the belly.

"Don't leave me over there for too long. Your grandkids are hellions," I teased.

He huffed out a laugh. "They take after their daddy."

"Hey!" Sebastian said indignantly.

I smiled and pressed my lips to his.

"Be safe."

Little did I know that those words would haunt me hours later.

***

"You have to tell her, Sebastian. She's going to figure it out eventually," Baylee hissed.

I woke from sleep almost instantly, but my years in prison had finely honed my faking sleep skills.

I knew that I'd learn more from them now by eavesdropping on their conversation while I pretended to be asleep instead of waking up and demanding they tell me what was going on outright.

Or, at least, that's how I'd get the most information from Sebastian.

Baylee would probably just tell me whatever it was that I wanted to know.

My stomach was in knots as I listened to the two argue back and forth.

"But we don't know anything. We only found his bike in fucking pieces. He's nowhere to be found," Sebastian said in exasperation.

But I heard the hint of fear in it.

And I knew fear when I heard it, believe me.

Sebastian was worried about something.

"Yeah, but if Silas' bike was broken up like that, then most likely Silas is too. Even if he's not actually at the scene of the crash," Baylee whispered a little too loud once again.

This time I knew she was trying to wake me, so I sat up, only opening my eyes once my feet were on the floor next to the couch.

"Tell me," I whispered.

Sebastian was across the room from me leaning against a wall in the kitchen.

Baylee was directly across from him standing beside the kitchen island staring at him like he was the school-yard bully.

Sighing, Sebastian leaned forward until both elbows rested on the countertop before saying, "Dad's bike crashed in between Longview and Kilgore. He left on his own while we were all doing our own thing around five this evening, and we haven't heard from him since."

My heart froze as I looked at Sebastian, hoping beyond hope he would tell me he was joking or that they knew exactly where he was.

But he wasn't and he didn't.

"You didn't have any GPS or anything on him?" I asked worriedly.

Sebastian shook his head. "No."

"But…but…what are we going to do? Are you going to look for him?"

Sebastian nodded. "We've been looking for him since we realized he left. Kettle was the one to find his bike. I've got a few friends working magic on their end, but dad's normally the one using his contacts to find people we need. We're not sure where to go from here."

My mind raced as I fought the bile rising up in my throat.

"You can't find whomever he worked with and talk to them?" I asked worriedly.

Sebastian shook his head. "No. We've been looking. I've never known anything about my dad's business. And not once, in all the years I've been alive, has he had a slip up."

My head hung. "I…I need to go home. I need to think. Maybe I can come up with something. Maybe he left me a note."

Sebastian looked at Baylee with pity, not holding back his worry about me.

Well, he could just take that pity and shove it.

I knew he wouldn't just leave without letting me know.

I knew it.

CHAPTER 23

Dear NASA, your mom thought I was big enough!
- Pluto

Silas

"That rifle shot that took your daughter-in-law out was meant for you. I lucked out that you thought it was a rock that hit her. Could've had me then, but you fucked up. You're getting soft in your old age," Shovel said snidely. "You almost lost her, and it would've all been your fault. All these years of you protecting them, and it wouldn't have mattered one single bit."

I couldn't breathe.

Not because of what he was saying, though that was significant.

But because I was fairly positive that the broken ribs I'd sustained after going down on my bike and having the shit beaten out of me were sinking through the tissue of my lungs.

I'd woken up like this nearly an hour before, and all Shovel had done since I'd woken was talk about the old days.

Him shooting Baylee was new, though.

We'd really thought the cut on her neck was due to a rock, or something that kicked up and taken out a chunk of her flesh while we were riding.

The bleeding had never made sense to me, though.

Now, knowing that Shovel had taken a fuckin' sniper rifle to her, it made sense.

"So what are you going to do to me?" Shovel asked.

What was I going to do to him?

I was the one that was tied up to a fuckin' chair.

Well, granted, I had wanted to be tied up.

I knew he'd take me if I gave him the chance.

Which was why I'd gone out on a ride alone.

I knew he couldn't resist the temptation.

And he was only one person.

He had my arms stretched upwards, tied to a pipe above my head.

But he'd made a mistake by not tying my feet.

I wouldn't escape…yet.

I'd wait until I had my chance.

Or possibly sooner if Sawyer found the note I left her.

"You know you ruined my life," Shovel said conversationally, pulling out a pocketknife and picking dirt from underneath his fingernails with it.

I raised a brow. "I did, did I?"

He nodded. "Leslie was going to be mine. She was going to be my reward. But then you came in, claiming her and jumping through every hoop I threw at you and took her right out from under my nose. I'd had my eyes set on her since I was sixteen, and you fucking ruined it."

That was new to me.

I'd just seen Leslie come in, and I hadn't been able to do anything else *but* save her.

It'd been her eyes.

The innocence in them.

I was drawn to that.

It drew me in every, single time.

Which had been the reason I'd fallen for Sawyer, too.

Now, though, I knew she was nothing like Leslie.

She was stronger.

She was someone I'd never in my life cheat on. She knew all about me, and I knew there'd never be a time that I kept a goddamn thing from her.

Hell, now that I had Sawyer, I realized just how much I *didn't* love Leslie.

Because what I felt for Sawyer, I knew, was real love.

It was unshakable.

This love…it would withstand the test of time.

She got me, and I got her.

Before her, every damn night, I'd dream of how my life could've been.

Now, with Sawyer in it, I dreamed of what our life *will be* like.

I didn't think in the past tense anymore.

I was now a future kind of guy.

And I knew Shovel hadn't picked up on that yet.

Because he wouldn't be talking to me right now about Leslie. He'd be trying to rile me up by threatening Sawyer.

Because if he wanted to see me break, that would be just how to do it.

He'd done it before.

Many, many times.

"Then you kept ruining my life by cleaning up my club, making me lose all that money. My gambling debts got out of hand, man, and every fucking day, every day, I worried about how I would pay those fuckers back. You did kind of solve that for me by sending me to prison, though. And I thought it wouldn't be half bad, except my parole was denied time after time, and I finally realized that something wasn't quite right. So I had some people start to dig for me. And what do I find when my people started digging into my club? I found you…the fucking president… living the high life while I suffered day in and day out," Shovel hissed, pushing his face into mine.

My body locked, and I didn't move a single millimeter back.

I had no room to move back from him. But mainly, it was because I wasn't going to flinch away from him. I didn't flinch.

Not from him, not from anyone.

"You ruined your own life, you piece of shit. You could've stayed just like the rest of us, but you chose to make a fucking mess out of everything. I cleaned your shit up. What I didn't do, but should've done, was fucking kill you. Then I wouldn't be in this predicament right now," I growled.

Shovel smiled.

"You know, I watched you drive to Huntsville," he said lightly. "Followed behind you the entire way."

I froze, eyes lifting up to look directly into his eyes.

"Yeah?" I asked, voice steady.

It didn't reveal outwardly what I was feeling, which was anything but calm internally.

"Yep. So I did some research into why you were there. Found four men that are fucking pissed as hell that they lost their jobs over a stupid piece of ass," he said lightly. "So I invited them back with me."

Then the doors behind Shovel opened, four men walking into the room.

Each one had a box in their hands.

"And they've got some entertainment for you. Each time you fail to show a reaction to what they're showing you," Shovel said, pulling out a lead pipe. "I'm going to introduce you to this lead pipe. And we're going to make you talk even if we have to kill you."

I doubted that.

It'd take a divine intervention to get me to react to anything.

Because as long as I knew they didn't have Sawyer, then they had nothing.

She was safe and that was all that mattered.

"This is the picture I took of our first encounter," the first man said.

He had blonde shaggy hair that fell over his head in a fucking mop of messiness. He had brown eyes that were dark, but not cold. Not nearly cold enough to get past my defenses.

The picture, however, wasn't anything I wanted to see.

"We took pictures of her every day for eight years," the man continued.

I clenched my jaw tightly as he showed me the first picture.

And I literally tasted blood as I bit into my tongue to keep from giving this creep a piece of my mind.

"Well, if that one doesn't move you…how about this one?"

Guess I didn't have the iron-willed control like I thought was the last thing I thought before a seething blind rage clouded over my eyes, and the only thing I saw was a broken Sawyer being violated by the pervert in front of me.

And although I went down hard as Shovel's lead pipe came down on the temple of my head, arms still tied above my head, I took pride in the fact that the man standing in front of me now had a knife wound in his heart courtesy of the one that slid out of my boot.

"Ohh," Shovel said, shaking his head. "That was very, very stupid."

Head pounding and the only thing holding me up was the rope around my wrists, I said, "Yeah, yeah, motherfucker."

The last thing I heard before I succumbed to unconsciousness was, "Tie his fuckin' feet."

***

Sawyer

"I have this note…" I said, handing Sebastian the note.

His brother Sam was in the room with him, and they were both staring at Silas' table with all of Silas' open cases laid out in front of them.

Sam and Sebastian looked up, their eyes so much like their father's that my heart ached a little bit.

"What note?" Sam snapped.

I held it out to him.

"What is it?" He asked, eyes scanning it quickly.

"Well, the other day when Silas and I were in bed…"

"Is what you're saying pertinent to what we're going through right now, or can we skip the life story?" Sam snapped.

I narrowed my eyes at him, but it was Cheyenne who set him straight.

"Sam, I realize you're worried, but being a dick to the woman isn't going to help. Get the fuck over it and let her speak," Cheyenne growled at her husband.

Sam's eyes closed, and when they opened again I realized that he really was worried, and covering his worry up with a bad attitude.

Just like his father did.

"Go on. I'm sorry," he said gruffly.

I shrugged. "Anyway, we were talking about gambling for some reason, and it kind of escalated to whether we actually had any 'bookies' in the area. When he said yes, I asked him to tell me where I could find one, jokingly, in case I ever needed one. And he told me all I would have to do was to look forlorn while gambling at the poker table at The Horseshoe."

Sebastian nodded. "Okay."

"So it kept going from there, but I finally got a serious answer out of him that a bookie's name in the area was 'Black Jack.' How a lot of people still owed him a ton of money and that he was a not man to cross. He said he'd seen Shovel nearly beaten to death over his gambling debts while he was cleaning up the club," I explained. "When I asked him whether or not Shovel still owed this man money, he said that he did. And if Shovel was smart, he'd never come back here. Because this 'Black Jack' guy knows every low life in the city, and if he ever got wind that he was back, Black Jack would let his underground army know, and they'd find him in a heartbeat. And that's what the note says."

Sam's eyes went to the note.

"21. Shovel. Horseshoe," Sam read. "So what, he wants us to go to The Horseshoe's black jack table and, what… ask for Black Jack?"

I nodded. "Yes, I think that's exactly what he wants you to do."

Sam shrugged, as did Sebastian.

"Ain't got nothin' else."

***

Ninety minutes later, I was down to my last fingernail when the two men came back to the house after a quick trip to the Black Jack tables.

"You were right," he said. "Old Black Jack was pretty happy to hear that Shovel was back in town. Apparently, not only does Shovel owe Black Jack money, but he'd also gotten kind of handsy with Black Jack's wife years ago. He wants Shovel to know that he hasn't forgotten."

Ouch.

That sucked for Shovel.

But if it got me Silas back, I didn't care who it hurt in the process.

"And? Where's Silas?" I asked worriedly.

Sebastian shook his head. "It's gonna take some time, Sawyer."

I wanted to yell, 'Silas doesn't have time!' but I just barely managed to hold it in.

I knew they were both aware, just as much as I was, that he didn't have a lot of time. Especially since he'd most likely had a motorcycle wreck before he fell into the hands of *that* man.

And I just knew it was Shovel that had him.

There was no other explanation for it.

I closed my eyes and thought about where Shovel might have taken them.

I came up with what I thought was a brilliant idea, but Sam shot it down almost immediately.

"What about the old clubhouse y'all used to have. Where's that? Shovel hasn't been out of prison very long, so I bet he hasn't had the time to replenish his money supply. So where would he go that wouldn't cost a lot of money?" I asked.

"This is the old clubhouse," Sebastian explained. "And the only place that has low income housing is by the interstate. But that was the first place we went when we started looking."

"Shit," I exhaled. "That sucks."

Both men nodded, and it was then that I realized that we were the only ones in the room. Several of the guys had stayed with me while Sam and Sebastian went to the casino. Now they were gone.

"Where'd everyone else go?" I asked.

The men didn't bother to look up.

"They're out looking. But you've been coming up with some really good ideas, so we've been staying here to help you jog your memory in that hopes that you'll remember something that might help," Sam said.

I nodded in understanding.

"Alright then, tell me what it is that you need me to do that'll get y'all out there looking for him. I'll stay wherever you want me to stay," I told them.

Both men looked at each other, but it was Sam who spoke.

"You know, we're not really used to dealing with understanding and compliant women. But what we really need for you to do is stay at the clubhouse until further notice," Sam explained.

I nodded, immediately getting up to head into the bedroom where I quickly packed a bag. I was back in the living room within five minutes.

"Ready when you are," I said.

They both acted so similarly and so much like their father that it hit me how close they could be, but yet weren't.

Did they even know how much Silas loved them?

I decided to ask them during the silence that continued in the truck.

"Do y'all know how much your dad loves you both?" I asked hesitantly.

A van passed us going at least ten miles an hour over the speed limit, and

I watched it while I waited for the two men in front of me to respond.

My question was met with silence.

Neither man said a word.

"He talks about you all so much. He's so happy that y'all are happy. Goes on and on about your kids, and how y'all include him in your lives when he doesn't deserve it. Loves your wives. Loves the fact that y'all are better fathers than he was. He's so proud he could burst. He has photos of y'all in his offices. Did y'all know that?" I asked in a trembling voice.

I don't know why I was telling them all of this, but I was scared, really scared.

And I wanted them to realize what they could be missing if he wasn't found alive and safe.

I knew Sebastian better than Sam, but neither one of them had a really 'close' relationship with Silas, and I that just made me really sad. They had no idea what they were missing out on.

I loved my father dearly, and I knew, if put into the position that Silas' had been in, he'd have done the same damn thing in a heartbeat.

Sam's phone rang, and he looked down as he pulled it out of his pocket just as we pulled onto the road that led to the clubhouse.

Had he not looked up just when he did, he never would've seen the body being thrown out of the back doors of a panel van. The same van that'd nearly cut us off earlier in the trip in its haste to get past us.

But he did.

And thanks to his quick reflexes, he was able to stop just in time to prevent his truck from running over the body that'd been thrown out of the back of the van directly in front of the clubhouse.

My eyes closed as my breath started to saw in and out of my chest.

And when I would've tried to get out, I was told to stay put by Sam as they both got out to look at the man that'd been thrown.

And I knew by the look on their faces, the devastation that completely took them over, that it was Silas.

Broken, bruised, and bloody.

I closed my eyes as fresh tears, not the first of today, started to pour down my cheeks.

They were gone so long that I couldn't take it anymore, and quickly opened the back door and circled it around to the front where both men were leaning over an unconscious Silas.

"Is he alive?" I whispered.

Sebastian looked up. "Yeah."

He didn't say more, but he didn't have to.

I knew it was bad.

Really bad.

I could tell that just by looking at him.

He didn't have a spot on his body that wasn't covered in blood or dirt.

His shirt was torn, nearly disintegrated in places.

His boots were missing.

His face so battered and bruised that he was unrecognizable.

His salt and pepper hair stained red from the copious amount of blood.

And he wouldn't open his eyes.

My phone was in my hand, and I had 911 on the line before I even realized I'd done it.

I handed the phone over to Sebastian when they asked to speak with someone who knew where they were exactly, and finally dropped down to my knees beside the love of my life.

"Silas," I whispered.

He didn't move. Didn't react.

I placed my hands on the side of his cheek, feeling the sticky wetness beneath my fingers, but not reacting like I normally would.

Instead, I leaned over him and prayed.

Prayed that he'd be okay.

And knew instinctively that it would be a long road to recovery ahead of him.

Because when he woke up, he'd be sore as fuck, and hell bent on vengeance.

And it'd be really, really hard to keep him there knowing that there were people out there trying to kill him.

"Y'all know you're going to have to take care of this, right? Because if you don't, he's going to kill whomever it was, whether he's up to it or not, and probably get himself killed in the process," I whispered to the two of them.

Sam's smile was a little bit unnerving as he said, "Oh, we'll take care of it. Don't you worry your pretty little head about that, Sawyer."

CHAPTER 24

Maybe it's not anger management that I need. Maybe you need to keep your stupid away from me.
-Food for thought

Sam

Four hours later

"You find him?" I asked my brother.

Sebastian looked up from his phone and smiled. "Got him. Let's go pay the fucker a visit."

I walked up to my wife where she was sitting in the plastic seats of the waiting room.

She had Sawyer's hand in hers as they both stared at the white doors where the doctor had come out earlier to let us know that there'd been more wrong than they'd initially realized, and they needed more time than they'd originally thought to examine him thoroughly and give us an accurate assessment of his condition.

That'd been over two hours ago, and I was getting anxious.

Anxious to find the man responsible for nearly killing my father.

And, I had to admit, to tell my father that I was sorry for being such an asshole.

I knew he didn't deserve it...*now*.

I'd had a long talk with my mother after my daughter's baptism, and I now knew what I didn't know then.

That, in my father's way, he loved me.

All the years that I thought my father was a bad person, he was actually taking care of me. Protecting me.

Doing the same thing that I would've done had I been in his position.

And that was a bitter pill to swallow.

I knew that I was running out of time to fix this, and it'd take a lot of effort on my part to heal that gap between us.

But the first thing I'd do would be to take care of the fucker that did this to him. That threatened his family, putting me and my family into harm's way.

"I think we should just go," Sebastian said at my side where I'd come to a stop just at the entrance of the waiting room. "There's no telling how long this will take, and if we don't hurry there'll be nothing left of him after Black Jack does his thing."

Fuck.

That I knew well.

I'd heard chatter about this 'Black Jack' person.

Knew he was a little less than savory in his dealings with people that wronged him.

I hadn't heard a single story him that indicated the man was capable of any kind of mercy in his retribution.

"Alright, I'll meet you out front in ten," I said, crooking my finger at my wife.

My life.

She got up after patting Sawyer's hand and started walking towards me.

Even after all this time, she still took my breath away.

"Hey," she whispered, walking straight into my arms.

I folded my arms around her. "We're going to go. Text me if you hear any news."

She looked into my eyes with those hazel eyes of hers and smiled. "Don't get arrested."

I grinned down at her. "Oh, I won't get arrested. Trust me, darlin'."

She laughed and pressed her lips against mine. "Go. Come back safe to me."

I pressed my lips against her forehead and nodded. "Will do, oh wife of mine."

She smacked my ass as I turned to leave, and I tossed her a wink over my shoulder, passing my brother speaking to his own wife as I went.

He broke off just as I reached the elevator, joining me as we rode the elevator in silence.

We didn't speak at all the entire way to the hotel room that Black Jack had said Shovel was occupying, either.

Both of us lost in our own contemplation of our lives.

And, in tandem, we breeched the room with guns drawn.

Shovel jackknifed off the bed, reaching for his gun but not making it.

I caught his hand with a bullet through the palm, causing him to freeze.

Sebastian was on him in the next second, and like true, good brothers, we took turns beating the absolute shit out of him.

Sadly, we weren't the only ones who wanted in on the action, and we stepped aside to allow some of The Dixie Wardens to get in on the action.

Three unconscious bodies hit the floor beside us, and I turned to find the three of the four guards that attacked Sawyer over the years, laying there where Cleo had unceremoniously thrown them.

"Caught them trying to round the back of the hotel," he mumbled, crossing his arms over his chest.

"How'd you get them over here?" I asked.

Cleo smiled. "Drug them by their feet one by one. Black Jack met me at the corner and helped."

I turned to find 'Black Jack' staring into the room with passionless eyes.

He was watching as Torren and Sterling took their turn.

"Can't believe he thought he couldn't be found. Fucking Silas trying to do everything himself. I told him weeks ago if he needed me, all he had to do was ask," Black Jack muttered.

"What's your real name?" I asked, looking over at the man next to me.

The man didn't even hesitate.

Smiling, he said, "Lynn."

"You work with my father, don't you?" I asked, not really surprised.

He nodded. "For a long, long time now."

"Are you really a bookie?" Sebastian asked.

He shrugged. "When I need to be."

"What are you going to do with him?" I asked, indicating to the man we'd just beaten the shit out of with our bare hands.

Black Jack, a.k.a. Lynn, just smiled. "Oh, I'm not nearly done with him yet. You see, boy, you've warmed him up. Given him a simple black eye compared to the beating he's about to receive from me. He's gone and done something real stupid, hurting the one man that has kept him safe all these years. If it wasn't for Silas' and that big heart of his, he'd have been dead a long time ago. I think it was all a because of a promise he made to a twelve-year-old boy that he would never hurt the man again."

Jesus. My father and his big heart.

Fuck, but do I have some serious groveling to do.

I'd been that twelve-year-old boy.

And it'd been because Shovel had thrown me down and hurt me that he'd beaten the ever-loving shit out of him.

And when I'd caught him doing it, I'd asked him to stop and promise never hurt him again.

Ahh, the naiveté of a twelve year old's mind.

"Well, consider that request rescinded. Do what you need to do."

With that, Sebastian and I left the hotel room and drove back to the hospital, yet again in silence.

And we sat, along with our loved ones, and waited.

CHAPTER 25

I wrote a song for you. It's called I don't like your face. I hope you like it.
- Sawyer's secret thoughts

Sawyer

I woke when something soft touched my face.

I blinked my eyes open and realized I'd fallen asleep in the chair again.

My neck hurt.

I stretched, pushing my arms up over my head.

They collided with something hard and I gasped, sitting up from my slumped position.

And stared right into the eyes of my brother.

The brother that wasn't supposed to be here yet.

Johnson was a sight for sore eyes.

"Johnson," I breathed, standing up and throwing myself into his arms.

Johnson caught me and pulled me tightly into his chest, burying his face into my neck as he hugged me hard.

"God, I've missed you so much!" I gasped as tears started to roll down my face. "How'd you get out so fast?"

"Family emergency. Called my CO and told him what happened; he told me to take off early," he told me. "I needed to meet this man that everybody keeps going on and on about."

I gasped and turned to find Silas's beaten face staring at me with his signature smile tilting up the corner of his mouth.

"Silas," I breathed, letting go of Johnson to rush to his side.

Silas smiled at me, then his eyes flicked up to my brother.

"Glad you made it home," he said roughly.

His voice sounded like he'd just gargled with gravel, so I immediately reached for my glass of water and brought it to him, bending the straw to his lips.

He rolled his eyes at me, but nonetheless drank deeply until he hit the end of it.

He'd been out for nearly a day and a half thanks to all the pain meds and antibiotics rolling through his system.

No wonder he was thirsty.

"Thank you," he said. "You okay?"

I smiled, placing my hand against his cheek.

"I'm perfectly fine, thanks to you. You, on the other hand, aren't so good," I told him.

He had eight broken ribs, a nearly punctured lung, and he was now spleen less.

"What's the verdict?" He asked.

I sat down gently on the edge of the bed, aware of the way that Johnson scrutinized us, but stayed silent.

"You had some internal bleeding. They had to remove your spleen. Your lung was nearly punctured; luckily, though, it wasn't. You've got eight broken ribs, though. Which isn't surprising considering you were beaten black and blue. Oh, and I'm pretty sure your nose is broken."

He grinned. "Do I still have all my teeth?"

I nodded. "Yeah."

He exhaled. "Well, at least that's somethin'."

I nodded.

"How long have I been out?"

"Little over twenty four hours," I answered.

He nodded.

"How're my kids?" He asked.

I smiled down at Silas. "They're all fine. Scared and worried about you, but fine."

He laughed, but then just as quickly grimaced. "I know that's a lie."

I shook my head. "Really, they've been in and out of here for the last day and a half, Silas. Even Sam."

He took a deep breath and sighed.

"All it took was me nearly dying to get them here," he laughed humorlessly. He looked at the man at my side. "Which brother are you?"

Johnson crossed his arms and smiled his usual smile.

"The best one."

Silas laughed softly, aware of the pain, but not letting it stop him from showing his happiness.

"This is Johnson. The smooth talker of the family. He's the easiest of my brothers to get along with," I informed my soon to be husband.

Silas offered his hand to Johnson, and Johnson took it, not softening his grip at all to give Silas a pain-free handshake.

No, Johnson gripped hard and shook away, and I could see Silas wince, but he let it happen.

"Johnson," I reprimanded my brother. "Go the fuck away and leave me alone for a minute."

Johnson grinned unrepentantly. "He'd have done the same to me had the positions been reversed."

Silas nodded. "Yeah, I would have."

I pushed my brother's shoulder. "Go. Tell the brunette at the desk that he's awake, will ya?"

Johnson nodded. "Sure thing, sis."

I rolled my eyes as he left the room but there was no real annoyance behind it. I was so happy I could burst.

Two more brothers home, and I'd be happier than I could remember being in years.

"Now that he's gone, you can go ahead and tell me all of it. What's the rest that you haven't told me," Silas said the moment Johnson cleared the door.

I looked at him, studying his face and body.

"Your sons' kicked the shit out of Shovel. And, um, three of the four guards that… well, you know… were also taken care of by the club. That Black Jack guy, though, he really came through," I informed him.

The man smiled.

Widely.

"Good," he said, leaning his head back and closing his eyes. "Good."

"Mr. Mackenzie," a nurse said, bustling into the room with a huge computer in front of her. "How are you doing?"

I liked Silas' nurse. She'd been his nurse the previous day, too.

"I'm fine," he said, not admitting to being in pain.

"He hasn't pressed his morphine pump yet, and I'm pretty sure he's in pain," I told her, knowing Silas would never admit to it.

Berty, the nurse, nodded. "Got it. Mr. Mackenzie, this is a morphine pump. You can press it if the red light is lit." She indicated by picking up a button Silas could hold in his hand and pressing it. The red light clicked off, and Silas' glared. "Don't worry. You can't over-medicate yourself. It'll only let you press it every fifteen minutes, understand?"

Silas nodded. "Good. I have a few medications to give you, and I can take your catheter out if you're interested."

Silas nodded again.

"Excellent. Let's take care of the catheter, first," she said, pulling out some purple gloves and slipping them on. "Ma'am, if you could step…"

"She's not going anywhere," Silas snapped.

Berty winked at me. "Alright then, let's do this."

I watched as, with able hands, she quickly and efficiently removed the catheter from Silas.

I smiled down at my hands as I saw how uncomfortable it made him to have some woman holding his dick.

"It's not funny," he mumbled once she was done.

I lifted up laughing eyes to catch his angry gaze, and shrugged. "I'm sorry. I can't help it."

"It doesn't feel right to have anybody touching it but you," he grumbled.

Berty grinned, but didn't look up from washing her hands.

I moved forward until I could place my lips on his. "I love you."

He grinned. "Love you too, darlin'."

And even though he was still hurt and had some healing to do, I knew everything was going to be alright.

Because Silas would make sure it was.

He'd never stop fighting for me, and I would do the same for him.

Because I loved him, and he loved me.

It was just as simple as that.

EPILOGUE

Old dogs know more tricks than you think they do.
- Silas to Sawyer

Silas

"I can't believe you're making me do this!" Sawyer grumbled under her breath as we made our way into the courthouse.

I shrugged. "It needs to be done. You deserve it."

She sighed and stopped protesting, even though I could tell she was still just as pissed now as she had been earlier.

I hired a lawyer to take care of Sawyer's restitution case.

The state had countered with an offer for $50,000. However, I still felt that wasn't nearly enough.

Especially considering how even after being released from prison six months ago, and with a full four months for the people in this town to absorb the knowledge that she'd been wrongfully charged, convicted and sentenced, everyone still looked at her differently. It broke my heart every single time I saw how it affected her and how she tried to bury and hide her hurt.

It'd been four months since I'd had my ass kicked by Shovel, and I still felt like shit some days.

It was harder to recover now from something like I'd been through than it had been for my younger body.

Bouncing back the next day just didn't happen for me anymore.

But I had the help of a beautiful woman, who was happy and doing something she loved with her life – training dogs.

She and Trance had teamed up after Trance saw how well she'd trained her puppy, and they were now well on their way to building a thriving business training dogs for people all over the Ark-La-Tex.

"It's not just for you, you know. The government makes mistakes just like real people do. If they made a mistake with you, then they need to realize that it's not okay. They can't just placate you with fifty grand and call it even. You can't really put a price on the years of your life that you've lost, but if you could, it certainly wouldn't be a measly fifty grand," I told her, once again telling her my feelings on the subject.

She rolled her eyes. "Whatever."

I knew she wanted it, though, just like I did. She was afraid.

Afraid that she'd not get what she felt she deserved.

Afraid that she would get even more attention for killing four people than she previously did.

Afraid that she'd be humiliated by the court.

All of those were very warranted concerns, but it didn't change the fact that she needed to do this.

"I'll be right here," I whispered. "Then afterwards we're going to get drunk."

She turned to me and laughed.

"We're getting married tomorrow. You most certainly are *not* getting drunk the day before. I want you to look good for pictures," she said, shaking her head.

I winked at her. "Darlin', I look good no matter what I do. Getting drunk the day before our wedding isn't going to change that fact."

She snorted.

"Whatever you say, Silas. I don't think that you can hack it anymore, though. You did say that you were getting too old for this shit to me just this morning," she teased.

I stopped and turned her to face me.

"That was because you wanted to have sex two minutes after I just came. What exactly did you expect me to do? I'm not fifteen anymore!" I laughed.

She giggled, and I wanted to spank her.

Alas, my damn cock-blocking, busybody bunch of children walked up at that precise moment.

"Dad, seriously? You can't say that stuff in a courthouse! Not to mention everything you just said echoed off the walls," Shiloh said, color blooming in her cheeks.

I grinned.

"Is that right?" I asked, offering one arm to Sawyer and the other to Shiloh.

"Yeah, that's right," Shiloh grumbled.

"I don't think I've heard this rule," Sam said from behind me. "Have you?"

"Nope," Sebastian confirmed.

I laughed as Shiloh started to turn to give her brothers a piece of her mind, but I held on tight and walked the two of them into the courtroom where we were scheduled to be in less than five minutes time.

"I can't believe it's come to this," Shiloh said, shaking her head as she took her seat.

Sawyer sat next to her, and I sat on the end, Sebastian and Sam filling up half the seats directly behind us as they waited for their wives to arrive.

“I can’t believe they all showed up,” Sawyer murmured, looking behind us.

I followed her gaze, looking over my shoulder at the men filling the seats behind my boys.

The Dixie Wardens were formidable in all their glory.

Each one of them had their cuts on, proudly declaring them as members of the Dixie Wardens.

They were getting the attention of not just us, but the entire courtroom.

“They love you, what can I say?” I asked, turning back around.

And they did.

Sawyer fit right in with the other women.

She helped out where she could, offering her support to all the other ladies.

She helped watch their kids, trained their dogs, and even helped with errands.

She was the quintessential lead biker babe, always there when you needed her.

And I loved the fuck out of her.

Loved that she loved my club just as much as I did.

“This is going to either go really, really well…or really, really bad,” she muttered under her breath.

I smiled and faced forward when the bailiff made his way to the front of the room.

“All rise,” he boomed.

We rose and awaited the decision that would affect the rest of Sawyer’s life.

***

"I can't believe you got all that you asked for," Shiloh squealed in excitement the next day.

I rolled my eyes.

The celebration last night had turned from just a small party to over a hundred Dixie Wardens strong somewhere after midnight. A thousand if you counted the families that belonged to those Dixie Wardens from the surrounding states.

I was now a married man, and the band on my finger had nothing against the strangle hold Sawyer had on my heart.

Curling my arm tighter around my wife, I turned her into my chest and said, "You think they'll miss us for an hour?"

Startled, she turned to me and asked, "What for?"

That was my woman.

Always ready to think the worst of things.

Leaning in close, I let my lips tickle her ear as I said, "So I can fuck you. I've been wondering what you had under that dress since I saw you in it twenty minutes ago."

But before she could answer her brothers were there.

I'd finally met the last two, Cole and Brody, and I liked them quite a bit.

In fact, I liked all of her brothers, even though they had no problem threatening my manhood every chance they got.

"Time for cake!" Brody yelled loudly, even though we were all standing right there.

Reba rolled her eyes, "Seriously, Cole?"

"I'm Cole. That was Brody," Cole said to his mother in exasperation.

"Just wait until you have kids of your own, then tell me if you care if you mix up their names," Reba grumbled. "Now, come on, my girl. It's time to cut your cake."

Reba was the impromptu wedding planner for our wedding.

In the beginning it'd started out as just her helping, but it quickly escalated into her taking over the whole show when we realized just how many people were coming.

Sawyer was happy that she didn't have to deal with it.

She had more than enough things on her plate without having to worry about that, too.

"Wait!" The photographer said. "I need to take a family picture! I don't want you to get cake on your wedding attire!"

I sighed.

My daughter had insisted on the wedding photographer, and although I did think it was a good idea to take pictures, I was down for the guests doing it with their own cameras, and sending them to me in an email or something.

This jackwad was like a man with a whip.

Although, I was fairly sure the pictures would turn out phenomenally.

But I was getting tired of having the man tell me when to kiss, and not to kiss, my wife.

Where to put my fuckin' hands, and how I should look at her.

One by one, our 'family' lined up and Gasten, the photographer's, mouth went slack.

"Uhh, I'm not sure how I'm going to be able to get all of you in the picture," he finally admitted.

I looked behind me at my children and their families. Then at Sawyer's immediate family. And finally at the rest of the Dixie Wardens and their families.

"This is our family. And not one of them better be left out of the picture or I'll shove my foot up your ass," I said. "Maybe you could take a panoramic or something?" I added as an afterthought.

It turned out to be a damn fine picture.

One I would cherish for the rest of my life.

***

Later that night

"Your mother's a fuckin' slave driver," I groaned as my back finally hit the bed.

I groaned when Sawyer followed me down.

"Sawyer," I said, finally striking up the nerve to ask her what'd been on my mind for months now.

"Yeah?" She asked, her face pressed into my chest.

"Do you want kids?"

I didn't know if I did want more, but I also didn't know if I didn't.

I just wanted her to be happy, and if that meant a kid for her, then I'd damn well do it.

"Yes, one or two," she admitted. "We'll just start with this one, first."

My lungs froze, and my breath seized in my chest.

"Say again?" I asked carefully.

I could feel her smile against my chest.

"Yep. You heard right. Exactly eight weeks," she said. "I was going to tell you tomorrow at the barbeque. Tonight was supposed to be just for us."

My arms went around her, and I pulled her in close.

"I'm going to die of a heart attack trying to chase after another kid," I told her my fear.

She sighed.

"Silas, you are the most in shape fifty-four year old I've ever met. Get the hell over it," she said in exasperation.

I thought back to the night I was guessing we'd conceived…it was the only time I'd ever gone without a condom since we'd been together.

It'd been the night I'd officially been released for work after my 'accident'.

In our exuberance to celebrate me being able to fuck my woman without a guilty conscience, I'd gone and forgotten my first rule of fucking.

Protection.

And I'd come inside her tight, hot pussy without a second thought.

Now, though, those repercussions made themselves known, and I realized that I wasn't upset about it in the slightest.

In fact, I was pretty goddamned excited.

I couldn't wait to raise a child the way I always wanted to raise my others.

And although my other children all ended up pretty fucking awesome, if I did say so myself, I still wanted a second chance.

And it was here, in my arms.

"I love you, Sawyer," I told my wife.

She hummed in contentment.

"I love you, too."

And we fell asleep like that, me holding the woman of my dreams in my arms and her arms wrapped me.

And not one nightmare made itself known throughout the entire night.

***

"What are you doing?" A voice asked from behind me.

I threw the last photo capturing Sawyer's torture at the hands of the four guards, photos they had taken during each attack throughout Sawyer's time in jail, in to the small fire I'd created at the side of my house sighing as it curled up and burned to ash.

"I'm getting rid of some stuff that's been needing to get gone," I told Dallas. "Why are you up so late?"

Dallas and Bristol were staying at his parent's lake house while they were away on vacation.

Their parents had remarried by the Justice of the Peace a month ago with all their family in attendance; this was their second honeymoon of sorts. Something they'd refused to take until they'd attended their daughter's wedding and saw her 'treated right.'

Dallas smiled. "I've been kicked out by my wife because she wants to wrap my birthday gifts."

I nodded. "Yeah, that tends to happen when they think you haven't seen the credit card statements and know exactly what they bought you."

Dallas and Sawyer had repaired the minor breach between the two of them, and their bond was even stronger now.

Dallas was over at my house, with his family, at least once a week when I got home from work, and vice versa.

And I was happy to see them happy.

Family was love, and you could never have enough love, especially someone like Sawyer.

"I never said thank you," Dallas said after a few long moments of silence.

I turned my gaze to his.

"For what?" I asked, wondering what I'd done to earn a thank you from him.

"For helping her when I should've been there doing the same. For being there for her, showing her she was worth everything and then doing whatever it took to give it to her," Dallas said softly. "I love her like crazy, and I thank God every day that she was okay after getting out of that hell hole."

Dallas had been over one night, staying late to play a game of poker with me, when we'd heard Sawyer screaming from the bedroom.

Dallas had gone deathly white when he heard what she'd been saying in her sleep, and after that, he had made it his mission in life to get her the help she needed.

I hadn't disagreed with him.

I'd been working on her for months to convince her to go talk to someone about it.

After a long, drawn out conversation with her brother on what was going on with her dreams, Dallas had finally been able to talk her into doing something that I hadn't been able to accomplish in months of working on her.

He'd explained it after Sawyer had gone back to sleep.

"You just have to play the pity card. Worked every time when I wanted the last cookie," he winked. "But it only works 'cause I'm her baby brother and I've been working that card for thirty years now."

"She didn't break, and she fights every day. You were able to get her to go to counseling sessions when I wasn't able to," I admitted. "I could be telling you the same right now."

His eyes clouded over, and I was sure he'd had something else to say, but a really shrill, "You didn't tell me you were pregnant!"

I smiled and looked down at the fire in front of me while Dallas stayed silent at my side.

"God help you, man. Because I can barely handle the two of my own."

And, for some reason, that admission from the man at my side didn't worry me a single bit.

In fact, it only gave me the motivation I needed to be what I'd never been before…a good father and husband.

Something that my other children had never gotten from me, but something I would spend the rest of my life trying to make up to them.

Something this child, the one that Sawyer carried in her womb, would know from me from the moment he or she took their first breath.

A promise I would keep until I took my final breath.

ABOUT THE AUTHOR

Lani Lynn Vale is married to the love of her life that she met in high school. She fell in love with him because he was wearing baseball pants. Ten years later they have three perfectly crazy children and a cat named Demon who likes to wake her up at ungodly times in the night. They live in the greatest state in the world, Texas. She writes contemporary and romantic suspense, and has a love for all things romance. You can find Lani in front of her computer writing away in her fictional characters world...that is until her husband and kids demand sustenance in the form of food and drink.

Made in the USA
Columbia, SC
14 March 2022

57665807R00189